C000271924

OF DUTCH DESCENT

Caroline Muntjewerf

€oinyard Publishing®

The right of Caroline Muntjewerf to be identified as
the author of this work has been asserted by her in
accordance with the Copyright, Designs and Patents Act
1988.

ISBN/EAN 978-90-833146-0-0

All Rights Reserved

No part of this publication may be reproduced, stored in a
retrieval system, or transmitted in any form or by any
means, without the prior permission in writing of the
author and publisher, nor be otherwise circulated in any
form of binding or cover other than that in which it is
published.

Any person who does any unauthorised act in relation to
this publication may be liable to criminal prosecution and
civil claims for damage.

Text Copyright © 2006 – 2013 Caroline Muntjewerf
Cover Artwork © 1949 Jan Muntjewerf

First edition January 2006
Second edition March 2013

Join the Readers List here and get your free Ebook:
https://cmuntjewerf.com

Other novels by Caroline Muntjewerf:

The Stories
Return to Les Jonquières
Bel Amour

Dutch:
van Hollandse Afkomst
Avondstond

German:
Holländische Wurzeln

Of Dutch Descent

1

'Ellie, Ellie, hurry up! We're going to be late,' her mother Rita calls out.

Ellie sits dreamily, staring at her adolescent face in the mirror, the notebook resting underneath her tanned hands.

'Ellie! Please ... ' Her mother hastily opens the door of the bedroom. The girl's pen drops on the floor and she reaches to pick it up. 'Ellie, do you want to come or not. We're leaving now ... '

Reluctantly Ellie stands up.

'Were you writing again?'

'Mm ... ' is Ellie's reply.

'I didn't know you had so many friends to write to.'

'I'm not writing to my friends, Ma,' Ellie says as she puts the pad in the drawer of her dressing table. She casts a glance in the mirror and brushes her hands through her auburn hair. 'OK Mum, let's go.'

Her mother follows her into the hallway. 'Aren't you pleased Opa and Oma are coming? We haven't seen them for so long,' Rita goes on as they hurry out of the front door, 'they won't recognise you anymore.'

'Hello Uncle Pieter. How are you today?' Ellie asks as she sees her uncle by the car.

'Fine,' he says. 'Get in, we're late.'

'I was just saying to Ellie,' Rita says as they drive off, 'how much she has changed. Just a baby when she left Holland and look at her now.'

'She's been saying that ever since Opa and Oma sent word that they were coming,' Ellie replies from the backseat. Pieter smiles and accelerates. The old Ford finds its way through the small town of Taihepe and on to the main road. 'Yeah, the old folks will be surprised,' Pieter mumbles and glimpses at Ellie's mother.

'Aren't you anxious to see them, Pieter,' Ellie asks, 'they're your parents.'

'Uncle Pieter,' her mother corrects her.

'That's alright, Rita,' Peter says. 'Well, I haven't seen them for so long … a lot of things have happened. And I wasn't exactly their favourite son.'

Each dwelling on their memories they drive on with the satisfyingly purring engine making the only sound. The hills in the distance are dressed in green forests, in contrast to the fields in front that are already showing signs of drought. The river beneath the bridge they cross only shows a trickle of water.

'Gosh,' Ellie sighs, 'we need some rain. Look at that river.'

'That one,' Pieter replies. 'That one's always low ... Ever since they put that dam up stream, this one hardly gets any water,' he mutters. Ellie wrinkles an eyebrow as if to show her disapproval.

'So, how's your boyfriend?' Pieter wants to know after a while. He looks Ellie in the eyes through his rear-view mirror.

'What boyfriend?' Rita asks. 'Ellie doesn't have a boyfriend!?'

Pieter takes another look at Ellie. She shakes her head at him in the rear-view mirror as Rita turns hers to see her daughter's face.

'He's just making a joke, Mum.' Now Pieter also turns his head.

'You keep your eyes on the road!' Rita says to him. 'Ellie? What is this about?'

Ellie's face displays an unwilling look. 'Nothing, Mum … like I said, he's just joking.'

'Mm,' her mother replies, seemingly satisfied with the answer. 'You don't have to keep anything from me, you know.'

Not many words are spoken as they continue their journey, until Pieter pulls up at a petrol station that has a small café beside it.

Rita wakes her daughter, who has nodded off, and they both go inside while Pieter has the tank filled up. A swift revolving fan in the ceiling keeps the heat from invading the small, basic eatery. Ellie looks around as her mother orders tea and some chips.

'Or would you like something else, sweetie,' Rita questions.

'No, I'm alright. Chips are fine.'

They take a seat at one of the tables next to the window in the otherwise empty room. A short while later Pieter joins them. The waitress carries in the tray with their order. 'Going far?' she asks.

'Wellington,' Pieter replies. 'We're picking up some relatives we haven't seen for years.'

'Oh, how nice. Do they live there?'

'No, they are coming all the way from Holland,' Rita replies in her unmistakably Dutch accent. 'We have not seen them since nineteen-fifty-one.'

'Oh, that's wonderful! You must be really excited. Well, enjoy your tea. Chips are the speciality of the house.'

'Yeah, I bet,' Ellie whispers under her breath as she takes one. 'You haven't seen Opa and Oma for a lot longer than that, aye Pieter?'

'Ellie, mind your manners,' her mother says.

'Yeah, not since forty-three,' he replies.

'Gosh, that's … almost twenty years,' Ellie quickly calculates. 'Oh, well. It's not *that* long ago. You haven't changed a bit, Uncle Pieter,' Ellie smiles.

'You didn't know me at seventeen. I was just a kid then.'

'You're still a kid, Pieter,' Rita says.

'Mum! Mind your manners,' Ellie reacts teasingly.

'You drink your tea, love.'

'Yeah, drink up,' Pieter says, 'we still have some miles to conquer.'

Ellie notices Pieter becoming somewhat nervous on their approach into Wellington and she wonders if he has lost his way, but Pieter claims he could find the Wellington Harbour even with his eyes closed. They soon catch a glimpse of the ship that brought their family safely across the oceans from Holland. Quay-hands are busy connecting the moorings.

Anxiously Rita peers at the ship's railing. 'Can you see them?' she asks with a slightly nervous tone in her voice. Ellie looks the other way. 'I think we can park over there … near the terminal,' she says calmly.

Pieter's eyes search for the empty spot, then drives the car towards the building. It is rather busy and hectic near the passenger terminal and they are lucky to find a parking space. Rita swiftly gets out of the car. 'Come on you two,' she says nervously, 'we don't want to lose them.'

'Please, Mum. How can we lose them, they haven't even left the ship yet.'

Rita does not go against her daughter and soon is steps away from Ellie and Pieter who composedly make their way through the groups of people. On entering the building an atmosphere of nervous anxiety sets upon them. Ellie moves closer and locks her arm around Pieter's.

'Don't worry, Uncle,' she says. 'Opa and Oma will love to see you again. You're still their son.'

Pieter glances at her with a surprised look on his face as if he wonders where she acquired such wisdom. 'And what about you, do you remember them at all?'

Ellie is indifferent. 'Nah ... It's been so long, and I hardly knew them before we came out here. Honestly, I don't understand why Mum is so ... all up on cloud nine about this.'

Pieter smiles as they walk along. 'Well, it's probably something to do with "the Dutch connection" she can't shake.'

Ellie looks at him. 'What trash, she's got us, right?'

'It's not the same. We've become too Kiwi,' he adds as he pinches her in the side. With a giggle, Ellie pushes him off. Before long they find a spot where they have a good view of the gangplank coming down from the ship.

'Why would they cover that gangplank?' Ellie wonders. 'It's not even raining.'

Rita's peering eyes start searching for familiar faces between the disembarking passengers. After a while, she sees them and starts waving her hands rapidly. 'There they are!' she yells.

Some people standing beside them turn their heads.

'Where?' Ellie asks.

'Over there,' Rita says as she points her finger.

Ellie tries to distinguish some of the faces passing underneath the marquee. Pieter follows the direction in which Rita aims. His strained face slowly relaxes when he recognises the elderly couple moving down from the ship. He bites his lip while Ellie looks at him.

'There they are, aye,' she softly says.

'He seems old ... and look at her,' he quietly states. There is hesitation as he waves at the people who are his parents.

'I think they haven't changed a bit,' Ellie says firmly.

'You would say that about anybody,' Pieter replies.

Rita grabs both her daughter and Pieter by the arm. 'Come on, let's meet them,' she says and urges them onward.

'Mum! What has got in to you?' Ellie says astounded. 'I haven't seen you so excited in all my life!'

They move along to the exit and wait.

'It's going to take a while yet, Rita,' Pieter says. 'Why don't we get some coffee?'

'What do you mean?' Rita asks. 'I'm going to wait right here.'

'It's at least another hour before they have sorted out their stuff and collected their luggage,' Pieter tries to convince her. Rita dithers for a moment but is determined to wait where she stands. 'You go, I'll wait.'

Ellie glances at Pieter and then the two walk off towards the coffee-stand. Rita looks about her at the many people swarming around the terminal. She smiles at some of them that pass by her.

After they finished their coffee Pieter and Ellie stroll back to where they left Rita.

'I remember when we first arrived here,' Ellie says. 'All those people. And I didn't understand at all why we had to come here.'

Pieter looks at his niece sideways as they walk along.

'I had a friend on the boat. Annie,' Ellie continues. 'I thought we would all live together, or at least in the same town.'

'But you never saw her again,' Pieter says.

Ellie shakes her head. 'No, but I suppose, that's how it goes.'

They join Rita who impatiently moves about as the

first passengers start to come through the exit doors. After some time the couple they have been waiting for emerges from the rest of the passengers. Mr Visser smiles when he sees Rita. His wife is a bit hesitant.

Eagerly Rita shakes the proffered hand. 'Oh. Oh, it's so good to see you, Father,' Rita says. She takes Ellie by her arm and pulls her closer. 'Look, this is Ellie. Hasn't she grown? Look Mother. This is Ellie.'

Mr Visser shakes Ellie's hand. 'What a pretty girl you are,' he says.

Pieter, who had kept a distance, moves closer and with an uneasy smile takes his mother's hand.

'Hello Mother.'

Mrs Visser looks at him with disbelief. 'Oh, oh Pieter ... It is you. I said to your father "that looks like Pieter", but he didn't want to believe me.'

Now Mr Visser turns his way. 'Pieter,' he utters softly. 'My boy.'

'Hello Father,' Pieter says and reaches for his father's hand, but the gesture finds no emulation.

'Pieter,' he utters once more and suddenly in a cheery, loud tone as if to convince his wife: 'It's Pieter! Boy, how ... look Mother.'

Mrs Visser just smiles, tears welling up in her eyes. Pieter pinches her hand that he is still holding. Ellie looks a bit uneasy at the sight of all that gladness.

'See, how good it is to see Opa and Oma,' Rita says and puts her arm around her daughter's shoulders.

'He looks so much like ... like Klaas ... Doesn't he, Mother?' Mr Visser says.

Rita lets go of Ellie and takes her mother-in-law by the arm. 'I think we should go, it's still an awfully long drive, and you must be tired.'

Pieter walks arm in arm with his mother with Rita on

the other side. Mr Visser and Ellie follow in their wake.
'Pieter does resemble Klaas a lot now,' Mr Visser
remarks. 'Don't you think so, or don't you remember your
father.'

'Oh yeah ... It's just that I never thought of it that
way.'

'And look at you. I wouldn't have recognised you
even if you would have passed me by in the street.'

Ellie shrugs her shoulders and glances around her in a
shy way.

'Are you still in school?'

'Uh, no. I've just finished, but I want to study more.'

'Oh, I wouldn't worry about that too much,' Mr
Visser says. 'You'll get married soon.'

Casually Ellie avoids her grandfather and stays
behind as they move through the crowds to find the car.
With a bit of contriving they all five fit in there, the two
men in front and the women in the back, as they embark
on their long journey home.

The following morning, the kitchen is filled with the smell
of freshly baked cake. Sunrays creep through the window
and onto the counter where Rita is just pouring hot water
in the teapot when Ellie enters. She wipes a hand over her
sleepy face. Still in her nightclothes, she sits down at the
table. 'Morn', Ma.'

'Morning,' Rita says. 'Don't you want to get dressed
first?'

'Why?'

Rita looks at her daughter and then turns to take some
cups out of the cupboard. 'Well, we do have guests now, I
think it's no more than decent.'

'Come on Mum. It's not the first time we've had
people staying and me walking around in my shorty

pyjamas.'

Rita sighs and calmly puts the cups and teapot on the table. 'Well, they *are* your grandparents,' she says as she checks the cake. 'They're not used to folks having their breakfast in nightclothes.'

'Well, they're in New Zealand now. They better get used to New Zealand ways,' Ellie replies with a faint irritation in her voice.

'Ellie ... ' her mother endeavours.

Ellie picks up the teapot and starts pouring.

'Where's Uncle Pieter?' she asks. 'I thought I heard his car.'

'Gone off again to get a paper and some more eggs. He's going to show Opa and Oma around a bit today. Would you like to come?'

'No ... Not really,' she replies and scoops some sugar into her cup. 'I'm still recovering from yesterday's ride.'

Rita takes the cake out of the oven, shakes it out of the baking tin and puts it down to cool. She then sits next to her daughter to drink her tea.

Stumbling in the hall indicates the guests have ended their first night's sleep in the strange country. Soon after, the toilet flushes and Dutch conversation starts coming from the bathroom. Ellie and her mother can't help but eavesdrop on account of their somewhat noisy home. They giggle at the remarks that are made about their house.

'You won't find that in Holland,' Ellie imitates her grandfather's loud voice.

Not long after Opa Visser enters the kitchen, with his wife following hot on his heels.

'Morning all,' he says.

The warm weather yesterday has made him not wear his jacket today, even the tie had to make way. Oma

Visser has followed Rita's advice and is wearing a thin, flowery summer frock but her straight and tight waistline shows the obvious signs of a corset underneath. Reservedly she follows her husband's example and sits down at the table. 'Morning,' she says in a soft voice.

'Morning. What would you like for breakfast?' Rita wants to know. 'I've made a Dundee cake and you could have toast.'

The couple looks around the breakfast-table. 'Oh, just bread will do, with some cheese,' Opa Visser answers at the recognition of the familiar products. Ellie picks up the teapot and pours them tea.

'Thank you, dear,' Oma Visser says.

Opa Visser takes a slice of bread and reaches for the butter as Oma Visser adds some milk and sugar to their tea.

'It's all so strange,' she says as she takes her cup. Rita slices the cake and puts it on the table. 'Here, try this,' she says.

'What is that,' Opa Visser asks.

'Dundee cake,' Ellie answers and takes a piece.

'Dun ... ' Opa Visser says, 'dun what?'

'Cake, Father,' Rita replies. 'Have a piece.'

Opa Visser finishes his bread and grabs a slice off the plate. He looks at it and then smells it.

'You can eat it with butter if you like,' Rita says.

Mr Visser casts a critical look at the piece of cake in his hand. 'We don't eat cake for breakfast in Holland,' he says.

Ellie looks at her grandfather with a reproachful expression in her eyes.

'Do you want it?' Opa Visser asks his wife and hands her the slice of cake.

'I will try, it looks nice.'

Oma Visser hesitantly spreads some butter on the cake and takes a bite. Opa Visser cuts off some more cheese to put on his next slice of bread.

'Tasty,' is oma Visser's reaction. 'Do you buy it at the baker's shop?'

'No,' Opa Visser says in his loud voice while he takes another bite, 'she made it herself, she just said so.'

'Oh ... but it is nice,' Oma Visser says. 'Did you bake it specially?'

'No,' Ellie replies, slightly irritated. 'Mum always bakes everything herself, also the bread.'

Opa Visser seems surprised and has another look at what is in front of him. 'Mm,' he mutters under his breath. 'She never baked in Holland.'

Rita sits quietly and finishes her tea. 'Better put some clothes on, Ellie,' she says in a soft voice; unlike her when they're together, in the English language. With a sigh, Ellie gets up and goes to the bathroom to freshen up.

'Does she always come for breakfast in her nightclothes?' Opa Visser enquires in an interrogative manner after Ellie has left. But before Rita can reply, Oma Visser wonders about Pieter.

'He'll be back soon,' Rita says. 'He wants to show you around today. It's good you put on something airy for it will be hot today.'

'I would love to meet little Ursula,' Oma Visser says.

'Oh, she's not at home,' Rita replies. 'She's with her aunt in Auckland at the moment.'

'Thank God,' Opa Visser mumbles with his mouth full.

An uncomfortable silence dominates the room while they continue their breakfast. They're almost finished when there's the sound of a car pulling up outside. A few moments later Pieter enters, clad in shorts and a short-sleeved shirt. 'Slept well?' he asks his parents.

He puts the eggs in the refrigerator and takes a cup to pour himself some tea. Mr Visser lets his eyes run up and down the attire of his son.

'Oh, we had a good rest,' Oma Visser says. 'We only feel a bit out of our element, still.'

'Do you always walk around like that?' Opa Visser asks Pieter with some disapproval. The latter glances at Rita who has started to clear the table. 'Well, uhm – ' Pieter commences.

'Do you want to eat something still, Pieter?' Rita interrupts him.

'Yeah, fine. Pop some bread in the toaster, thanks.'

He turns to his mother: 'I think I'll take you over to William and Grace's. I worked for them when I first came out here. Rita did too. They're good people, you'll like them.'

'Is that far?' his father asks.

'No, not too far,' Pieter replies as Rita gives him his toast and places the butter and jam in front of him.

'I have my property there as well. You can have a look there too.'

'I could make you some eggs, if you like,' Rita addresses Pieter.

'No, I'm alright, thanks. Better get ready. Is Ellie coming?'

Oma Visser gets up, wondering if Rita needs a hand but Rita won't hear of it. She calls out to Ellie that they'll be leaving soon.

Ellie, wearing her shorts and sleeveless top, strolls outside to see the rest of the family off. She observes Opa Visser opening the front door of the car on the right side and intending to get in.

'Do you want to drive today?' Pieter asks him.

Puzzled, his father looks at the wheel. 'Oh, hell. I forgot you drive on the wrong side.' He promptly closes the door and walks around to the other side. Pieter re-opens the car door to sit behind the wheel.

Ellie watches them all get into the car and waves at them from the veranda when they drive off.

Inside the car, Opa Visser turns his head to address Rita. 'I don't see why you let your daughter walk around like that,' he condemns. 'Hardly any clothes on.'

'That's how they dress here, Father,' Pieter replies. 'It's too hot to wear a lot of things.'

'Yeah, look at you,' Opa Visser criticises. 'You can hardly say otherwise, can you?'

Pieter steers the car onto the main road and points out to his mother the hall where the women of the town do their quilt making once a week.

'I'll take you there one day, if you like,' Rita tells her mother-in-law. The latter seems surprised.

'Is that allowed?' she wonders. 'Don't you have to be a member?'

'No, it's fine. They love it when people come to have a look. They sell them too, you know.'

Oma Visser nods approvingly. 'That's nice,' she says.

'Fields are dry,' Opa Visser comments and points at the arid fields where cattle are trying to find green succulents. 'They can have some of our rain.'

Oma Visser laughs at that remark. 'Do you get any rain in this country?' she asks.

'Oh yeah,' is Pieter's reply, 'but the hot weather dries the land up real quick.'

'We had a lot of rain ... uh, two weeks ago,' Rita explains. 'Didn't we, Pieter?'

Oma Visser takes a roll of peppermints out of her purse and offers Rita one. 'From Holland,' she says, 'nice against a dry mouth.'

'Oh, thank you,' Rita says.

'A shame Ellie didn't come with us,' Oma Visser continues and hands the peppermints to her husband in front of her, 'but I suppose she would rather go out with people her own age.'

'She was a bit tired still,' Rita states.

'I was saying to Father last night who she resembles,' Oma Visser goes on. 'She doesn't look like Klaas.'

Rita sits back and folds her hands in her lap. 'Well, people say she looks like me,' she replies.

Oma Visser faces sideways to have a closer inspection of Rita's features and makes an agreeing sound. 'Apart from the hair,' Oma adds.

William and Grace's farm is only an hour and a half away but to Mr Visser, it seems like another boat journey all the way from Europe and he inquires of his son what his idea of "not too far" is.

Shortly, they enter a gate and drive up the gravel road to the house, leaving a trail of dust clouds behind them. The house is surrounded by trees, which partly clothe the dwelling in a blanket of shade. Pieter honks his horn when he notices William, way in the field.

Grace appears on the veranda where some children are frolicking about with a ballgame. As soon as the car comes to a halt Rita steps out and warmly greets Grace who has come down from the veranda.

'What a surprise,' Grace says cheerfully and hugs Rita. 'Hi, Pieter, how are you today?'

'Fine, thanks,' Pieter replies and walks to the fence to meet William.

'Look Grace, these are Pieter's parents,' Rita says.

Mrs Visser comes closer to meet Grace. Mr Visser doesn't seem to know where to turn and looks out at Pieter.

'No English … ' Mrs Visser explains as Grace and she shake each other's hand.

'That's alright,' Grace says, 'Rita will translate. So you came all the way from Holland? Long journey.'

Opa and Oma Visser follow Rita and Grace into the house while talking to each other in Dutch. The children look up at them, making tittering sounds with their little hands over their mouths.

In the kitchen Grace starts tending to her unexpected guests. 'We had Ellie visiting last week,' she says with some pride, 'it was lovely to see her.'

Rita motions the elderly couple to sit down. 'Yes, she really enjoyed that,' Rita replies, 'she'd wanted to go for some time.'

'So, what do you think of New Zealand?' Grace asks the Vissers.

Mr Visser looks at his wife. 'What does she say?' he asks.

'She wants to know what you think of New Zealand,' Rita answers.

'Oh. Oh, yes, uhh, a bit hot,' Mr Visser says in his best English and blows out a gasp of breath as if he's very warm. Grace smiles and pours the boiling water into the teapot. 'I hope they won't mind a hot drink,' she tells Rita.

'Ellie is a good friend of Chrissie's, William and Grace's daughter,' Rita explains to her in-laws. 'Chrissie got married a few months ago and also lives in Taihape.'

Mrs Visser smiles at Grace with some kind of familiarity. 'They have a son too,' Rita goes on. 'Jody, but he's away now, in the services.'

Footsteps stumble onto the veranda and a moment later Pieter and William enter the kitchen. William nods his head at the strange visitors. 'Pieter's parents, aye,' he says and sits down at the table. Pieter hands Rita some flowers. 'These were still in the car.'

'Oh, completely forgot,' Rita says and gets up. 'I brought some flowers for you, Grace, from the garden. I'll put them in water straight away.'

'Oh, they are lovely,' Grace says admiringly. 'My favourite roses.'

With the men at the one end of the table and the women at the other end, they soon engage in familiar conversation. Oma Visser occasionally asks Rita what's being said while Opa Visser listens intently to the men discussing the problems on the farm.

'Is it going well here?' Mr Visser finally gathers some nerve to ask his son as the party follow William outside to one of the paddocks. 'I listened to you talking but I didn't understand a word.'

'Oh, there were some problems with disease,' Pieter replies, 'we lost a few.'

'Cows?' Mr Visser wants to know.

'Yes, Father. This is a dairy farm.'

'Yes, I know that,' Mr Visser says defensively.

William opens the gate and they go into the paddock. The dogs that caught up with them, slip through their legs and make a run for it.

'Do you want me to go in here too, Pieter?' his mother asks him as she looks at her good shoes and the dry mud in front of her.

'If you like,' Pieter says.

'I'll get my shoes all dirty,' Mrs Visser says.

'Don't whine woman,' Mr Visser says.

'You can stay here, with the women, Mother,' Pieter suggests, 'and we'll drive down to my house later.'

That sounds more appealing to Mrs Visser and she makes her way back to the house.

'Don't you have problems now with the milk production?' Mr Visser asks Pieter.

'What do you mean?' Pieter asks.

'Well, with these sick cows.'

'The sick ones are gone,' Pieter says.

Mr Visser becomes slightly impatient. 'Yes, but wasn't it contagious, for the rest of them?' he questions.

'No,' Pieter replies

William points in the distance. 'They broke through the bloody fence back there,' he mutters to Pieter.

'Where? Over there?' Pieter mumbles back. He wipes some of his blond hair off his sweaty forehead and puts his hat back on.

'Yeah ... Bloody broke the fence poles too.'

Mr Visser tries to make out what they are saying but has to resort to Pieter for an explanation. 'Was there an accident?' he asks.

'No, the fence is broken.'

'Hell. Did they have burglars?' his father wants to know.

'No, Father,' Pieter replies, 'it's only the fence, it needs fixing.'

The dogs wait patiently at the entrance of the milking-shed and follow William as he goes in. Two farmhands are busy clearing the shed of some equipment. William starts explaining the way his husbandry works and with Pieter translating it soon meets with Mr Visser's approval.

On the veranda, the women have made themselves comfortable to have a cool drink as the children are enjoying their lemonade. With some enthusiastic arm movements, Mrs Visser tries to explain to Grace what a nice house they're living in.

'Yes, yes it is a comfortable home,' Grace admits and hands them their drinks.

'And the garden, so nice,' the older woman says in her Dutch language, to Rita's amusement who finds Grace's understanding of Oma Visser's sign language rather amazing.

Oma Visser waves her hand in front of her face to keep the warmth off.

'You shouldn't have worn that corset,' Rita remarks.

Oma Visser looks at her with a startled face. 'Oh, does it show?!'

'Mother,' Rita says calmly, 'for as long as I've known you, you've worn one, but you don't need it here.'

'Of course I do!' is the reply. 'Where will I connect my stockings to if I don't wear my corset?!'

Rita lifts her skirt slightly and shows off her bare calves. 'See, you don't need to wear stockings in these temperatures.'

'I cannot do that,' Mrs Visser replies. 'It's not done! Besides, I need it to support my back. My back is not that strong anymore like you young ones',' she justifies herself.

Rita smiles as her eyes stray to the men who are coming back from the field. Mr Visser seems to be having problems with the hot weather, wiping the sweat from his face with his handkerchief. When they have reached the veranda he jadedly drops himself in one of the chairs while the dogs seek the shade underneath. As Pieter pulls up another chair William goes in to get a few cold beers. 'You found it interesting?' Rita asks Opa Visser.

'Oh, yes. But it gets so damn hot here.'

As soon as William has handed Pieter his beer one of

the children crawls onto Pieter's lap and tries to get a sip of the beer, but Pieter won't let him.

'Will you be staying for lunch?' Grace inquires while they are finishing their drinks.

'No. Thanks Grace. I'll take them over to my place,' Pieter replies as he puts the child on the floor. 'Shall we go?'

Mr Visser looks at his wife and reluctantly rises from his comfortable spot. Mrs Visser follows his example. She shakes Grace's hand and thanks her for their hospitality. They say their goodbyes and with the children in their wake, they walk to Pieter's car. Rita thanks William and Grace while the children badger Pieter to take them for a drive.

'Hey, you kids,' William calls out, 'go play your own games.' The children get off the car and stand to watch the guests get in.

'Next time, don't wait so long to call!' Grace cries out as they drive off.

'Come to town Grace, come visit us one day,' Rita calls back and waves at her.

In a cloud of dust, Pieter drives the old Ford to the road that leads to his farm. His father next to him opens the car window to let the breeze in.

《　》

It must have been just after my fifth birthday. I had already gone to sleep but something had woken me. I crawled out of bed to ask my mammie for some water. When I quietly walked along the lit landing, I heard my mother and father arguing. Clutching onto the balustrade I went down the stairs when all of a sudden Papa yelled out. The sound was so loud it almost made me lose my balance.

Halfway down I sat on one of the steps and peeked through the balustrade. The living room door was ajar and I could see my father making wild movements with his arms, with my mother trying to outscream him. Mammie yelled he was drunk, but I didn't know what that was then. Papa was yelling back at her in such an unfamiliar, strange voice it frightened me.

A loud noise of something breaking made me shrink back.

Another horrible scream blew out and the door flew open. Papa staggered out and made his way to the kitchen door. When the door was slammed, the breaking of glass sounded.

Trembling, I sat there in the eerie silence that had descended inside the house. Waiting, for my mother to appear. It wasn't until I heard a soft moaning coming from the living room, I dared to get up and carefully move down the stairs. With caution, I entered the room. My mother was lying on the floor as if she had fallen asleep right there and then. I started shaking her and calling for her. She moaned a few times and then, to my relief, she opened her eyes. I remember asking her why she was sleeping on the floor. Slowly she got up and I saw some red stuff on the carpet. I put my finger in it, but Mammie told me off. She held her hand at the back of her head and went to the kitchen. I went after her. The curtain was waving because of the wind blowing through the broken window.

'Why was Papa yelling?' I asked her, hanging on to her skirt.

'Papa is a bit upset, he doesn't know what he's doing,' she answered. She put a wet cloth against her head.

'He broke things,' I told her.

'That's alright, sweetie,' she said. 'Papa is clever, he can fix it again.' My mammie was right. Papa was clever. He made toys for me, the nicest toys in the whole street. Many children came to play with me because they liked my toys so much. And once papa fixed my doll that had lost an arm. 'When is Papa coming back?' I asked her.

'Go to bed,' she said. 'I have to clean up this mess.'

'But, Papa – '

'Go to bed, Ellie. I don't have time for that now,' she said as she began to wipe up the glass. 'Or do you want your papa to cut his feet when he comes back!'

I didn't want to upset my mother so I did what I was told, but I didn't sleep well because I was worried about my father not being home.

The next morning the window was all pasted up with cardboard so Papa must have come back to fix it. Mammie said he had gone out when I asked her where he was.

She took me with her to the doctor's a few days later because her head kept aching, so I told her she should not have slept on the floor, that's too hard. She couldn't leave me at home she said, because there was no one there to look after me and Papa had gone out again.

Mammie had to rest a lot after that and I was sent to stay with a neighbour. I didn't like that because the lady was old but she had a dog I could play with. My mother didn't want me having a dog. The cat that Papa had brought home one day had gone to live at another house after a while. That's what my mother had said.

When I came back from the neighbour's I was relieved to find my papa was home, but he didn't pick me up like he always did and he didn't call me his favourite girl. I asked him if he was still upset but he said he wasn't. So I asked him if he was angry with me because Mammie had been ill and he said that had nothing to do with me.

That summer we went to visit Oma and Opa.
Mammie said I had been to their house when I was a baby
but I only remember them of the few times they came to
visit us. Papa's sister was having a party because she was
going to get married soon. My mother made me a new
dress and she said I looked like a princess when I tried it
on.
Opa and Oma lived in a big farmhouse with a stable
at the back. In the winter the cows used to be there. Now
they were grazing in the meadow. There were not as many
cows as before, a friendly man told us, because, in the
war, the Germans ate them all. I remember asking him if
they were hungry and the man started laughing. 'No,' he
said. It was because the Germans were bad people; they
stole a lot of things from our country. Then he turned to
my mother and asked if she had told me anything about
the war. Mammie shook her head and said that that was in
the past and pulled me along to have something to drink.
The friendly man was the fiancé of Papa's sister, my
mother explained. She said it would be nice for me to stay
with them when they were married for they would be the
only aunt and uncle I had then.
It was a fine sunny day so we were all outside to have
cake and coffee. I was the only child there so I sat on the
grass and played with my doll. They were talking about
some new country. I looked up when Mammie and Papa
said they should go there. Oma wasn't pleased but Opa
said it was a lot better than staying in Holland where Papa
could not find work. My aunt looked at me and said with a
smile she would take me to live with them. But I didn't
like that and jumped up.
I grabbed on to my papa, but he said to go to my

mother.

Oma was sad when she heard that my mother and father wanted to go away. She held on tightly to my aunt's arm. Opa told her not to be so childish. She should want what was best for her children. I asked Mammie if I had to stay alone in our house when they left but she smiled.

'Of course not, you're coming with us,' she said.

On the bus, on the way home Mammie and Papa were talking about moving to this new country. I told Papa I didn't want to go because all my playmates lived here.

He said to be quiet so I sat still, holding on to my doll and looking out of the window. I saw cows in the meadows. These bad people probably only ate Opa's.

2

I remember well the day I arrived in this new country, only six years old, clutching on to my mother's hand. I remember the warmth of the sun when I, still unsteady on my feet after the long boat journey, moved off the ship. There seemed to be a rush for my mother was pulling me by the hand hissing through her teeth to hurry along. We came to a big hall and there were a lot of people milling around. Looking up at all these strange people, I only saw one I recognised from the boat. I started feeling very tired for we had to wait a long time. I sat down on a crate that, like me, seemed to be lost. My mother told me not to move from there. She said she was going to collect our bags. I just sat there between all those busy people passing by me. I did not dare to get up, afraid my mother wouldn't find me anymore when she came back. When she finally showed up, I felt very relieved. I took hold of her skirt when we went to leave the hall because she needed both her hands to carry our bags.

There was a man standing by the exit doors, peering through the crowds. He seemed to recognise us for he was waving and had a big smile on his face. When we were outside on the quay he picked me up and said he was so pleased to see us. He tickled me on my side, but I looked at my mother with fright. I didn't like him then, he spoke Dutch with a funny accent. He gave my mother a big kiss on her cheek, again saying how glad he was. My mother looked pleased.

'You will have to learn English now, little one,' the man with the funny accent said. He grinned at me.

'That is your uncle, sweetie,' my mother explained. 'You know, I told you about him. Papa's younger brother.'

The uncle didn't look like my papa at all. Papa had dark hair.

All of a sudden I missed my father terribly and wished he was there with us. 'Where is Papa, Mammie?' I remember asking my mother. The uncle put me down. I looked up at my mother. She didn't say a word but took me by the hand. 'Come, we will go with Uncle Pieter now,' she said. Holding my mother's hand, I looked up from one to the other and did not understand why neither of them would tell me where my father was. I looked over my shoulder when we moved away from the last thing that had been familiar to me.

This country appeared strange, the surroundings looked like something out of a book a man on the boat had shown us. On the boat, where people had spoken the language I understood.

Just before we had to go into a car I saw my friend Annie. We had been almost inseparable on the boat. I started yelling out to her. She turned. I called out her name again and pulled towards her but my mother grabbed me by the arm.

'We have to go now, Ellie,' she said. I tried to explain to her that I wanted to talk to my friend but she was unrelenting. 'We have to go now,' she said once more.

Annie looked at me, smiling, holding on to her parents. Like us, they were with some stranger. The uncle lifted me and put me in the car. As we drove past I despairingly waved at the only friend I'd had for many weeks. Tears filled my eyes when I looked out of the rear window and saw Annie's sad eyes looking back at me. I knew then that I would never see her again.

Sitting in the backseat I saw treetops quickly moving

by. There were no houses. I wondered where all the people were. My mother didn't seem to notice there was no one living here. She was too busy talking and laughing with this new uncle of mine. Who was I going to play with? Annie was gone and there seemed to be no children living in this country.

I suddenly felt all alone.

I wished we had never left Holland.

We should never have left at all. We hadn't even looked for my father. He should have been here with us.

I don't know how far we drove that day. I was lifted out of the car when darkness had fallen. I heard my mother whisper that we had arrived. She carried me into a house, the uncle behind her with our suitcases.

We went into a room where she put me on a bed. She undressed me and put the covers over me.

Sunrays beating down on my eyelids woke me the next morning. I turned my head and saw my mother lying next to me. She was fast asleep. I always knew when she was, for she had her mouth slightly open then. Silently I crawled out of the bed and went to the window. Looking through it, I saw I had been right, there was nothing out there. Everything was bare. Nobody did live here.

We were all alone.

Disappointed I put on the dress that my mother had folded over the chair the night before and went to see where Uncle Pieter had gone.

Cautiously I opened the door and peeped through. There was a hallway and I was surprised to hear voices. Following the sound, the smell of freshly baked bread came my way. All of a sudden I realised how hungry I was and tried to remember when I had last eaten. I remember my mother giving Annie and me a large apple not long before we were separated on the boat and I had wondered how she had come by it. We hadn't seen an apple tree for weeks.

Watchful, I looked around the room. Strange faces turned my way. There was no sign of Uncle Pieter.

A tall woman with a friendly smile stood by a stove and said something to me I couldn't understand. The man at the table had a big grin on his face.

'I want Uncle Pieter,' I told them.

Again they spoke in a strange language. The woman came towards me and took my hand. She motioned me to sit at the table. I felt afraid and ran out, back to the familiarity of the bedroom, but my mother was still sound asleep. I sat down in the chair and wondered if I should wake her to tell her about those strange people and that Uncle Pieter had disappeared, just like Papa.

Sadness overcame me.

I don't know how long I'd been sitting there when there was a knock on the door. Relieved, I jumped to my feet when it appeared that Uncle Pieter was still here. The one who would understand me. He picked me up and tickled me. This time I didn't mind.

'I see your mother is still asleep. She was very tired last night. And how about you?' Uncle Pieter said.

'Who are all those strange people?' I asked.

'The ones in the kitchen? They are Grace and William. I work for them.'

'Do we have to live here now?' I wanted to know.

'For the time being, yes. Your mother has a job here until you two get settled.'

I looked at him. 'Why isn't Papa with us?'

He put me down. 'You must be starving,' he said. 'Come, Grace has made a wonderful big breakfast.'

He took my hand. 'You will like Grace. She is very

kind. Have you met the children yet?'

I looked up at him in amazement. There were children here? Now I would have someone to play with.

In the kitchen, Uncle Pieter lifted me onto a chair. The kind woman put a plate with bread in front of me and said something in her strange language. The grinning man was gone.

'You will learn English soon enough,' Uncle Pieter said to me. He drank his coffee and pointed out what I was eating.

'Cheese,' he said in this strange language, 'and this is "bread", almost the same as in Dutch: 'brood.'

He must have noticed the sad look in my eyes for he smiled at me and said I would soon love this country once I got used to it. 'And you will go to school soon. There you will learn the language and in no time you will speak it better than I do.' He smiled and took a few slices off the plate. 'I will prepare some bread for your mother, she'll want something to eat when she wakes up,' he said.

Uncle Pieter had been right. We must have only been in this country for a few weeks and I could speak to anyone in their language as if I'd always lived here. I heard Grace once tell my mother how quickly I had picked up the language. She'd never seen that happen before.

My mother seemed to be happy here and had lots to do on the farm helping Grace with all sorts of things.

During the day I went to school with the other children who lived on the farm. There was another Dutch girl at school. I loved talking to her, but she had never heard of Annie. She had been here a year she said.

When I was alone I missed my papa and wondered where he was but my mother always avoided my questions when I asked and Uncle Pieter didn't seem to know. One night I heard my mother and Uncle Pieter talking of my papa and about how bad the war had been for him. I wasn't born then so I didn't ask my mother about that because I didn't want to upset her.

I always had a lot of fun when Uncle Pieter took us and the other children to visit the town. When we had collected the groceries we all went for ice creams. I only ever had ice cream once before when we were still in Holland.

I found it even stranger that it was going to be Christmas soon because it was summer, but my mother said it would only be Christmas after Saint Nicholas had been. I found that strange, too, because how was Saint Nicholas going to find us on his grey?

Holland was very far away.

One night we went to see the Dutch family and found that Saint Nicholas had brought the presents to their house. I was very happy that night, knowing that even though my mother and I were in this far away country, Saint Nicholas still had managed to find us and bring us gifts.

I was certain that my papa must have told him.
One day before Christmas William came home with a big tree that he had chopped down in the forest. Chrissie, Jody and I sat down one afternoon in the shade of a large tree to make colourful decorations to put on the Christmas tree that evening.

Grace lit some candles and Uncle Pieter took me on his lap and made me sing Dutch Christmas songs. I didn't want to at first but everybody seemed so happy to listen that I didn't mind.

Later that evening I told my mother that I wanted Papa to be with us and that I wanted him to come and live with us. He would like this country very much for I remember him taking me to the beach one day when it was very warm -that was before we had to go on the boat- and he told me how much he liked the sunny weather. I remember everybody in the room fell very quiet after I'd asked her and Grace telling my mother she shouldn't keep it from me any longer.

That night before I went to sleep my mother told me that my papa was no longer with us. That he had gone to heaven, that he was with the angels now, just like Jesus. I asked her why he hadn't told me before he left but she didn't know. He'd probably forgotten, she said, because he had gone so suddenly.

Ever since that day I always talked to my papa before I went to sleep just like I talked to Jesus sometimes.

I wasn't the only child in the world without a daddy but there were days when I felt very sad about him not being there. One day I didn't feel well and was allowed to stay home from school. With all the others working and no one to play with, I, barefooted, wandered off in the field leading up the hill. My mother had told me to wear my shoes that day because of my cold but I didn't like shoes on my feet. None of the children here wore shoes very often, only when it began to be too cold and I had told my mother that we were not in Holland. She became a bit upset with me then and put the shoes on my feet herself but I had taken them off and hidden them when she had gone back to her chores.

Some curious cows followed me up the hill. I picked some flowers that were lining the field, pretty bright yellow and white ones. At the top, I climbed a fence and ended up in the forest. There was an open spot where I sometimes went to when I wanted to be by myself. It was my special place no one knew about.

The soil was moist beneath my feet as I walked along. I reached the grassy sunny patch and took the photo of my daddy that my mother had given me, out of my skirt pocket. I sat down in the middle of the patch and let the sun warm my skin. Protected by the surrounding trees, their tops slowly waving in the breeze, I placed Daddy's photo in front of me and put the pretty flowers around him. I then sang to him, a song he always liked me singing, about the goblin sitting on a toadstool until it breaks and the goblin goes "hoopla!" with his little legs in the air.

When I used to do "hoopla!" I threw my arms in the air and jumped. My daddy always burst out laughing when I did that.

But this time it didn't work, not really. His eyes in the picture kept their same expression, his mouth showed the same wan smile. I gently brushed my finger over the face in the photograph and tried to remember my daddy's happy laughter. I lay down and closed my eyes. With the sun's warmth on my face and my daddy safe beside me I imagined us on that beach in Holland walking barefoot along the tide-line. My daddy had his trousers and shirtsleeves rolled up and held my hand as I reached for pretty shells. He knelt beside me to admire them. I still remember his smiling eyes at my keenness. In thought, I smiled back at him and with the sound of the surf in my ears I dozed off to sleep.

I was already wet through when I realised it was the rain that had woken me. I jumped up and looked at the dark clouds above me. All of a sudden I remembered Daddy's photograph. It was lying there in the wet grass, raindrops all over Daddy's face. I quickly reached for it and picked it up. Then I started running through the fierce rain, climbed the fence and ran down the hill, through the paddock and into the yard. Shivering, I entered the kitchen where Grace was standing by the stove, cooking.

'Child!' she shrieked. 'Look at you!' She wiped her hands on her apron and grabbed me by the arm. 'Do you want to die of pneumonia! Quick, get out of those wet clothes.'

'Where is my mother?' I asked.

'Be glad your mother doesn't see you like this,' she said as we marched towards the bathroom. 'She's found your shoes, you know.'

She turned on the tap to let the bathtub run full of warm water. 'Take off those wet clothes,' she demanded.

I put Daddy's photo on the windowsill and swiftly did what I was told.

'Now, you get into that water and don't come out until you're warm all through again, and then you are going to spend some time in your bed, young lady,' she said, shaking her finger warningly.

She grabbed the wet clothes off the floor and marched back to the kitchen.

That evening I woke to find my mother sitting on the side of my bed. She was holding Daddy's picture.

'I'm afraid it's a bit wrinkled up, because of the rain.'

She always spoke Dutch when we were by ourselves or with Uncle Pieter.

'Well,' she sighed, 'I suppose we could keep it between a book.'

She looked at me. 'Papa wouldn't have liked what you did today, going against my will.'

I felt bad when she said that. I pushed myself up on my pillow. 'I'm sorry, Mummy. I didn't mean to.'

There was silence for a while with my mother

looking at the photograph.

'How did Daddy die, Mummy?'

She sighed and for a moment I thought she wouldn't tell me. 'Accident,' she said and turned to me. 'A very bad accident. That's why we thought it would be better for you not to know about it at first. It would have only upset you more.'

I remembered I was sent away for a couple of days to stay with a friend of Mum's when we were still in Holland.

'Would Daddy have come with us if he hadn't died?'

Mum paused for a while. 'He was meant to come. We were supposed to go together, Papa, you and I.'

She stood up. 'Are you hungry? Would you like Mummy to get you something?'

《 》

When the heat has been chased away by cool evening breezes, whiffs of air carry the spicy scent of honeysuckle and the smell of sweet roses. The small house is surrounded by twilight when Pieter and Rita enter the garden and stroll through the sound of chirring cicadas up the veranda. Pieter pulls up a few chairs and sits down.

'I'll make us some tea,' Rita says. Pieter leans back in his chair and yawns. 'Good idea,' he says, only to seize Rita by her arm as she wants to go through the door. She looks him in the eyes until he lets go.

'Yes,' he says, 'a cup of tea will be fine.'
A subtle secretive smile is showing on Rita's face as she goes in. A moment later followed by Pieter.

He moves up behind her and lets his hands slide around her waist as she reaches for the cups. She silently gasps for breath as he strokes her breasts. Gently he kisses her on the neck. His hands search for the buttons on her blouse and start undoing them. Rita turns to face him.

'Not here, Pieter,' she sighs but he caresses her cheek and kisses her lips.

She can no longer resist his arousing ways and she eagerly accepts his passionate kisses. Pieter leads her into the hallway and opens the door to her room.

'This good enough for ya ?' he asks mischievously.

'Well … It has to do,' she says with a giggle and starts undoing his trousers.

With his feelings kindled he grasps her and kisses her passionately. Clothes whirl to the floor and soon they find themselves on the bed, between the cool sheets, which do nothing to quench the fire of their lovemaking.

The room is darkened when Rita opens her eyes. She lets her hand search for the body beside her. She turns and finds Pieter's face close to hers. He is fast asleep. Softly she places a kiss on his lips and slides out of bed. She drapes her dressing gown around her naked body and walks to the kitchen where she switches on the light. The kettle is still steaming on the stove and Rita quickly removes it. It makes a sizzling sound when she pours cold water in it. Humming a song, she places it back on the stove. She is just scooping some tea out of the jar when the sound of footsteps on the veranda makes her turn around. Amazed, she looks at her daughter walking in.

'Hi Mum.'

'Uh, hi dear,' Rita replies as her eyes drift to the open hall door. 'What are you doing here?'

Surprised, Ellie looks at her mother. 'I live here, remember?'

'No, no that's not what I mean,' Rita replies as she casually closes the door to the hall. 'But I thought you were spending the night with friends.'

'I said I *might* stay at Chrissie's,' Ellie corrects her mother. 'but, why are you making tea in the middle of the night?'

Rita looks at the clock. 'Oh, is it that late already? Well, I was just thirsty. Would you care for a cuppa as well?'

'Sure, now that you've made some,' Ellie says and sits down at the table. 'Oh, look, Uncle Pieter forgot his hat.'

'What?!'

'God Mum. You're edgy tonight,' Ellie says, putting the hat on her head. 'We had such a laugh, Mum. You wouldn't believe. I really needed that after we had those old grumps staying here.'

'Ellie! Don't talk about Opa and Oma like that,' Rita rebukes her, putting the tea on the table.

'Well, they weren't exactly your average pacemakers, but it was lovely to see how Oma liked to be with Pieter, aye Mum.'

'Yes, that really cheered Pieter up,' Rita says and takes a sip. 'It did his heart good.'

'But those weird remarks about Uschi,' Ellie says. 'That really put me off.'

Rita agrees. 'As if she can help it that she has some German blood in her. Well, I suppose Pieter was right about them being prejudiced.'

'Yeah, Opa is a bit crazy,' Ellie says while she examines the inside of her cup as if to check the level of the tea. 'When will they be back?' she asks.

'Oh, I think Father mentioned something about two, three weeks. Depends on how long those friends in Auckland can put up with them, I suppose.'

'Mm,' is Ellie's reply. She gets up and empties her

cup in the sink. 'I shouldn't have too much of this or I'll be up all night to pee.'

Rita follows her example. 'Yes, bedtime.'

'Did you wash those pink shorty pj's today, Mum?' Ellie asks as they walk into the hallway.

'No dear. I didn't do any washing today.'

'Oh well, then I need to borrow some of yours for I'm not wearing that other sweaty thing again,' Ellie says and grabs the door handle to her mother's bedroom.

'I ... I ... I'll get it for you,' Rita is quick to say and gently pushes her daughter aside. 'You run the tub, alright?'

Ellie looks slightly surprised at her mother's reaction but does not oppose her. Rita holds the door closed until Ellie is inside the bathroom. She then enters the room, swiftly takes a nightgown from her wardrobe and takes it to Ellie. After they have said their goodnights Rita goes back into her room and locks the door behind her. With a relieved sigh she takes off her dressing gown and crawls between the sheets to nestle herself in the warmth of Pieter's body.

In the quiet of the morning, the sun silently sends her gleaming rays over the range in the distance and radiating lines stream through the bushes in the garden that is occupied by chirping birds.

Clad in her dressing gown, Rita opens the door to the veranda. With a contented look on her face, she stretches out and lets the soft morning light brighten her features. When she notices a neighbour across the street she waves at him before going back into the kitchen where the kettle is already boiling on the stove. While she takes out the things for breakfast, Pieter enters the kitchen.

'Morning, darling,' he says, putting his hands around

her waist and kissing her. For a moment she allows herself to be held in the embrace but then releases from Pieter's grip.

'Ellie came home last night,' Rita says with some remorse in her voice.

'Oh? Did she?' Pieter replies and sits down. 'Then she must be asleep still because I didn't run into her in the bathroom.'

'Well, then luckily she is still asleep. She almost caught us last night, you know,' Rita says and places the toast on the table.

'Rita, don't get all wound up about it, she's not a child anymore.' He spreads some butter on his toast and dips it in the baked beans on his plate. 'Father and Mother must be enjoying themselves there in Auckland ... in the Dutch shop.'

Rita smiles wanly and pours the tea. 'Or would you rather have coffee?' she asks.

'Well, yeah, but don't worry,' he says and gets up. 'I'll make it myself.'

'Did you give them the address of Birgit's sister, so they can see their granddaughter?' Rita enquires.

Pieter pours hot water on the coffee before he answers her question. 'I slipped it to Mother but I doubt whether they'll go there. There's no way Father would set foot in a *German* household.'

'I cannot recall Father being like that,' Rita says with some disbelief in her voice.

'I can,' Pieter says and resumes his seat at the table.

'Will you be going back today?' Rita asks.

'Not necessarily. I got all my work done last week.' He looks at her. 'Why? Did you have something in mind for today?'

Rita chews on a piece of toast. 'Well,' she says a

moment later, 'Ellie really wants to get some nice clothes. I thought maybe we could go to Palmerston North.'

Pieter nods his head. 'Fine, I suppose my farmhand won't miss me for another day.'

With a satisfied smile, Rita finishes eating her toast.

A door slams in the hall and a moment later Ellie walks in. 'Morning all,' she pronounces, imitating her grandfather.

'Hi Uncle,' she says and rubs her hand through Pieter's hair, 'you call early today ... Mummy,' she adds and kisses her mother on the cheek.

Rita gazes at her daughter with a questioning look. 'You're cheerful this morning,' she says. 'What's the occasion?'

Pieter glances at his niece and gets up to check on his coffee.

'Well,' Ellie says, 'it's so nice to have my room to myself again, and I slept like a log.'

'Good,' Pieter says and gives Rita a brief look.

'No offence, Mum,' Ellie adds.

'Pieter is going to take us to Palmerston today,' Rita says and gets up to have a bath.

'Are you?' Ellie asks her uncle. 'Oh, that's great! Then I can get this nice dress that I wanted, aye Mum!' she calls out to her mother and quickly makes herself something to eat.

'No need to rush,' Pieter says, 'we still have all day.'

Before long, they have finished their breakfast, with Ellie all freshened up in a matter of minutes.

'I'll just walk down to old George's to get the car,' Pieter says when Ellie comes out of the bathroom.

'The car? What do you mean?' Ellie wonders. 'How did you get here just now?'

'Uh, I drove in,' Pieter hastily replies.

Ellie shakes her head with a puzzled look on her face. 'Why would you want to take your car to old George's that early?'

'Uhmm, it needed fixing,' Pieter says and quickly walks to the kitchen door.

'I didn't know old George fixed cars,' Ellie mumbles and goes into her room to finish getting dressed.

« »

For some reason, my mother and I had to move away from the farm after a couple of years. That's when we went to live in a tiny house in a small town. It upset me very much because it meant moving away from my friends, Chrissie and Jody, and I wouldn't see Uncle Pieter that often anymore.

My mother said there was no other way. The cottage where we'd been living in was given to another farmhand and with Grace's children growing up there wasn't enough work for my mother to do on the farm. Uncle Pieter had bought his own farm by then, so he could stay.

I wondered why we could not live with Uncle Pieter but Mum said that was impossible.

'Uncle Pieter has found himself a woman,' she said, 'and Uncle Pieter's house is just not big enough for the four of us.' My mother seemed just as sad about the move as I was but still, we had to go. Uncle Pieter and a few farmhands loaded our possessions onto a truck. I cried when we drove away from the house and off the farm. I didn't want to see anyone, so I sat in the backseat with my head down.

Soon after, Uncle Pieter married this woman. We had to go to the wedding and Mum put on a pretty dress. I didn't want to come with her but she said we had to; we

~ 42 ~

were the only family he had here. I had never seen Uncle
Pieter's woman before and I didn't like her when I did see
her, standing next to Uncle Pieter in her silly suit. She had
weird hair and an ugly face and she wasn't friendly. I
didn't understand why Uncle Pieter wanted to live with
her instead of us. It felt as if he had betrayed us. Mum
didn't seem to think he had, she didn't have any reason
not to like him anymore. That confused me even more.
Mum told me that he had met his woman when he was on
a night out in Auckland. Uncle Pieter tried to be nice to
me that day and he said I was still his little princess but I
didn't want to talk to him. He came to visit us, even after
he married his woman but it took me a long time to
forgive him for not letting us live with him on the farm. I
had to go to a different school while Mum was working in
her new job during the day.

Sometimes William came to the village and I was allowed
to come back home with him to stay with them so I could
play with Chrissie and Jody. I never went to Uncle
Pieter's house then because he was living there with that
unfriendly woman. One day I came for a visit and she had
had a baby, Grace told me. 'Don't you want to go over
and see them?' she asked. 'You have a cousin now.' But I
didn't feel like it. I also had cousins in Holland that I'd
never seen. That's what mum had told me.
    'You shouldn't be so bloody-minded,' Grace said to
me. 'Pieter's wife is not as uncivil as you think, you
know.'
    It wasn't until Chrissie told me how sad Uncle Pieter
was about me not calling when I was on the farm that I
went over and came across him, working in the field. He
just smiled when he saw me and I told him I wasn't angry
with him anymore. I asked if he was pleased with his new

baby and he said he was. 'Then you don't need me anymore,' I told him, 'you've got your own little princess now.' I had read that in a book once and I only said it to cheer him up but he wasn't thrilled. He was silent for a moment and shook his head. He put his hand on my shoulder and told me that nothing had changed. 'I see you every bit as my little daughter as I do my own,' he assured me. 'We're still one family, your mother, you and I. Only now with a few new members.'

I asked him if he liked his new woman and Uncle Pieter had to laugh. 'Wife,' he said, 'yes, I like my wife. Don't you want to come and have a cup of tea?' Uncle Pieter didn't seem to mind when I told him I wanted to go back and play with Chrissie.

'Well, maybe next time,' he said and drove me back to the main house on his tractor.

The next time Uncle Pieter came to visit us he brought his wife and little daughter. His wife's name was Birgit. Her parents were German. They had named the baby after her mother who had died a year before, Ursula. I'd never heard such silly names and I felt sorry for the little baby.

Mum was quiet after they had left. Maybe she didn't like Uncle Pieter's wife either.

'Uncle Pieter says he likes his wife,' I told my mother, 'and that we are still a family.'

She just looked at me and told me to clear the table.

It happened a few times that Grace was looking after Uncle Pieter's baby when I came to visit. That was when he had to take his wife to the hospital in the city. Birgit was not well Grace told us. Chrissie and I didn't mind because then we could play with the baby. She was lovely and we gave her all sorts of names, for we didn't like that silly German name. It became even more fun when Julie, as we named the baby in the end, started taking her first steps. We took her all around the house until Grace said that it was enough and put her back in her playpen.

But Julie was only a small baby when Uncle Pieter's wife became ill. I felt sorry for him because I had never seen him so sad. I felt bad because of it. He said there was nothing I could do when I offered to help them. One day Chrissie, Jody and I were sent to stay with a family that lived near the farm. That was when my mother and William and Grace went to Auckland with Uncle Pieter for Birgit's funeral. They took the baby with them. I told the others that my daddy also had a funeral and that he lived with the angels. Chrissie felt very sorry for the baby because she no longer had a mother. I said to her that Julie had us and Grace and she still had her daddy, but Chrissie said that that was not the same. She asked how I would feel if my mum was dead. I couldn't imagine the world without my mother and I suddenly missed her terribly and wanted to go to her, but that wasn't possible the lady said. I didn't sleep well that night. I dreamt that the car with my mum and Uncle Pieter crashed on the road and I woke up screaming for my mother.

A day later my mother came with William to collect us. Uncle Pieter had gone to his house already. Mum said it was best to leave him be for a while. Grace was going to look after the baby when Uncle Pieter was working.

I thought it would be a good idea if we moved back to the farm now that Uncle Pieter's wife was gone. Mum said to put those silly thoughts out of my mind. It could not be.

We didn't see Uncle Pieter for some time after that and I started missing him. One day, when my mother and I went to visit William and Grace I left the house and wandered off to Uncle Pieter's. I found Julie playing by herself on the veranda. I picked her up and started looking for Uncle Pieter. He wasn't inside the house. I went over and found him fixing some machines in the shed. He was very pleased to see me and said I had grown since he'd seen me last. I told him he should not leave his baby by herself. Grace had said it was not good to leave babies by themselves. He wiped his greasy hands and walked out of the shed asking if I would like something to drink.

Julie became heavy in my arms, she had grown too, so I asked Uncle Pieter if he would take her but he said she could walk on her own feet. That confused me. 'Don't you love your baby?' I asked him. He stopped and turned. Then he took Julie from me and walked on to the house. He never called the baby by her name, even though it was a silly German one. He never called her by any name.

He gave me a drink and we sat down on the veranda. I noticed his eyes were sad when he looked up.

'How have you been?' he asked. 'And how's your mother?'

He let the baby play at his feet.

'Why don't you come to visit us and you'll know,' I told him.

'Always the smart-arse, aye,' he said, but luckily he was smiling again.

'Why don't you come now? Mum's here too,' I said. He seemed surprised. 'Is she?' he asked and I thought I saw a twinkle in his eyes.

'Oh, I don't know.' He picked the baby up when it started crying. 'I think this one needs a feed.'

'She needs a change, Uncle Pieter,' I told him.

'Does she?' he asked. 'Well, since you're so good with babies,' he said and handed her over to me.

I went into the house and looked around for Julie's things. Uncle Pieter called from the veranda that they were in the bedroom. I noticed he kept a photograph of Birgit and the baby on a dressing table.

After I had changed Julie I told Uncle Pieter he should come with me to the house to see all the others. He was reluctant and said he had to feed the baby.

'Grace keeps Julie's food too, you know,' I said to him.

'Julie?' he asked astonished.

I must have blushed. 'That's how Chrissie and I always call her,' I explained.

He took the baby from me. 'Her name is Ursula,' he said sharply.

I looked up at him and said that that was the first time I ever heard him mention his baby's name. He looked at me and I thought he was going to tell me off but instead, he walked down the steps of the veranda. 'Let's go,' he demanded and I was more than happy to follow him to the main house.

We didn't live long in the tiny house in the village. After about a year we moved in with an elderly couple who lived in a huge house on the edge of town. They were a bit eccentric, as Mum called it, but at least we had more space there. And we had our own bathroom. The only thing my mother had to do was keep the house clean and I helped her. Some days Mum worked in her job at the dairy. They created a small tea-shop there too, for people passing through who wanted a drink. I soon made new friends at school but Chrissie and Jody remained my best friends, although Jody was playing more and more with his friends. We didn't see much of him anymore.

The fun thing about the big house was that it had

spare rooms and Chrissie could come and stay with us sometimes. We even had Uncle Pieter's baby a couple of times. Mum was babysitting her when it became too busy on the farm. The old couple, who we called Nana and Granddad, had two cats we loved to play with. One of them was very old and one day the cat lay dead under a bush in the garden. Granddad took a shovel and dug a hole to bury him in. Chrissie was very sorry that she'd missed that funeral. She picked some flowers to put on the cat's grave when she came visiting again. Nana missed that cat very much for she had had it for years but she said she didn't want another. 'It might outlive me,' she said, 'and who will look after it then?'

I said we would, and that we would also look after Granddad, as we sometimes looked after Uncle Pieter's baby who didn't have a mummy anymore. That was a very comforting thought for her, she said.

Granddad had a lot of treasures that he kept in the big living room downstairs. One day he showed us all his medals from the wars. He said he'd also been in Europe where Holland is, but he hadn't fought in the same war as my father. Nana and Granddad once had a son, but he was killed in a war. Now they only had a daughter who lived all the way in some American country. They had not seen her for years but Nana always kept a picture on the cupboard so they could see her and the grandchildren when they were having their breakfast.

One day my mother came home very upset and nervous. Grace had sent her a message that Uncle Pieter had been in an accident on the farm with William. Uncle Pieter was sent to the hospital and Grace was looking after the baby. I became very frightened and started crying. Mum wanted to go and see Uncle Pieter straight away but she didn't drive a car and the bus had already passed.

Nana told her to be calm. Things would be all right, she said. Mum could go to see him in the morning. I wanted to know if Uncle Pieter was going to die too, but Mum didn't want to hear about that. 'People don't just die,' she said.

'Yes, they do!' I cried. 'Daddy did, and Uncle Pieter's wife did.'

She told me to be quiet, that she couldn't handle my crying. Mum herself was close to tears but she said that was because she was so nervous. The next morning Mum had a ride with someone from the village to see Uncle Pieter in the hospital. I didn't have to go to school and stayed with Nana that day. To keep my thoughts busy she read me stories that she wrote herself. Nana always did a lot of writing on her old typewriter. She told me that I should write things down too. 'You must have had an interesting life, Ellie, even though you're still a child,' she said. 'Born in a faraway country, a long boat-journey and all of a sudden you were in this strange land.' She had a bit of a mischievous smile on her face when she said that. Nana had such a way of telling stories that she drew my attention away from the bad thing that had happened to Uncle Pieter.

Mum came home late that evening but I was glad to see her cheerful. 'Uncle Pieter is going to be all right,' she said when she came to tuck me in. 'He broke his arm, rather badly, so it will take some time to heal. But he was making jokes already when I was there so, that's a good sign.'

The next day when I came home from school Nana handed me a notebook. She called it a *journal*.

'A small gift for you,' she said, 'now you can write your own stories.'

It was a beautiful pad with a picture on the cover. A picture of Nana when she was younger, standing under a tree that was in full blossom. The picture was taken in India where Nana and Granddad had lived because Granddad was stationed there. I was thrilled with my present and after I'd been thinking about what I should write, I started my journal that evening.

《　》

It isn't until Pieter is halfway to his farm when he hears something moving in the backseat. He slows the car down on the dark road and looks behind him. He pulls a blanket aside and staring back at him in the darkened car are Ellie's remorseful eyes. 'Ellie, what are you doing there?' he asks, stunned. Ellie looks at him searchingly.

'Oh, c'mon Ellie, don't play dumb.'

Ellie straightens herself. 'I've had a row with mum,' she softly says.

'Well, these things happen. Care to tell me what it was about?'

Ellie is reluctant.

'If you don't want to tell me, you don't have to,' Pieter says and starts turning the car around.

'What are you doing?!' Ellie yells.

'Taking you back, what do you think?'

'NO! I'm not going back!' Ellie cries out.

Pieter is unrelenting and accelerates.

'STOP THE CAR!' Ellie cries out again. She opens the car's backdoor and tries to get out.

'Bloody ... ' Pieter utters and jams on the brakes. He jumps out, grabs Ellie by her arm and pulls her out of the car.

'Now maybe you can pull those tricks on your mother, but don't try them on me,' he threatens. 'What an idiot you are,' he hisses through his teeth. 'Do you want to get us killed?!'

Ellie turns her back on Pieter and buries her face in her hands.

Pieter crosses his arms and waits patiently.

'I'm waiting for an explanation,' he says after a few moments.

Ellie sobs but then, in a soft voice tells him that her mother found out about her boyfriend and that she has forbidden her to ever see him again.

Pieter sighs. 'Is that all,' he says. 'Is that what the fight was about?'

For a moment, they are highlighted by the headlights of a passing car. 'You don't understand,' Ellie sobs and kicks some dry mud away from her feet.

'Try me,' Pieter replies.

'I love Bob,' Ellie says while wiping the tears from her cheeks, 'but, what does mum know about that. She's just jealous because she doesn't have a man in her life,' she adds angrily. 'She hasn't had a man for as long I can remember.'

'Hasn't she?' Pieter asks.

'Well,' Ellie continues, '… apart from that guy who owns the hardware-store – '

'Did she?' Pieter seems surprised.

' … But she probably felt sorry for him,' Ellie goes on, 'because his wife left him with all the kids.'

Pieter lifts his eyebrows and walks back to the car.

'Get in,' he orders and opens the door.

'No, Uncle Pieter, don't make me go home,' Ellie grumbles.

'Stop whining Ellie and get in … You can sleep in Uschi's room tonight,' he softly adds.

Without further protest, Ellie takes the seat next to Pieter and they drive on, home to the farm.

Ellie puts a handkerchief away. 'When will Uschi be back?' she asks.

While keeping his eyes on the road Pieter replies he'll collect her tomorrow. 'And I'll drop you off on the way.'

Ellie looks at him. 'Oh, can't I come with you? Then you can drop me off after.'

'Don't push your luck,' Pieter remarks.
She sits back and stares at the beams of the headlights, which light the road ahead.

While making a cup of coffee in the kitchen Pieter walks in.

'Where did you go?' Ellie asks.

'I went over to ask Grace if she could phone someone in town, to let Rita know where you are.'

'Oh.'

'She'll be worried sick, you know,' Pieter says reproachfully.

Ellie shrugs her shoulders. 'Would you like a coffee, too?' she asks.

Pieter looks at her. 'Don't be so bloody indifferent, Ellie,' he says, sounding annoyed.

'I'm sorry,' Ellie mumbles.

'Are you?' Pieter wonders.

'Yes!' Ellie cries out. 'I'm sorry, I'm sorry, I'm sorry! Why doesn't anybody take me seriously?!'

She points at Pieter. 'And you ... You are just as bad as my mother!' She tries to run outside but Pieter stops her in her tracks. 'Alright,' he says to calm her down, 'just, sit down and tell me what this is all about.'

'I don't want to sit down!' she yells back at him, runs to the bedroom and slams the door behind her.

Pieter shakes his head in despair. He then starts making himself a coffee and sits down to read the paper, but with Ellie's sobbing sounds coming from the other room he cannot concentrate and takes his paper out onto the sparsely lit veranda.

After some time a door opens and reluctant footsteps approach the kitchen door.

Ellie spots him outside on the dimly lit veranda. 'Are you still angry with me?' she asks sulkily.

Pieter looks up from his paper. 'You're the one who's angry around here.'

Ellie sits down on the floor and rests her back against the wall. Her eyes are still red from crying. 'I think I should go away for a while,' she says.

'What? You mean, to the city.'

'No, away from this country,' she quietly states.

'C'mon Ellie. The fight you had with your mother can't have been that bad.'

Ellie shrugs her shoulders. 'I still don't see why she's so terribly against it. Me having a boyfriend I mean, and Bob is the nicest bloke in the whole town.'

'I bet he is,' Pieter says.

'You know Bob, aye? His father sometimes works for William.'

Pieter lowers his paper. 'Yeah, I saw you with him. He looks like an OK chap to me.'

'He's adorable,' Ellie muses.

Pieter casts a thorough look at Ellie. 'So uh, how serious are you with this bloke?' he wants to know.

'Well, serious enough ... We go out together and ... uhh ... '

'And what?' Pieter asks.

'Well ... you know ... '

'Have you slept with him?'

'No!' Ellie shouts.

Pieter utters a sigh of relief. 'So what's the big deal

with Rita then?'

Ellie shakes her head. 'I don't know. She kept yelling that I didn't know what I was doing, that I was far too young ... all that trash. So I ran out of the house. I wanted to go to Bob, but, then I saw your car in town and crawled in ... Wanted to run away.'

Pieter shakes his head. 'I don't know what it is with you women,' he says. 'I sure hope my daughter is not going to play up like that when the time comes.'

'Uschi doesn't have a mother she'll have to fight,' Ellie says, instantly realising what she just said.

'Oh, I'm sorry Uncle Pieter!' she says regretfully and grabs hold of his arm. 'I didn't mean that. Oh, why am I always doing the wrong things,' she adds with despair and covers her face in her hands.

'Comes with your age,' Pieter says. 'It's called puberty.'

Silence sets in with Ellie staring into the dark night.

'It's not just puberty, Uncle Pieter,' she answers after a while. 'I've always felt a bit, left out. Maybe it's because this is not my own country. Maybe a part of me is still Dutch.' She looks up at Pieter. 'Don't you ever have that feeling, that you don't belong here?'

Pieter shakes his head. 'No,' he says, 'not really. I've got all my friends here, my daughter, you guys and, after my parents' visit, I know for sure that here's where I belong.'

'Don't you ever want to go back to Holland, on vacation?'

'That's likely to happen, one day, when the time is right.'

'I want to go now,' Ellie says. 'I'm going to look for a job and when I have the money I'll go.'

'That's a noble pursuit, but what about your studies?

Or do you want to end up like most of them, married with children.'

Silently Ellie shakes her head and for a while, they just sit and listen to the sounds of the late evening that interpose their conversation.

'Maybe I could study first,' Ellie says quietly. 'Holland won't run away ... Maybe I could do both, study and work at the same time. Then, when I've finished I will have the money to go to Europe.'

Pieter nods his head. 'That sounds like a better idea.' He reaches out and pats her on the shoulder. 'You'll get there,' he says encouragingly. 'Now, let's get some sleep. The sun will rise again tomorrow.'

3

After the rainstorm has subsided, Ellie pulls her jumper over her head and says goodbye to her boss. Opening the door of the corner dairy she peers at the sky where the last dark clouds make way for the late afternoon sun. A few lost raindrops still catch her hair as she makes her way across the street.

There's a car slowing down beside her. 'Hey! Ellie!' a young man yells out. Ellie waves at him. 'G'day,' she says as she reaches the pavement. 'How are you?'

The man stops the car next to her. 'Need a ride back to town?' he asks.

'Well uh, I hadn't really planned on going home tonight, Bob,' Ellie says.

'Is that right? So, where were you going to stay then?'

'I have a few school friends here where I stay,' Ellie replies, 'so I don't have to go up and down every day.'

Bob looks disappointed. 'Well ... that's a shame. I thought maybe we could do something together tonight.'

Ellie is feeling a bit indecisive. 'What do you have in mind then?' she asks.

'There's this band playing at the Barn, thought we might go together,' Bob replies.

Ellie's eyes light up. 'Sounds good, but I am working tomorrow. So ... '

'That's OK. I'll run you back.'

Ellie hesitates but then gives in. 'Won't your father mind you borrowing his car?' she asks as she gets in. Bob waves that remark aside. 'He'll be away for the weekend, goes fishing with his mates.'

Trying to avoid muddy slabs, he drives the car down

the road that is still damp from the afternoon showers.
'It's good to see you, Ellie,' Bob says. 'How do you like your job?'

'It's OK, I'm meeting interesting people.'

'Thought you were going to Wellington, to study,' Bob says.

'I am, I've passed the exam,' Ellie replies.

Bob glances at her. 'Congratulations,' he says, 'and also, happy eighteenth.'

Ellie looks at him. 'You remembered,' she expresses, 'but, you didn't show.'

'Yes, sorry 'bout that. I was out of town.' Bob keeps his eyes focused on the road as he reaches out and touches her thigh. 'You know, you don't need to move away and study, we could – '

'I need to,' Ellie interrupts him and takes his hand off her leg. 'We've been over this before, Bob. Don't start again.'

'I'm sorry ... I didn't mean to upset you.'

'Dinner at my house?' Bob asks when they've reached Taihepe.

'Sounds fine,' Ellie replies and a few minutes later Bob parks the car beside the small house.

Bob's father is just making something to eat for himself when they enter the kitchen. He looks up when he notices his son has brought his girlfriend home.

'Well. Ellie. How are you?'

'Fine Mr Swanson. How about yourself?'

Bob checks the refrigerator for something to eat and pulls out some cheese and a few eggs.

'This OK with you?' he asks Ellie.

'C'mon son,' his father says. 'Ellie here would like something better than that, won't you, love.'

'Whatever's in the house is fine with me,' Ellie replies.

'Go get some fresh veg from the garden, son,' Mr Swanson tells Bob. 'Make her a nice salad.'

Bob seems a bit indecisive but nevertheless complies.

'I'll do the eggs,' Ellie says.

'Cup a tea, love?' Mr Swanson asks and takes another cup off the tray.

Ellie nods as she watches the butter melt in the pan.

'Haven't seen you around for a while,' he says. 'Did you move out from your mum's?'

'No Sir,' Ellie replies, 'it's just that I have this job in Ohakune now and I usually stay there with friends during the week.' She breaks a few eggs and lets them slide into the melted butter.

'Wellington off the books?'

Ellie shakes her head as she takes a few plates from the cupboard. 'No Sir, I'm going next year.' She looks up when Bob enters the kitchen with his arms full of fresh produce.

'This should make a nice salad,' he states.

There's a chill in the air when they stroll home from the venue and Ellie snuggles up to Bob to stay warm. 'Great evening, Bob. Thanks,' she says.

He kisses her. 'We could do this more often if you want.'

Ellie shrugs her shoulders. 'Yeah ... maybe.' She turns to him and gently kisses him on his lips. 'Why don't you come with me to Wellington?' she asks.

Bob shakes his head, says he cannot leave his job and his father all by himself.

'You can get a job in Wellington,' Ellie replies, 'and you're not wedded to your father. You can go whenever you want.'

He looks downwards. 'You know it's not that simple, Ellie. We could get married,' he goes on, 'but you don't want to.'

'I don't mind being married and living in Wellington. I told you that before,' Ellie replies. 'But I need to do what I feel is best.'

'Come on, Ellie. And you're always telling me that I am pig-headed!'

Ellie is silent for a moment and then takes him by his arm. 'We'd better go home,' she says, 'before we freeze to death.'

They continue along the dark street when, suddenly, Bob draws her closer, pulls her into a store doorway and starts kissing her. Ellie playfully punches him in the side, only to put her arms around his neck a moment later. For minutes they caress and taste each other's kisses.

'Where are you sleeping tonight,' Bob says in a quiet voice.

' … At Mum's,' Ellie replies, 'what do you think?'

He pulls her closer. 'Well, I thought … ' They hold each other close for a while. When footsteps approach in the empty street they silently stand, pressed against the wall. After the person has passed, they disengage from the darkness and walk on. In front of Ellie's house, they kiss goodnight. 'And don't forget,' Ellie says in a hushed voice, 'I have to be at work at ten.'

Bob waves back at her as she enters the garden. She quietly walks into the darkened house and notices a familiar hat on the kitchen table.

'Uncle Pieter'll forget himself one day,' she quietly mumbles and stealthily walks into the hall.

She hesitates when she sees her mother's bedroom door ajar and peeks through, wrinkling her eyebrows at the sight of something uncommon. Slowly she pushes the door open a bit further and tries to determine what it is that has captured her attention. In the dark, she silently moves towards her mother's bed, but a soft moaning makes her stop.

Her mouth falls open at the recognition of the person who just turned over. In a reflex, she puts her hand before her mouth and quickly withdraws from the room. In the hall, she leans her back against the wall and lets out a gasp of breath. After a few moments, she rushes back to the kitchen and goes outside, silently closing the door behind her. With an uncomprehending expression on her face, she stops on the veranda, staring into the garden, which is only lit by a vague shine of the moon. Until the cold winds playing around her slender stature make her come to her senses. Gradually she moves down the few steps and walks back into the street.

In dead of night, she finds herself in front of Bob's house and walks alongside it until she reaches his bedroom. She knocks on the window and in a subdued voice starts calling his name. When there's no sound she tries again. After a few moments, there's a stumbling noise and the curtain is pushed aside.

'Ellie? What are you doing here?' he says somewhat stupefied and opens the window a bit wider.

'Can I sleep here?' Ellie asks. 'I'll sleep on the couch.'

Bob notices the desperation in her voice. 'What happened? Why ain't you at your mother's?'

'Please, Bob. Please let me in. I'm freezing.'

'It's OK,' Bob says, 'go 'round the back.'

When Ellie enters the house Bob is just taking a few blankets from a closet. He hands her one when he sees her shivering. 'So, why ain't you at your mother's?' Bob wants to know.

Ellie shakes her head. 'I can't sleep there,' she says and sits down on the couch. 'Please, don't ask me why.'

Bob puts his arm around her and feels the chill of her body. 'You're cold through,' he says. 'Take my bed, I'll sleep here.'

'No, no ... I'll sleep here,' Ellie insists.

'Ellie, my bed is nice and warm. You can have it.' Ellie looks him in the eyes. 'We could also, both sleep in your bed,' she says softly. 'Then you can keep me warm.'

'Are you sure?'

She nods. Bob's father calls from his room what all the noise is about but Bob assures him everything is fine. Bob takes Ellie's hand and they walk into his room. Ellie pulls her jumper over her head and takes off her slacks before crawling between the warm covers. Not long after she falls asleep in Bob's loving embrace.

« »

One day Granddad became very ill and I wasn't allowed to visit him in his room. My mother said it would give me a scare to see Granddad the way he was. A nurse came every day to look after him for it was too hard on Nana, who walked around all day with a very sad face and when I asked her something she didn't seem to hear me.

After a while, my mother took me to see Granddad. I hardly recognised the man lying there in that bed, his face very thin and grey. Mum said it was because he hadn't been eating well. He opened his eyes when I took his hand; it was all bony with blue veins across it. I asked him if he was still feeling sick but he just looked at me. Mum whispered that Granddad was paralysed on one side, that he could not speak well anymore. I wanted to know if he was deaf too, but Mum said he could still hear us. I started telling Granddad about my days at school and that we were going to do a play but Mum hushed me, it was too tiring for him. But I saw Granddad smile before we left the room.

The nurse told me that it was not likely that Granddad was going to be well again. 'We can clap our hands in glee if he even gets out of bed,' she said.

Now that I was allowed into granddad's bedroom I went to see him every day and told him about school. I read him stories from my books, sometimes I told him my own stories that I had written. He didn't say much but I could tell by his eyes that he liked my stories. Nana was with Granddad a lot too, she was a bit more cheerful now that he was doing better. She helped Granddad with his food because he could not hold the spoon himself.

One day a lady came to the house, she was going to teach Granddad to speak again. Nana was very happy about that.

'Is Granddad going to be all well again now?' I asked her.

'We can only hope, dear,' she said. 'We can only hope and pray.'

At a given moment, the nurse found it time to take Granddad out of his bed for a short while. 'To let his blood flow in a different direction for a change,' she said.

Granddad looked a lot better when he was sitting up. His face wasn't that grey anymore and even when he attempted to speak we could understand what he tried to say. The nurse took Granddad from his bed every day since then, and slowly he became better.

A large van stopped in front of the house one day and the men took out a big chair. 'That's Granddad's wheelchair,' Nana explained. It was a real nice chair, it had wheels so we could take Granddad out in the garden and push him around. And Granddad liked being outside again after so many months. The nurse used to ride him to a sunny spot where the gazebo was so he could see all over the garden and smell the pretty flowers. Then Mum and I would take out the tray with tea and biscuits and we'd all sit and keep Granddad company and drink tea. Those were the nicest times of the day.

Although Granddad's speech became a bit better he was never able to go without the wheelchair. The nurse helped him take a few steps every day but he could never go by himself anymore. After a while the nurse only came in the morning and my mother helped when he had to go to bed at night.

'Isn't it a miracle that granddad is still with us,' Nana said to me one day. She had tears in her eyes. 'I thank God every day that I am allowed to keep my Henry a while longer.'

Mum was very busy at that time, working at the dairy, helping with Granddad and then Uncle Pieter came to collect her so she could help Grace out on the farm. I could always stay at home to keep Granddad company. One day during the school holidays, Uncle Pieter brought Chrissie with him. She stayed with us for a week. We had a lot of fun with Mum not being there. We drove Granddad around the garden, we helped Nana in the house and helped the nurse make the beds. We even baked biscuits one day to have with the tea. Chrissie and I knew how because our mothers had taught us. Nana was really impressed with our biscuits, she said she couldn't have done a better job herself.

One day on a Sunday we all went to church and took Granddad with us in his wheelchair. The people were all very pleased to see him, even the grumpy old man who lived at the other end of the village. They all shook Granddad's hand and the Minister let him sit in front of the church.

That afternoon Nana had a lot of people over to have tea in the garden and Chrissie and I made a new friend, Martin, but everybody called him Marty. His mother was Dutch and his father was from England but he was born here. With so many people helping Nana, we had all the time to play around the house. Chrissie and I showed Marty where Granddad kept his treasures and Nana's writing desk where she wrote all her stories. I also showed him the journal that Nana had given me. In my mother's room, we found a photograph of her with Uncle Pieter. It was between a book that fell on the floor when Chrissie bumped against the chest. Marty said he knew the people in the picture, that he sometimes saw them at the coffee-bar. I said to him that it was not true. 'My mother always tells me where she's going,' I told him.

'Yeah,' Chrissie said, 'and right now she's on the farm where I live, to help my mother.'

Marty claimed he was sure that he had seen them before, for his parents owned the coffee-bar. I took the picture off him and put it back in the book. 'Let's go outside and play,' I said.

I never did ask Mum if she often went to town with Uncle Pieter and not telling me. Marty probably had them confused with another couple. When Mum came back that evening she gave Nana a few jars of marmalade that she and Grace had made. Sadly, Chrissie had to go back with Uncle Pieter.

It was on a rainy day when my mother and I left the house to take a train to the city. I asked her why Uncle Pieter didn't take us in his car but she said he was too

busy. It had sounded like an adventurous journey and I
didn't have to go to school, but the train ride was long and
I was very bored in the end, looking at the raindrops
rolling down the windows. Mum didn't really want to say
why we were going to the city. 'You will see when we get
there,' she said. That day, she wasn't the nice mother I
knew.

When we finally reached the city it was still raining.
Luckily Nana had given us an umbrella just before we left
the house. We walked through the rain to a building where
Mum needed to talk to a gentleman. When I saw him I
didn't think he was gentle, I thought he was a grump. He
told my mother that children weren't allowed to go in. I
had to wait outside the office and play with a few
magazines that were there but I just sat still and watched
people going in and out.

My mother took a long time. I became bored and
stood up to look out the window. We had to go up a few
stairs when we arrived here, so now I could overlook the
street and the harbour. I had never seen so many people
together since we had left Holland. My father took me to a
big market on a rainy day in Holland once; it was in a big
city too.

It seemed so long ago, so far away. I could hardly
remember what happened that day, maybe I had been too
young to remember. I wondered how my friends in
Holland were. I didn't think I could ever see them again. I
wondered how little Lucy Bakker was. We called her little
Lucy because she was the smallest of all of us, but that
was because she was always ill. Maybe she still was ill,
maybe she was dead, too.

A door opened and my mother came out, she didn't
look pleased. I asked her if the man had been angry with
her but she took my arm and said we still had other things

to do. She was in a hurry to get down the stairs. 'We have to take a bus now, to another building,' she said and pulled me along. I splashed with my shoes through the puddles of rain that were on the pavement. We had to wait a while before the bus came. I remember there was a nice smell of chips and I asked Mum if we could not have some but she said we were going to have something to eat later. The bus didn't take long to get us to the other building. Mum pointed to the flag that was flown from the building. 'Look, the Dutch flag,' she said with a smile. Some people here spoke Dutch and my mother had to go into an office again. Again I had to wait outside the office but there was a nice lady here who talked to me and let me tell her all about where we lived and what I did in school and that I wrote things down in a journal. She was very surprised when I told her that. 'I've never heard of a child keeping a journal,' she said.

'Nana taught me how,' I said.
When Mum came out of this office she looked happier. 'Now that we've got that out of the way, let's have something to eat,' she said. She thanked the lady and we went outside. We didn't take a bus but walked back, under the umbrella that protected us from the rain. Even though it was raining, there were still a lot of people in the street. When we came to the shops Mum looked for a nice place to sit and have something to eat. When we were inside, Mum had coffee and I could have lemonade with the sandwiches. I said to Mum that we looked like two rich ladies having tea in a restaurant.

She smiled. 'You and your imagination,' she said.

A woman stopped at our table and started staring at my mother. I pulled Mum's sleeve and said that the woman was staring at her. Mum looked up and said she knew her.

'Rita?' the woman said. 'Rita Visser?'

My mother nodded. 'Yes?'

'Tine Vermeer,' the woman said.

A big smile appeared on Mum's face. 'Yes, of course! I'm sorry I forgot your name. Come have a seat, please.'

The woman sat down next to me. 'It's been a long time, Rita.' She turned to me. 'And is this little Ellie?'

'Well, not that little anymore,' Mum said, smiling, 'she'll be eleven next week. Ellie, this is Tine Vermeer. We were in school together and during Hunger Winter we volunteered for the Red Cross.'

'It's so good to see you,' Tine said. 'I heard about your husband. I am sorry ... But, I didn't know you were in New Zealand.'

'Yes, we live in a small town east of Taranaki. What about you?'

'My husband and I came here four years ago,' Tine told us. 'Henk works as a carpenter, and we live right here, in Auckland.'

Mum and Tine were surprised to discover that Tine and her husband arrived in New Zealand less than a year after we did. They arrived in July 1952. My mother and her friend talked a long time about what they did and about all the people they knew in Holland. They had a lot of fun and I just listened to their stories. About American soldiers, they dated during the war and how amusing they were. I asked Mum if Daddy also had a lot of fun in the war but Mum said Daddy had been somewhere else, in a bad place.

Tine mentioned she had never heard of Greg and Billy anymore. 'Well, we all went back to our own lives once we were liberated, I guess,' she said.

After some time my mother and Tine exchanged

addresses and Tine asked why we didn't go with her, for a visit. Mum didn't think that was a good idea, we needed to catch the train back. Tine tried to persuade her. 'You can stay with me tonight. Then you can go back tomorrow, all refreshed.'

I said to Mum that it was a good idea, and I didn't have school the next day. She agreed. 'But I will have to let Nana know that we won't be back until tomorrow.' Tine said that Mum could make a telephone call from their house. And, now there was still enough time for Mum and me to buy everybody at home a little gift. After that, Tine drove us in her car to the railway station so Mum could change our tickets and then we went to Tine's house.

She lived in a house with a lot of Dutch things on the wall and she had a nice garden. I really liked her house and Tine was a nice lady. She had blonde curly hair, almost like gold. Not like my mother's. Mum's hair is sand coloured and she always keeps it out of her face with a few hair clips.

Tine took a photo album from a closet to show Mum and me. Mum recognised a lot of the people in the photographs, most of them were from Holland. She became all swoony over a photograph of her with a soldier. I asked her who the soldier was.

'Greg,' she said, 'and this is Billy, Tine's friend.' She pointed at another picture. 'How nice that you kept these photos,' Mum said to Tine.

I wondered if my father would have also liked the photos because there were so many people in them that Mum knew. Daddy must have known them too.

After a while, Tine's husband Henk came home and Tine started cooking dinner. She made an old fashioned Dutch dish with all that cool winter weather outside. My mother helped her in the kitchen and I read a book that

Tine had given me. Henk was reading a paper. He said he was tired because he had worked so hard. Even though there were no children of my age -Tine and Henk didn't have any- I enjoyed the evening very much. We were like one big family. I was allowed to stay up later than usual, I went to bed at the same time as my mother did. We both slept in the spare room and Tine gave us some nightclothes to wear. Mine was a bit too big but I liked it just the way it was.

The next morning after breakfast Tine drove us to the railway station. I didn't want to go home yet, I wished we could have stayed longer but for some reason, we had to go back. I think my mother was worried about Granddad. Just before we went on the train Tine gave me a present. 'For your birthday, but don't open it before then,' she said. I thanked her and gave her a kiss. I was so happy with the present with its colourful wrapping. Mum looked pleased too.

When the train slowly moved out of the station we waved until Tine was completely out of sight. She had promised to visit us one day when her husband had a few days off. Mum had a happy smile on her face when we rode back. 'Wasn't it wonderful?' she said. 'One moment you're having all these problems and the next you run into a dear friend and have a great time.' She put her arm around my shoulder. 'A great time,' she said once more.

The ride back was a lot less boring with the rain out of the way. We enjoyed the scenery that passed by with Mum pointing out some houses that she liked. 'We can't stay at Nana and Granddad's forever,' she said. But I wouldn't mind.

When we reached home Uncle Pieter was there with the baby and Grace. That was unusual because Grace had never visited us before but she had heard so many stories about the house from Chrissie that she had to come and see for herself, she said. Nana was rocking Uschi on her lap; she always was fond of her. Uncle Pieter brought Uschi to ask Mum if she could look after her for a couple of days because he had to go to the South Island. Mum didn't mind of course but she had to ask for a few days off work. Uncle Pieter didn't want to tell me why he was going to the South Island, but later on, I heard him say to Mum he was thinking of buying a property there.

I told Nana, Granddad and Grace all about the nice time we had in the city and how Mum had met her old friend. Uncle Pieter didn't seem to be interested; he was outside talking to my mother.

For the first time since we came here, Uncle Pieter missed my birthday because of his trip. I was very excited that morning for I could finally open Tine's present. It was a beautiful book with lots of different stories and lovely pictures and inside was a handmade bookmark with my name on it.

'And I thought my present was special,' Nana said. She also gave me a book, but it only had one story and not that many pictures.

'You'd better write Tine a note to thank her,' Mum said. My mother gave me some new clothes but that's what she always did.

It was really nice to have Uschi staying with us for almost a week but one morning she was gone. Uncle Pieter had come late the night before to pick her up. I hadn't even said goodbye to them. But he did leave me a small present, a few pens to write with and a notebook.

Mum didn't look pleased when she said that Uncle Pieter might take the baby and move to the South Island. She said he might leave soon when he has sold the property he had here.

'Who will look after Uschi when he's working?' I asked her. Mum said he was thinking of hiring someone. 'Typical Pieter,' she said, 'never appreciates what he's got. Taking little Ursula away from us and letting a stranger take care of her.' She walked out of the kitchen and slammed the door. Nana looked a bit disapprovingly when she did that. I didn't understand Uncle Pieter, abandoning us again and taking Uschi with him. But there was nothing we could do, Nana said. She was his daughter.

« »

Ellie walks up the dirt road towards the house to find Grace beside it, hanging out the washing. The wind almost rips the sheets from her hands. Ellie hesitates for a moment but then comes nearer. 'They will soon be dry in this weather,' she says.

Grace looks surprised when she sees Ellie emerge from the trees. 'G'day love. What brings you here?'

'Oh, I didn't have a lot to do so I thought I'd drop in,' Ellie replies as she takes part of the sheet Grace is trying to hang up. 'Did you come in with Pieter?'

'No, I hitched ... had a ride with the neighbour,' Ellie says.

With only the sound of the wind blowing they hang out the rest of the washing and after the job is done they start walking to the house. 'How's Rita?' Grace asks.

'Oh, Mum's fine ... keeping busy.'

She picks up her bag that she left on the veranda and takes out a small tin. 'I brought you some chocolates,' Ellie says and hands Grace the tin.

'Oh, lovely, dear. Thank you.' Grace glances at her.

'Time for a cuppa?' she asks.

'Sure. Thanks,' Ellie replies and sits down at the table.

She follows Grace's movements as the latter puts the kettle on and takes a few cups from the cupboard to put on the table. 'Grace?'

'What dear?'

'When my mother comes to help you out, does she stay here? In the house?'

Surprised, Grace looks at her. 'Of course, where else? I don't put her in the doghouse, you know,' she adds laughingly.

Ellie suppresses a smile. 'No. I just thought, maybe she sometimes stays with Uncle Pieter.'

'Oh, she did, sometimes, when Uschi was smaller.'

Ellie casts a questioning look.

'To help out,' Grace continues. 'You know yourself how clumsy he was with the child.' She pours the tea. 'Mind you, she hasn't been around for some time now.'

'Well, like I said, she's keeping busy,' Ellie says.

Ellie seems lost in thought. She stares at her teacup.

'Grace?'

'Yes?'

'Grace ... have you ever noticed Uncle Pieter dating another woman after Birgit died?'

'Child, what on earth is going on in that head of yours?' Next, she shakes her head. 'No, I haven't noticed. But I don't know what he's up to all the time. I'm not his keeper. Why?' She takes Ellie's hand for a moment and smiles: 'Do you think it's time for him to remarry?'

Ellie looks somewhat abashed.

'He'll be alright. Don't you worry about him,' Grace says. 'And Uschi turned out a wise little girl. They'll be fine.'

'Have you ever wondered why my mother never remarried?' Ellie asks.

'What are you implying, Ellie?' Grace wants to know.

'Oh, nothing,' Ellie replies, bemused by Grace's reaction. 'It's just ... well, you know.' She puts her cup down and gets up. 'I'd better go,' she says.

'Don't be silly, child,' says Grace. 'Sit back down ... You shouldn't let your imagination run away with you. There's nothing going on between those two.' Grace pours them another cup and pulls the biscuit tin nearer when their attention is drawn by the sound of a car outside and Grace gets up with a curious look on her face.

'That could be Chrissie and Marty,' she says. Ellie follows her example and walks to the door, too.

'Hi Mum,' Chrissie says when she steps out of the car.

'Marty not with you?' Grace wonders.

'Ellie! I just saw you in town this morning,' Chrissie says. 'How'd you get here?'

'She hitched,' Grace replies, still checking the car for her son-in-law.

'I dropped him off with Dad, by the cows,' Chrissie says. 'You hitched? Why didn't you call on us, we could've given you a ride.'

Ellie shrugs her shoulders. 'Sorry, but, it was just a spur of the moment thing.'

Chrissie grabs a large parcel from the backseat and they walk back into the house where she puts the parcel on the kitchen table and explains that she wasn't able to get the design her mother wanted but hopes that this colour is alright. Grace rips the brown paper off. 'Oh, look at this,' Grace says contentedly as she inspects the material, 'but this is fine. This will go perfectly with those other curtains. Thank you, dear.'

Chrissie takes a bottle of juice from the refrigerator and pours herself a glass. 'And how's everything between you and Bob?' she asks Ellie. 'I hear you're seeing him again.'

Ellie looks at her in a questioning way. 'What gave you that idea? All we did was go to the Barn together the other night.'

'Well?' Chrissie insinuates.

'Nothing else,' Ellie replies.

'He's a good boy,' Grace responds, 'you shouldn't let him slip through your fingers.'

'Why don't you just marry him?' Chrissie suggests. 'You know he wants you.'

With some uneasiness, Ellie moves about in her chair.

'Chrissie,' her mother soothes, 'that's something that cannot be forced.'

'Well, I just want what's best for her,' Chrissie reasons. 'It did me good, so why not Ellie?'

'You're older than she is,' Grace replies, 'maybe Ellie is not ready for commitment yet.'

'No, it's not that – ' Ellie begins.

'But you need to go to Wellington and study,' Chrissie interrupts her. 'I still don't see why you want to do that. Get a bloke and let him do the work and you look after the babies.'

'I don't want any babies,' Ellie replies.

'Of course you want children,' Chrissie says. 'Remember the way you were always dragging Uschi about?'

'That was different, we were just children then,' Ellie says.

'Oh, c'mon girls,' Grace says, 'let's not squabble

about it. When the time is right Ellie will get her turn, just like any other woman.'

'Oh Mum,' Chrissie sighs.

Soon after the last streak of daylight has disappeared behind the hills Ellie withdraws to the spare room and takes her journal from her bag. Staring through the window at the dark skies beyond, she contemplates what to write down on the paper in front of her. With her pencil, she starts drawing scenery, which does not characterise the familiar surroundings of New Zealand. Contours of dunes with sturdy Lyme-grass appear on the paper. Seagulls hovering over them look so real, their obtrusive crying can almost be heard. In the distance, a windmill, surrounded by outstretched meadows. A longing expression arises in her eyes when she gazes at the finished product. With a sigh, she turns the page and starts writing. She is so engrossed with her story that she doesn't hear the knock on the door and someone entering. Chrissie moves up behind her and furtively looks over her shoulder. 'Would you like to have a cuppa with us,' she asks a moment later.

Alarmed by the sudden voice, Ellie shrinks back.

'Christ! Chrissie! Can't you knock first!' Ellie calls out.

'I did. And don't use the Lord's name in vain.'

'Since when do you worry about that?'

'What are you writing?' Chrissie asks.

'Nothing much, it's not finished yet,' Ellie says. She turns around on her chair. 'Chris?'

'Yeah.'

'Oh, I'm not sure if I should tell you this, but … No, it's better – '

'Oh, c'mon Ellie, we never had secrets before. Tell

me.'

Ellie looks directly at her. 'As long as you don't mention it to anyone.'

'I won't.'

Ellie notices the door has been left slightly open and she gets up to close it. 'It's my mother,' she says.

'What's with your mother?' Chrissie asks, a bit worried.

'And Uncle Pieter.'

'What about them?'

Ellie presses her lips firmly together.

'What Ellie?! Oh, come on, you're not saying that ... ' They look at each other in silence.

'I had to let someone know,' Ellie says in a soft voice. 'Have *you* ever noticed anything between them?'

Chrissie shakes her head. 'No, can't say I have.'

'Don't tell anyone,' Ellie pleads with her. 'What will people say?'

'You can trust me, you know that,' Chrissie assures her. 'But, why don't they just come out and get married?'

Ellie shrugs her shoulders and shakes her head. 'And I don't dare ask either.'

'Well, maybe they will. Soon. Let's just wait and see,' Chrissie says. 'I can't think of any reason why they shouldn't.'

'It's just that, it bothers me,' Ellie says. 'Here's this mother of mine telling me what I should do and what I shouldn't. Even forbids me to have a boyfriend! And in the meantime – '

'Did you actually, see them, together?' Chrissie asks. Ellie nods her head. 'Oh. I don't understand,' she replies irritably, 'and Uncle Pieter doesn't make things any clearer, just like Mum. Two peas in a pod.'

'Well,' Chrissie says, 'if you look at it that way, then

they're made for each other. Let's go and have that cuppa before it gets cold.'

Slowly Ellie rises from the chair and follows Chrissie out of the room.

The following morning before breakfast William calls Grace to the shed where one of the cows is in distress trying to give birth. Gladys wonders if he has contacted the vet.

'Sent Marty off to get him, he's at the neighbour's house,' William replies.

'What's he doing at the neighbour's?' Grace asks as she quickly follows her husband to the shed. 'He could've phoned from here.'

'The bloody vet is at the neighbour's,' William explains.

Rushing after them, are Ellie and Chrissie, who is still braiding her long hair.

'Good lord,' Grace says when she sees the cow moving about nervously in her confined space.

'Don't go near her,' William warns. He tries to grab the rope that dangles down from the cow's neck but the cow kicks back.

'Dad, shall I try from this side?' Chrissie asks her father as she ties a piece of elastic around her braid. Taken aback by the cow's low mournful sounds, Ellie keeps her distance.

William climbs the fencing and aims for the rope once more. Suddenly the cow turns and with its massive behind presses William against the wall.

'Dad!' Chrissie cries.

'William! Get away from her!'

William gives the cow a hard slap on her side and yells out. The animal is startled and that gives William just enough time to rapidly move away and jump back over the fencing.

'Dad! Are you all right?' Chrissie calls out.

William takes another rope and motions Grace to divert the cow's attention.

'I'll help you Mum,' Chrissie says.

'No. You stand back,' William says, 'cow's edgy enough as it is.'

With soothing sounds, Grace tries to calm the animal while William sneaks up and with a sudden move manages to get the rope around the neck. He pulls the cow to the wall and ties her up.

'I wish that vet would get here,' Grace says while she's making an effort to give William a helping hand as he's coming back over the fencing. 'She's not going to last long like that.' The cow pulls at the rope, her eyes turned white with fright and discomfort.

'Poor thing,' Ellie says.

'How long has she been like this?' Grace asks.

'A while, pulled her out of the field like that,' William replies.

'Do you think it's coming?'

'No. It's dead.'

'How's it going,' Pieter's voice sounds as he walks in.

'Dead calf,' William grumbles.

'I just saw Jack drive up,' he tells William.

Ellie has her eyes subtly fixed on Pieter; she quickly glances downwards when he turns her way. 'How are ya?' he asks her. 'Haven't seen you for a while.'

'Mm, been around, working,' Ellie unwillingly replies.

The cow gives another pull at the rope.

'Go see if Jack's coming,' Grace tells Chrissie who

straight away walks out of the shed only to come back a moment later with Jack and Marty following behind.

William and Pieter stand on either side of the animal to keep it secure while Jack slides his hand and then his arm inside the cow's behind. He tries to turn the calf around, and after a while, succeeds.

Ellie pulls a wry face at the sight of the animal in distress. The cow stands petrified while Jack pulls the dead calf out and with strips of bloody tissue it falls in the sawdust amongst the stench of cow-dung. 'Ooh,' Ellie says with a twisted face. 'Poor thing,' Chrissie says.

Jack is feeling the inside of the cow, with William and Pieter still keeping the animal under control. Jack pulls his arm out and makes it clear to William that the animal should be alright now. William pets the cow on her side and loosens the rope around her neck while Pieter sends Marty to fetch a wheelbarrow to remove the dead remains. The cow turns her head and sniffs at the lifeless lump that should have been her calf.

A curly-haired girl runs across the yard towards the shed. One of the dogs is playfully jumping beside her. Pieter stops her when she asks about the new-born calf. 'Don't go in there,' he tells his daughter, 'the calf is dead.'

'How can it be dead? Did you see it, Ellie?' Ursula asks.

'We all did,' Ellie replies, 'and it was not a pretty sight.'

'Have you finished your breakfast?' Pieter asks his daughter. 'School bus will be here soon.'

'Are you going to bury the calf now?' Uschi asks.

'We'll – ' Marty commences.

'Yes,' Grace says. 'He'll be given a nice little grave.'

'Can I watch?' the girl asks.

'You don't have time for that, young lady,' Pieter

says. 'You have to go to school.'

Ursula doesn't look pleased. 'Why can't I just stay home today?' she whinges. 'Grace, can I stay with you?' she asks as she follows the grown-ups to the house.

'Uschi! Quiet!' Pieter yells.

Disapprovingly, Ellie glances at her uncle and takes her cousin by the hand.

'Breakfast anyone?' Grace asks. Pieter follows the others into the house, while Ellie walks Ursula to the end of the dirt road to await the school bus. A few minutes later Pieter emerges from the house to follow behind Ellie and Ursula. He catches up with them at the end of the road.

'You behave yourself in school today,' he says and kisses his daughter on her cheek. 'No whingeing.'

'OK, Dad,' Uschi replies. 'You tell me all about the calf's burial tonight?'

Pieter nods. 'Sure,' he says and lends a hand as she boards the bus. Ellie and Pieter wave at her when the school bus drives off and then retrace their tracks, back to the house.

'When'd you get here?' Pieter asks after a few moments.

'Yesterday.'

A subtle insight shows on Pieter's face as they walk along. 'Rita tells me you enjoy your job,' he says.

'Did she,' Ellie replies. 'So when did you speak to her?'

Pieter raises his eyebrows and makes a vague gesture with his hand. Ellie glimpses at his face. 'You forgot?' she asks.

'What do you mean, I forgot.'

'When you spoke to mum.'

'I saw her last week,' Pieter admits, 'but you weren't there. She said you'll be going to Wellington soon.'

'Oh, did she?' Ellie reacts. 'Well, then she knows more than I do. I wasn't planning on going until next year.' She looks at him. 'Anything else I should know?'
Pieter appears a bit indifferent. 'I'm only telling you what I've heard.'

Slightly disillusioned Ellie looks downwards. 'Maybe she wants me out of the house but doesn't have the nerve to tell me,' she says.

'Oh Ellie, don't start that.'

'Maybe she thinks it's time I should be on my own,' Ellie goes on, 'so she can have more privacy.'
Pieter looks at her. 'Where'd you get that idea? You know that's not true.'
Ellie stops in her tracks and fiery-eyed cries out to Pieter not to be such a hypocrite. 'What kind of idiot do you take me for? I asked you if there was anything else I should know about!'

Pieter is surprised by her sudden outrage and tells her to calm down but Ellie punches him on his arm. 'How long has this been going on between you and my mother?!' she yells.

A slight tenseness shows in Pieter's attitude. He faces Ellie as he ascertains that Rita probably never told her.

'HOW LONG?' Ellie cries out again.

' I ... I think you should talk to your mother about this,' Pieter says and walks on. 'You're being hysterical.'

Ellie grabs him by his arm and makes him turn around. 'How long were you thinking of living this lie?' she asks with suppressed anger in her voice.

'Oh, shut up Ellie,' Pieter says annoyed. 'Don't be so dramatic.'

'Have you ever considered what people might think?' Ellie goes on. 'You can't keep this quiet forever, you know.'

'I've had enough of this. You,' he cautions her, 'talk to your mother.' He turns and takes to his heels.

'And what about Uschi?' she yells after him. 'How would she feel when she finds out she has a whoremonger for a father!'

Pieter pauses for a few seconds but then continues across the field.

Still filled with anger Ellie follows the path back to the house as Marty and William emerge from behind the compost heap. 'What was that all about?' William asks Ellie but she shakes her head and walks up the steps and into the house. She doesn't pay attention to the others in the kitchen and walks straight to the spare room.

'What's with her?' Grace questions.

'Yelling and screaming at Pieter,' William condemns and sits down at the table. 'Someone should tell that girl off.'

'She's not a girl anymore, Dad,' Chrissie says.

'I wonder what's going on in their household,' Grace remarks as she puts the bacon and eggs on the men's plates.

'Trouble, nothing but trouble,' William says, 'single mothers with children.'

'William! Rita's a widow,' Grace rebukes her husband. 'How can you say that?'

Chrissie is helping Grace to clear the table when Ellie appears from the spare room. 'When are you going back to town, Chris?' she asks.

'Eat something first,' Grace says, observing Ellie's sad face. 'Chris and Marty won't be going until ten anyway.'

Ellie takes some leftover toasted bread from the countertop and sits down. Sluggishly she spreads the jam on her toast.

'How come you had a fight with Pieter?' Grace wants to know while she's making fresh tea. 'You always get along so well with him.'

Chrissie winks at Ellie that she should tell but Ellie shakes her head. 'I think, it's better you ask Pieter,' she answers. 'I don't want anything to do with it anymore.'

'To do with what?' Grace asks. 'Don't be so mysterious, child, you know I can't stand that.'

'I don't want problems Grace,' Ellie says. 'Please. Ask Pieter, he'll probably love to tell you.'

Grace looks at her. 'OK, I will,' she says and puts a fresh pot of tea on the table.

From the car Chrissie watches Marty pay the petrol bill. 'I don't think it's a good idea to fight over this with Pieter, Ellie,' she says. 'He's always been so good to you.'

'I can't stand the way he's avoiding the subject,' Ellie replies.

'What do you mean?' Chrissie asks. 'Did you confront him or not.'

'Oh, I did, but he just doesn't want to admit to it. Told me I should talk to my mother.'

'That's strange. So, will you ask her?'

'I don't know,' Ellie quietly replies. 'Maybe I should just wait until she tells me. Maybe, Pieter will talk to her now.'

'Well,' Chrissie sighs, 'to be honest, I think they would make a nice couple.'

'You know,' Ellie utters a moment later, 'I have a feeling that ... ' She is interrupted by Marty jumping back into the car. He throws a newspaper in the backseat and pulls away from the petrol station.

'Dad wasn't pleased about losing another calf,'

Chrissie says after a while and takes a few chocolate bars from her bag. She hands Ellie one.

'Has he lost more then?' Ellie asks.

'Yes, and last year those cows, remember?' Chrissie replies and offers Marty a piece of chocolate. 'They say it's something genetic.'

'Where did that dead calf end up?' Ellie asks Marty who is just stopping at a crossing.

'We dumped it, back of the field,' he replies.

'Nice grave,' Ellie remarks.

'It's alright, William will burn it,' Marty says as he pulls up.

'Yes. I hate to tell you, Ellie,' Chrissie says, 'but that's how they also got rid of our dead pets when we were small.'

'I wonder what Pieter will tell Uschi tonight about the "burial",' Ellie mumbles and looks out the car window.

'Mm, yummy chocolate,' Chrissie say as she experiences the satisfying taste of it, 'this is like the chocolate Nana used to give us. Good old Nana. How is she doing, Ellie?'

'Well, Mum has just been to visit her. She's coping, but it must be hard now that Granddad is gone. Her daughter is with her now. I think she's going to stay.'

'Is she?' Chrissie replies. 'I sometimes had the impression they didn't get along. She hardly visited.'

'Well, America is a long way. An expensive journey,' Ellie says. Chrissie waves that remark aside and says that money was never an object in that family.

'She's come back more often after she divorced her husband,' Marty says, 'that's what Dad said.'

'Well, I'm glad Nana has someone to look after her,' Ellie says. 'I hated leaving their home. They were the sweetest people.'

'Why did you move away from there, anyway?'
Marty asks.

'Rita wanted to be on her own. Independent,'
Chrissie answers.

'She probably wanted more privacy, for herself,'
Ellie mumbles from the backseat.

'What?' Marty asks.

'I really miss Granddad,' Ellie says. 'But I'm pleased
he's not suffering any longer.'

'Yeah,' Chrissie agrees. 'He was such a far cry from
the strong man we knew. Well, here we are,' she
continues. 'Are you staying for lunch or do you want us to
drop you off at your mum's?'

'I'll come with you,' Ellie replies.

《 》

Soon after a disturbing letter had come from Holland my
mother and I moved out of Nana and Granddad's house. It
was all rather sudden and Nana wanted to know if it had
anything to do with the letter but according to Mum that
was not the case. She said that as long as we had been in
New Zealand, we had never had a place of our own and it
would be better for me to change houses now that I was
going to secondary school. But I didn't see what
secondary school had to do with moving to another house.
I hated to leave. One day, I sneaked into my mother's
room to look for the letter. I found it lying on her dressing
table. It was from my aunt in Holland, but before I could
read it, I heard my mother in the hall and I quickly put the
letter back.

Nana was very sad my mother wanted to leave.
Granddad didn't say a word; he just sat there. One evening
I asked my mum why she was so upset about the letter but

she said there was nothing to worry about. 'It's not your problem.'

She had bought a small house in another town and one day Uncle Pieter came to help us move our possessions. When we arrived at the house it already had some furniture in it. I didn't like the house at first. It was a lot smaller than Nana and Granddad's and the garden wasn't half as big. I sat on the bed in the room that Mum had pointed out to me as 'mine' and looked at the bare walls. It had a closet for my clothes, but not even a writing desk. Mum said I could use the kitchen table to write at, but for me that was out of the question. I was angry with her for bringing me here, even further away from my friends and away from Nana and Granddad. I tried to get used to my new surroundings, but missed the big house, with its spirited atmosphere very much.

One day, instead of going home after school, I strolled along the road until I saw someone I knew from Nana and Granddad's village and asked for a ride.

They were very pleased to see me. Nana wasn't even upset with me, but picked up the phone and called someone in town to let my mother know where I was. I was so happy to be with them again and I asked Nana why I could not live with them. I could take the train to go to school. But Nana said that it was not for her to decide. 'A child should be with its mother,' she said.

I didn't agree. 'Mum has her own place now, I could visit her and live with you,' I said. Granddad smiled but Nana said to be realistic. 'Life isn't all a bed of roses, unfortunately. It's a learning-game and that also includes the less pleasant things.'

I thought about that and said that every time something nice happens, my mother makes sure that it doesn't last long. But Nana said I misunderstood. 'You're looking at it from the wrong point of view,' she said. 'Look at all the nice people you've met so far. If it hadn't been for your mother, you would never have met them.'

If it wouldn't have been for my mother I would still be with those nice people, but I kept that to myself.

That evening I listened to one of Granddad's many stories. He still had a slurred speech, but I always understood what he tried to say. He was telling me about this boy in India who lived at their house when they were there. His name was Vijay and no one knew who his parents were. He worked a bit around the house and he was taught to read and write by Nana, who also taught their own children. One day when they were having something to drink outside, in the late afternoon, Vijay's face became all frightened and he looked as if he had seen a ghost. 'His eyes were almost falling out of their sockets,' Granddad said, 'staring at that corner of the veranda.'

'Don't tell her that story,' Nana said, 'she won't sleep a wink tonight.'

But Granddad went on in his slow speech. He said that Vijay claimed to have seen a ghost, his grandfather's. 'Of course, we had always thought that his family were all dead and that Vijay very likely never had met his grandfather, but he said it definitely was his grandfather because he had made himself known, in dreams that Vijay had had.'

I thought the whole story became a bit eerie but still wanted Granddad to continue. According to Vijay his grandfather came to collect him. 'I still remember the look on Nana's face when he said that,' Granddad went on. 'So I asked him where he got that idea. He said his grandfather had beckoned with his hand to follow him.' Granddad gave me a meaningful look and I got goosebumps. Nana told him to stop but Granddad never left a story unfinished. I asked him if they saw the ghost as well but he said it was just Vijay who saw him. So I asked Granddad how they knew he wasn't lying. 'You wouldn't ask that question if you had seen his face,' Granddad said. 'India is not like the West, those people there are very spiritual. They see things that we cannot see.' Again Granddad had this meaningful look on his face. I felt a chill going down my spine. It was silent for a moment until Granddad said: 'Sadly ... a couple of days later, Vijay was dead. Run over by an ox-cart.'

Nana said that that was the saddest event, the servants mourned the boy for days on end. Granddad nodded his head. 'Tragic,' he said. 'But that wasn't all.'

Nana told Granddad that I had heard enough for tonight, but when she went to the kitchen to make us all a hot chocolate, Granddad continued. 'Vijay came back, to visit us.'

'He was dead,' I said. 'How could he visit you?'

'His ghost,' he said.

I asked Granddad if they could see his ghost like Vijay could see his grandfather's.

'No. But he was in the house. We could feel him. And things were moving sometimes ... ' Granddad told about a scare their son had one day. He was in his room when the pieces on the chessboard all of a sudden started moving about. 'Vijay loved a game of chess,' Granddad said. And then there was their dog. Ever since the boy had died he would bark at a corner of the living room. Every night at the same time, always at the same corner.

'There's Vijay again, we used to say. Waiting to hear his goodnight-wish.'

That sounded funny to me but Granddad was serious for after they had said "goodnight Vijay", the dog would stop barking and lay down in the very same corner.

I still had to smile about that but Nana, who had brought in the hot chocolate, was serious too when she said that it was no lie. 'And I have seen Vijay on several occasions after he died,' she said.

Granddad looked surprised.

'I just never told anyone, not to distress the family.'

Granddad said that that must've been the best-kept secret in their marriage and smiled.

'Well, how would you have reacted if I had told at the time, you used to be the last one on earth who believed in ghosts.' Nana told me that Granddad used to be very sceptical about wandering spirits. 'He has mellowed quite a bit over the years,' she said. She saw Vijay sometimes drifting through the garden just before dark and one time he was sitting at the kitchen table and waved at Nana.

'Yes,' Granddad said, 'that boy was certainly happy at our house. So tragic he had to die so young.'

Nana stood up and started looking in the chest of drawers. She said there were still some photographs somewhere of the boy. She took out one of the photo albums; it was one I'd never seen before. After she had flicked through some pages, she pointed at a photograph. 'Look, this is Vijay,' she said. I curiously gazed at the dark-skinned boy in the picture, his black hair in strong contrast with his white teeth, standing tall and proud in front of a tree. 'How old was he when he died?' I asked.

'No one knew exactly,' Nana said, 'but we think he must've been eleven or twelve. He was a bright little chap.'

Nana flipped over a few more pages and showed the rest of the photos, some with the boy, others with their family and servants. They lived in a big house surrounded by large trees in a big garden. The house was built in a beautiful colonial style, as Nana called it.

'And here, this was in Simla.' Nana pointed out a few other photographs. 'Beautiful place, way up in the mountains. Hill-stations they called them. We used to spent holidays there to escape the heat of the city.'

Granddad said that India was his favourite country on earth and if their health had been better it would have been India where they would have spent their old age. Nana nodded in agreement; there was a yearning in her eyes for that far away country with all its mysteries. 'We were very happy there,' she said, while she held the photo album against her breast. 'But, after Independence, everything changed.'

We drank our cocoa and Nana suggested that when I had grown I could go to India and see for myself but I said I wanted to go to Holland.

'Fair enough,' Granddad said.
The evening was very enjoyable, dwelling in Nana and Granddad's presence. I slept in my old room since there was no one else living in anymore after my mother and I had left. Granddad's story about the boy in India hadn't frightened me enough so that I couldn't sleep. Instead, I slid off in dreams about faraway places and cultures unknown to me.

The next morning I rose early to have a nice long breakfast with Granddad and Nana before I went to school. A nurse came to help Granddad and after breakfast, there was still some time left to push him around the garden in his wheelchair. But then it was time to take a train. Before I got on I promised Nana and Granddad I would visit them as often as I could.

'But not without your mother's permission,' Nana said. I told her Mum wouldn't mind and waved at them until they were out of sight.

That day I had a thing or two to tell my classmates but they weren't too impressed, they thought I was making things up. Even my new best friend Mary didn't believe what Granddad had told me the night before. 'My mother says ghosts don't exist,' she said.

What did her mother know anyway, she'd never been to India. I wished Chrissie were there, she would have believed me. When our homework that day was to write a paper I knew what mine was going to be about.

After school, I had to face my mother, but surprisingly she wasn't angry with me. She only warned not to ever accept a ride with strangers. We sat down to have a cup of tea and she wanted me to tell her all about Nana and Granddad and how they were. I asked her again if we couldn't live with them but Mum said it was about time for us to be independent.

When we were given our papers back a couple of days later I had the best mark in the class and our teacher said she was very impressed.

« »

'Are you sure this is the right way?' Chrissie asks Ellie as they walk along a narrow mountain track. Ellie looks confident. 'As long as we follow the path, what can go wrong?'

Chrissie stumbles over a rock but can keep her balance. 'It's just that ... ' she starts. 'Oh, hell.'

'What?' Ellie queries as she turns around. 'Are you OK?'

'Yeah, I guess.' Chrissie lifts her foot while holding on to Ellie. She pinches her ankle and pulls a painful face. 'Rotten ankle. I must've twisted it.' Chrissie takes her shoe off. 'Maybe if there was some cold water around I could soak it,' she says.

'Well,' Ellie replies, thinking, 'we passed that spring a while back.'

'Oh, forget about that,' Chrissie says. 'That was at least half an hour ago.'

Ellie takes her scarf off and pours some water from her water bottle over it. 'Here, put this around. Tightly.'

'Thanks.' Chrissie cautiously wraps the cloth around her sore ankle and with Ellie looking on, she wriggles her foot back in the shoe. 'That should do it,' she says. After she has tried a few steps she is ready to continue the hike. Amidst the green of the surrounding mountains, they walk onward through the gentle freshness of the moist forest. The path is narrowing and at places so overgrown, they have to find their way through the trees in order to continue. 'It looks like no one has been here for ages,' Chrissie says, slightly worried.

'Not many people walk this track,' Ellie replies assuredly. After they have struggled their way through another dense part of the bush Chrissie expresses that she wished they had Marty and Bob there with them instead of having them do the other trail.

'Well, that's what they wanted,' Ellie says. 'We could not "*possibly do that difficult track*",' she imitates Bob.

'Sure,' Chrissie says as they push through the thick undergrowth. 'I wish they could see us now.'

Rather abruptly Ellie halts. Chrissie, who was looking downward so as not to stumble onto any obstacles, bumps into her. 'Jesus,' she utters.

Ellie looks concerned. 'I think we have moved off the track,' she sighs. 'This doesn't look like a beaten path anymore.'

'It never did look like a beaten path, Ellie,' Chrissie says.

'Let's go back,' Ellie says.

'We could also walk around, maybe the path is right there,' Chrissie suggests, whisking at some sand flies. They make a right and slowly walk on until they come to a small clearing. 'Maybe this leads somewhere,' Ellie says and points at a narrow trail going back into the bush.

'Probably an animal track,' Chrissie says. She looks up at the clouds disguising the sun. 'Let's try it,' she says and they follow the trail that gradually winds up the mountain.

'Which way are we going, anyway?' Ellie asks.

'Haven't got a clue,' Chrissie replies. 'As long as we end up in the land of the living again.'

The bush around them becomes darker and more dense. After a while, they stop and sit down on a fallen tree to have a rest. Ellie pulls her jumper out of her bag and puts it on. 'How's your foot?' she asks.

'Fine,' Chrissie replies. 'How much food do we have still? I'm getting hungry.'

Ellie inspects her bag and takes out a few apples. 'And you still had some sandwiches,' she says.

Chrissie opens up her bag. 'You're right,' she replies. 'Had. They're gone. We ate them when we stopped at that stream.'

Ellie hands Chrissie an apple and takes one herself. They sit there in silence and listen to the wind playing through the treetops. The sound is only interrupted by the occasional cries of birds.

'Do you recall which way we came?' Ellie asks after a while. 'I think we should try and find that path.'

'I have a hunch we've been walking up hill,' Chrissie replies. 'Let's find a way down, maybe we'll end up on that track again.'

Chrissie unties her jacket from her waist and puts it on before trying to find the way down. With Ellie following close behind she struggles through the thick shrub.

Too late Chrissie notices she is on the edge of a slope. Trying to keep her balance she slips and with a scream, she slides down the steep cliff.

'CHRIS!' Ellie cries out. 'CHRISSIE!'

In horror she sees her friend swiftly rolling further and further into the gorge, struggling to grab hold of branches and scrubs to break her fall. After a few moments, she disappears from Ellie's sight, who again cries out for Chrissie. She bends over to have a better look, holding on tight to a few branches. 'CHRISSIE! ... Oh, God.'

Only the rumbling of falling rocks rolling down the slope and the sound of breaking branches can be heard. A dull blow emerges from below and a frightful silence sets in. Fearful, Ellie looks down and tries to determine where her friend is, but she can only see a stream running through the steep mountain slopes. 'Chris?!' she calls out once more. When there is no sound she cautiously puts her feet where Chrissie so abruptly went down a few moments before. She holds on tight to every branch she can reach while treading warily down the steep hill. Now and then she glances over her shoulder while she slowly makes her way downwards. At a given moment she sees a piece of cloth hanging on the branch that she just took hold of. She reaches out and manages to grab it. She puts it in her bag that's dangling from her shoulder and once more she calls out Chrissie's name. Again there's no answer and Ellie painstakingly continues. The mist has taken over most of the daylight in the gorge and the atmosphere becomes cold and grey. After a few more metres of clambering down, someone cries out. Ellie startles at the sudden noise and clutches on to a rock. 'Chrissie! Is that you?!'

A soft moaning not far from her makes her look down. 'Chris!' Ellie calls out with joy. 'Chrissie! Are you all right?'

'I will be when you take that foot off my hand,' Chrissie replies with a painful voice.

'Oh, God. I'm sorry. I never even noticed you.'

Ellie cautiously takes a few more steps and kneels next to her.

'Hi,' Chrissie says. 'What happened?'

'Don't you know?' Ellie wonders. 'You fell down that slope.'

She wipes some of the blood off Chrissie's scraped hands.

'Did I?'

'Yes. You gave me an awful fright. How do you feel?'

Chrissie looks up. 'Well, alright I guess. Where are we?'

Ellie tries to see in the distance to ascertain where they are but the fog doesn't give away much of the surroundings. Only the trickling water of the stream below can be heard.

'Now I remember,' Chrissie says. 'I slipped. God, what a fright. I couldn't break my fall.' Suddenly tears start rolling down her face. 'Oh, Ellie, what are we to do? Everything hurts.' Ellie takes Chrissie's scratched hands in hers and tells her that everything will be all right. Chrissie tries to push herself up. 'Let me help you,' Ellie says.

When Chrissie is leaned against the rocky wall of the gorge, they start realising the damage the fall has done to her body. Apart from severely scraped hands and face, her leg has taken a blow and her knee is so swollen, the leg of her slacks is tight around it.

'I hope it's not broken,' Ellie says. 'We should try and make our way further down.'

'I can't do it, Ellie. You go ... Oh, why didn't we take the men with us.' Her tears are washing away the blood on her cheeks.

Ellie puts her arms around her and says that there is no way she is going anywhere without her.

'We have to be realistic, Ellie. Look at this leg. I can't climb down a cliff with this.'

Ellie sits down next to her while the chill creeps in on them. 'We'll have to think of something,' she says while looking at the misty clouds that surround them.

'I think it's best that you go down and follow that stream, it must lead somewhere,' Chrissie says. 'You have to get help.'

'I don't think that's a good idea,' Ellie replies. 'We can hardly see in the distance as it is. What if I walk the wrong way?' Chrissie moves up closer to Ellie to stay warm. 'We have to do something,' she says. 'We'll freeze if we stay here all night.' The chilled wind blows wafts of fog past them, while they contemplate what to do.

'I could go down and see what that stream looks like,' Ellie says. 'Maybe it has a good walking track beside it.'

'You go then,' Chrissie suggests.

Ellie gets up and looks over the edge of the rock to see where there is a way down, then takes hold of a branch and Chrissie sees her slowly disappear over the edge. 'Keep talking to me,' she says.

'OK ... I'm going down.' Gradually Ellie finds her way through shrubs and dense ferns, feeling with her feet for solid ground.

'Are you OK?' Chrissie yells out to her.

'Yes. Still going down ... I can hear the water coming closer.'

It isn't until Ellie is a few feet away from the stream, when she sees there's no path alongside the water. The moss-covered rocks reach into the stream. She stretches out on an overhanging branch and takes her water bottle from her bag. Reaching over, she fills it up with the fast-moving water of the stream and then puts it back in her bag. Instead of going the same way she came, she goes a bit further to the left and makes her way along rocks and low bushes. 'Chrissie!'

'Yes, still here!'

'I'm going to check a bit further on! There's no access here!'

'OK ... Be careful!'

Ellie climbs over a few rocks, following the water downstream. After a while, the stream becomes calmer. She stops and looks around. There's a small path going up against some rocks and back into the bush, she follows it for a few minutes. Then, she walks back the same way she came.

'I've found something!' she yells up to Chrissie.

There's no answer. 'Chrissie!'

Silence.

'CHRISSIE!' With a frightful look on her face she nervously scrambles up the rocks to where she left her friend. When Ellie looks over the edge, she sees her, sagged against the cold wall, her eyes closed. Quickly she moves up to her and shakes her. 'Chrissie. Chrissie! Wake up!' With both her hands she holds Chrissie's pale face. 'CHRIS! WAKE UP!'

A soft moan sounds. 'Chrissie! Open your eyes!'

Slowly Chrissie comes to again. She manages a faint smile when she sees Ellie's face. ' ... I'm sorry ... I must've dozed off.'

'The hell you didn't. You passed out,' Ellie says in a worried voice. 'And you're so cold.' She sits down next to her and wraps her arms around Chrissie's shoulders.

'There's no way I'm leaving you behind like this,' she says. She rubs Chrissie's arms, trying to get her warm.

' ... I'm OK,' Chrissie says. 'How did you do?' she wants to know. 'Is there a path?'

'Yes. A bit further down, going back into the bush. We have to find a way to support your knee so we can go down together.'

Ellie doesn't listen to Chrissie, who expresses her reluctance, and stands up. She breaks off a few branches. 'We need some pieces of cloth to tie them to your knee,' Ellie says. 'Maybe the scarf that's around your ankle.' Then she notices Chrissie's torn bag. After a closer inspection, Ellie rips it apart further and with caution she attaches the pieces of wood on either side of Chrissie's wounded knee. Chrissie pulls a painful face. 'It hurts like hell,' she says. 'There's no way I can walk with this leg.'

'I will help you, don't worry,' Ellie replies. 'Now. Maybe you could slide to the edge.'

With a tormented face, Chrissie manages to slide over the edge with Ellie holding on to her tightly. 'Grab hold of anything that can give you support,' Ellie encourages her. Descending is hard on Chrissie; seeking spots to put her healthy leg down while holding on to branches with her sore hands. Ellie does all she can to help her and eventually they succeed in reaching the point where the branch overhangs the stream.

'I'm dizzy,' Chrissie says in a soft voice.

'It's just the exertion,' Ellie says. 'Take it easy.'

She hands her the water bottle and Chrissie takes a sip.

'Where's the path?' she asks. Ellie points out they have to climb over the rocks a bit further on before they reach the trail.

Desperation shows in Chrissie's face. 'I can't do it,' she utters discouraged. 'Look at those rocks, all wet and slippery.'

'You have to, Chris. You did it so far,' Ellie says. She takes Chrissie's hand. 'You can do it. I'm here. We'll do it together.' A tear rolls down Chrissie's cheek, then she nods. They wait a while for Chrissie to gather more strength before they continue. Ellie goes in front to give Chrissie as much support as she can. With her sore leg, Chrissie tries to find a little hold to keep her balance, but it gives her so much pain she has to give up. She crawls from one rock onto another until they finally reach the trail. Chrissie lets herself fall to the ground in agony and takes hold of her painful knee. 'I can't walk anymore, Ellie,' she cries. 'Please. You have to find help without me.'

Ellie sits down beside her. 'Just rest a bit. It will be dark soon. I can't leave you here by yourself.' She takes her jumper off and puts it underneath Chrissie's head. 'Here, rest a little,' she says. 'And then we'll start again. We will probably run into the others soon.'

'Oh, be realistic,' Chrissie laments. 'They don't even know where we are.'

'We should've been back hours ago,' Ellie states. 'They're probably out looking for us by now.'

Chrissie closes her eyes. 'Just let me rest,' she mumbles.
Ellie looks at her and then gets up. She follows the path for a while and checks the surroundings. Rubbing her bare arms against the chill she walks back.

'Chrissie,' she says, shaking her shoulder. 'Chrissie, wake up. We have to go.'

Chrissie opens her eyes and shivers; her face is pale. Slowly she sits up and looks about her. Ellie takes her jumper and wants to put it back on. 'Are you warm enough?' she asks. Chrissie doesn't pay attention; she carefully strokes her wounded knee.

'Chris, are you warm enough? Do you want to wear my jumper?'

'My knee must be broken,' Chrissie says. 'It hurts so much.'

Ellie puts her jumper back on and looks around for a stick. She finds a few and tries them out. 'This one will do for a crutch,' she decides and hands it to Chrissie.

She helps her friend to her feet. Chrissie holds on to Ellie's shoulder and uses the crutch to support her wounded side. Slowly they continue their way into the forest. 'It's going well,' Ellie says. 'Just, lean on me.'

The path they follow gradually goes down and after quite some time they come to a clearing, it's lit up only by the last streaks of daylight. Ellie looks up at the sky with a worried expression on her face and then turns to Chrissie. 'Are you OK?' she asks.

'Mm,' is the mumbling answer. 'Let's have a rest for a while.' Gently, Ellie leads them to a spot across the clearing where they can sit down on part of a broken fence. They both drink some water from Ellie's bottle. ' ... I feel sick,' Chrissie says.

Concerned, Ellie looks at Chrissie's white, sweaty face when suddenly Chrissie bends over and vomits on the ground.

'Oh, Chris. You're not at all well,' is Ellie's worried reaction. Chrissie wipes her mouth and sighs. 'I'm sorry,' she says.

'Do you feel better now?' Ellie asks. 'We really have to get you to a doctor.'

There is little response from Chrissie, who just sits and rests her head against the fence. 'I don't know, Ellie. I'm exhausted.'

'We can rest a bit more before we go on,' Ellie replies.

'It will be dark soon,' Chrissie says in a soft voice.

'You rest while I have a look around,' Ellie says and wanders off. She follows a path that leads back into the bush, but it's a dead end. Turning back, she notices a side-track and starts following it, when shortly after she sees a little wooden structure between the trees. Inquisitively, she walks towards the shack and cautiously opens the door. There are a few chairs and a table. On a shelf, she finds a loaf of bread wrapped in a piece of paper.

Sudden voices make her turn around but before she can leave the small shack a man enters. 'Look what we've got here,' he says. A younger man, following behind, only smiles.

'Lost, are we?' the man says. 'Or did you just want to have a bite to eat?' nodding at the loaf that Ellie is still holding.

'No, no,' Ellie is quick to say and places the bread on the table. 'Oh, I'm so pleased to see you! You have to help me,' she says to the men. 'My friend and I, we are lost and Chrissie broke her knee!'

The men look at one another.

'Come with me!' Ellie says and grabs one of them by his sleeve as she leaves the shack. 'Do you have a car or something?' she rambles on. 'My friend can't walk.'

The men look at her. The younger one tells her to calm down for a minute. 'How on earth did you get out here?' he asks. 'This part of the bush is not open to the public.'

'Let's just follow her, Simon,' the other man says as he sees the distress on Ellie's face.

'She's at the clearing!' Ellie cries and runs back into the forest.

'What clearing? Come back!'

Ellie stops in her tracks and turns towards the men.

'Now, let's see,' the older man says. 'Are you sure this is the right way? 'Cause there's no clearing up this way.'

Nervously, Ellie looks around. 'Yes.' She's starting to doubt. 'No. No. I couldn't see the door from here.' She turns around indecisively.

'Don't worry,' the man says, 'we'll find your friend.' He turns to Simon. 'She probably means that old paddock. You get the tractor down there while we try to find this friend.' They walk back to the shack and enter the darkening forest on the other side of it as Simon goes down the track to get the tractor.

'Come along, uh … What's your name?'

'Ellie ... Oh, I hope we're not too late.'

'I'm Pete.' He quickly walks on with Ellie following close behind. One time he stops to see if they are going in the right direction with the forest almost dark, but they are soon on the trail that leads them to the clearing.

'I left her by a fence,' Ellie says in a nervous tone.

When they reach the clearing Pete starts looking around but Ellie walks passed him, straight to the spot where Chrissie was left. 'Come on! Here she is,' Ellie says. In the vague light of dusk, they find Chrissie sitting on the ground with her back leaning against the broken fence. Her chin resting on her chest. 'Chrissie!' Ellie screams. 'Chrissie! Wake up!'

Pete, who is right behind her, takes one look at

Chrissie and then pushes Ellie aside. 'Come on, girl!' he yells as he slaps her cheeks. 'Open your eyes!'

With a shock, Chrissie opens her eyes. She shows a faint smile when she notices Ellie. 'Hi ... what kept you so long?' she says softly.

'How long has she been like this?' Pete wants to know but before Ellie can answer he adds they need to get her to a hospital. He looks up when he hears the tractor approaching. A moment later headlights light up the clearing. When the tractor has come to a halt, Pete and his colleague lift Chrissie up and place her on a small, improvised seat at the back. They rest her hurt leg on a few old rags. Pete tells Ellie to stand beside her and make sure she doesn't fall off. He gets behind the wheel while Simon stands next to him, holding on to the front seat.

Ellie tries hard to keep her balance with the tractor driving along the uneven forest track. At the same time, she holds Chrissie in the seat, as she convinces her that everything will be all right.

It seems to last forever but after an unsteady drive, they finally come to a paved road. In the shine of the tractor's headlights, Ellie notices a car parked by the side of that road. Pete stops the tractor and he and Simon, lift Chrissie off the seat and put her on the backseat of the car. 'Hang in there, love,' Pete says. Ellie sits down beside Chrissie while the men take their seats in front. 'I'm so tired,' Chrissie softly sighs as she leans her head against Ellie's shoulder. ' ... So tired.'

'It'll be all right, Chris. We'll get you to a safe place.' Ellie turns to the younger man, wanting to know where they'll be going.

'New Plymouth is the best place, I reckon,' he replies. 'That's where the nearest hospital is.'

'How did you two end up at that godforsaken spot?'

Pete asks.

'We must have taken a wrong turn, I guess. And then Chrissie fell down that gorge.'

'She did what!' Pete says in a loud voice.

'She fell, quite a long way down,' Ellie replies. 'I was so frightened. I thought she ... '

'No wonder she passed out,' Pete expresses. 'You must have walked a long way through the bush to get to where we found you.'

Exhausted, Ellie sits down on a chair in the waiting room while Chrissie is being examined. She looks up at Pete. 'I'm so glad you were still there, in the bush. I don't think we would have made it if it hadn't been for you,' she says and gets up to shake his hand. 'Thank you so much.'

'It's alright, love,' Pete replies. 'I hope your friend will be better soon.' He walks out and a moment later his colleague enters. He hands Ellie a sandwich.

'Thank you,' she says gratefully.

Simon sits down next to her. 'That's quite an ordeal you two must've been through.'

'I was so frightened,' Ellie says in a soft voice, staring at her sandwich. 'But, I'm pleased Chrissie is now being looked after. She's not at all well.'

'The doctors will know what to do,' Simon says. 'Come, eat up. You won't help your friend by starving yourself.'

Ellie manages a smile and takes a small bite from her sandwich.

'Where do you live, anyway?' Simon asks.

'Taihape.'

'Is that so? How come you came here to go hiking?'

'We'd never been here before, thought it would be nice.' Ellie's face clouds over.

'Just the two of you?'

'No, Chrissie's husband and my boyfriend also came ... But, they went off, to do another trail.'

'Why would they want to do that?' Simon wonders.

Ellie looks at him. 'They thought that the one they wanted to do was too difficult for us.'

'Well, they will eat their words now, won't they? So, where are they now?'

Ellie shrugs her shoulders. 'Probably still waiting, in this town where we were supposed to meet.'

'Don't you think you should get in touch with them?' Simon suggests. 'Let them know where you are?'

Ellie gazes down at the sandwich that she has hardly touched. 'I don't know how. We were camping, you see,' she replies, 'and I don't have a phone number. But I did talk to Chrissie's parents, on the phone just now. They are coming right over, they said.'

Simon takes Ellie's hand when he sees her close to tears. 'Everything will be fine now,' he says. 'I'll wait with you till they get here.'

'Oh, you don't have to do that,' Ellie says. 'You and Pete have done so much already.' Her attention is drawn to the door that opens. A nurse enters the waiting room.

'Ellie Visser?' she asks as she notices the only woman present.

'Yes, that's me,' Ellie replies and jumps up. 'How's my friend, how's Chrissie?'

'Well, she's been asking for you all the time. She's fine now, considering the circumstances.'

Ellie lets out a relieved sigh.

'However,' the nurse continues, 'she needs an operation on her knee. Does your friend have family?'

'Her parents, they're on the way,' Ellie says.

'That's fine then,' the nurse says. 'I take it they will

sign a consent?'

'Yes, of course,' Ellie says. 'Can I see her now?'

The nurse is silent for a moment. 'I suppose that'll be all right,' she then says. 'Just don't tire her too much.'

Ellie turns to Simon. 'Thank you very much for all you've done,' she expresses.

Simon gives her a smile. 'Don't worry about it. Go on, go to your friend.'

Ellie swiftly follows the nurse out of the waiting room and goes into a small side room the nurse pointed out, where she finds Chrissie in her hospital bed, attached to an iv-drip.

Carefully Ellie approaches the bed as Chrissie opens her eyes. 'Hi,' Chrissie says. Ellie takes her hand. Most of the blood has been removed but the scratches can still clearly be seen. 'How do you feel?' she says in a hushed voice.

'Well ... an awful lot better than when you dragged me through the bush,' Chrissie replies with a grateful smile.

Ellie smiles back at her, a tear appearing in the corner of her eye. 'I'm sorry,' she says. 'But I had to.' Looking at the equipment by Chrissie's bed Ellie wonders what it is for.

'Don't really know,' is the reply. 'Fluid they said.'

'Are you in pain?'

Chrissie shakes her head. 'No, they gave me something. Did she tell you about the operation?'

'Yeah,' Ellie replies.

'Have you talked to Marty and Bob?'

'No,' Ellie says. 'Don't know where to phone them.'

'I hope they're alright,' Chrissie says with a sigh.

'Oh, Chris. You think about yourself now for a while, OK? Your mum and dad will be here soon.'

They both turn their heads when the door opens. A doctor enters the room. He looks at Chrissie and asks her how she is feeling.

'Not bad,' Chrissie replies, 'with all those painkillers they gave me.'

'A few more tests came back,' the doctor says, fumbling through the file he is holding. He looks at Ellie and asks Chrissie if she wants her there when he gives the details.

'Of course,' Chrissie says. 'Why on earth not?'

'Alright then. Apart from the fracture on the left knee and a sprained ankle, we found a small fracture of the skull as well.'

'What does that mean,' Chrissie questions.

'A lot of bed rest,' the doctor replies with a quick smile. 'But that's OK, it will be good for the other thing we hadn't bargained for.'

Ellie faces him. 'What other thing?'

'The foetus.'

Chrissie looks at him. 'What do you mean?'

'Your baby,' he replies as he checks the iv-drip. 'Or didn't you know?' he adds when he sees her incredulous face.

'A baby!' Ellie calls out. 'You're having a baby!'

'Well, not for a while yet,' the doctor says. 'But as far as we could tell, all is well and healthy.'

Confused, Chrissie looks at Ellie, who is very excited.

'Quieten down a bit,' the doctor says. 'No strain on you, Mrs Woods.' He hesitates before leaving the room, making sure the two regain their former composure.

'A baby,' Chrissie whispers.

4

Mum was very thrilled when Tine Vermeer sent word that they were coming for a visit. Even though we had been in New Zealand for about seven years by then, for some reason my mother liked being among Dutch people. She was rather close to the Dutch lady at the dairy but Tine was Mum's old, and best friend.

Tine and her husband drove down one day in spring just before Mum's birthday. When I came home from school they were sitting outside, having a lot of fun. I took a drink from the kitchen and joined them, listened as they were telling Dutch jokes to each other, about the Germans. I thought the jokes were very funny but had to think of Uncle Pieter. I bet he wouldn't have liked them, but he wasn't there. Tine thought it would be a good idea to visit the National Park. 'Have you ever been, Rita?' she asked my mother.

'No, never got around to it,' my mother replied.

'You don't drive either, do you?' Tine said. 'Why don't you learn?'

Mum didn't seem to be too passionate about the idea, she just looked a bit disinterested. 'I never knew how to drive in Holland, so I don't see why I should learn it here,' she said.

Tine said that that was not the same. 'You can be very isolated here if you don't drive.'

Mum admitted that she was right about that. We always relied on others, usually Uncle Pieter, to take us places. 'But, what do you think a car costs?' Mum said. 'And I just bought this house.'

Tine agreed. 'It must be hard for you,' she said and added with a smile that we should take advantage of the fact that they were here now, so we could go places together.

Mum cooked a really nice dinner that evening, "something from the motherland" and Tine made the desserts. We were just like a real family with Henk and Tine present. Henk helped me with my homework later on, so I would have plenty of time to go with them on the weekend. Mum suggested we should also go and visit Nana and Granddad. We missed them still.

'Ellie even ran away from home once to visit them,' she said.

'Did she?' Henk asked.

I felt a bit embarrassed when she said that because I hadn't run away. 'I just wanted to see them again,' I explained.

'They must be lovely people,' Tine said. 'I can't wait to meet them.'

The following morning, Mum had laid a little table on the veranda so we could have our breakfast outside in the morning sun. We had a nice long breakfast and afterwards, Mum and Tine packed us lunches to take with us. I showed Henk around our garden and cut some flowers to take to Nana and Granddad. I told him that they had lived in India and about the house in which they had lived, where there had been the ghost of a young boy. Henk didn't seem impressed, he said he had heard stories like that before from an old army friend he had. 'He was in the Dutch East Indies and also experienced these things,' he said.

I asked him if he believed in ghosts. 'No,' he replied and said it was about time to go.

Mum and I sat in the back of the car, but I thought it would have been better for Tine to sit in the back with my mother because mum and Tine were constantly chatting to each other with Tine half turned towards her. When we reached Nana and Granddad's we came upon Nana in the garden with her daughter Gwen, who had come all the way from America. Granddad wasn't well and confined to his bed. He suffered from influenza Gwen said. I wanted to go and see him straight away, but Nana thought that was not such a good idea. 'He's sleeping now,' she said. 'Let him rest, dear.'

Mum was worried too and talked to Gwen about Granddad's condition. Nana invited us all in for coffee. She was pleased to meet Tine and Henk from whom she had heard so much. We had coffee and cakes in the pleasant lounge with all the Indian crafts. Although Henk didn't believe in ghosts he was really impressed and asked a lot about their stay in India. Nana told Tine and Henk all about India with Mum listening intently.

I sneaked out and went upstairs to see if Granddad was all right. I was very quiet when I opened the door to his room but he must've been awake for he had his eyes open when I approached his bed. He gave me a bit of a fright when I noticed him looking at me, but when he smiled I knew he was OK. He moved his lips, but there were no words. I told him it was all right and said hello to him, too. I took his hand, it felt clammy but that probably was because of his illness. He soon closed his eyes. I just stood there holding his hand, wondering if he was would be well soon so that we could go out in the garden again. After a while, I heard someone coming in. It was Gwen. 'We thought you were up here,' she said.

I asked her whether Granddad was going to be well soon. She replied that the doctor gave her father all the care he could and that she would stay with her parents for as long as it took. Her husband didn't mind her being away for so long.

'And what about your children, who's looking after them?' I asked her.

'They're in college now, they look after themselves now.'

We waited until we were sure Granddad was peacefully asleep. I kissed him on his cheek before we left the room.

'You're very fond of my parents, aren't you?' she said when we went downstairs. 'Do you have grandparents in Holland at all?'

I told her I only had Opa and Oma Visser but that I hardly knew them. My mother's parents died when she was young from some kind of disease or something. In the lounge, the others had finished their coffee and went outside to have a look at Nana's garden. Nana took me by the hand and asked if we were doing well in our new home. I assured her that it was fine but not the same as living with them. I told her that I had brought my journal. 'It's full, and I would like you to read it, Nana,' I said to her. 'I also wrote about you and Granddad.'

Nana said she would be very interested and 'honoured'.

'And maybe you can give me some more tips.' I felt a bit cheeky when I said that but Nana is such a good storyteller herself, she would know. She smiled and said that she would have a look and make notes, if necessary, before she joined the others who were admiring the rosebushes. I noticed Nana's cat having a snooze in the gazebo and I sat down next to her. Nana had told me this one was getting older too, but she still looked all right to me. I suppose you can't really tell with cats, they don't turn grey or get their face full of wrinkles.

It was almost lunchtime when a doctor came to call

on Granddad and Mum decided that it was time for us to go. I thought we could have lunch here, in Nana's garden, but my mother didn't want to intrude any longer and soon we were all back in the car. We almost drove off when I remembered my journal. Quickly I took it from my bag and jumped out of the car. I heard my mother yell after me not to be so foolish but I went back into the house where Gwen was talking to the doctor. I put the journal on the table after Gwen told me Nana had gone upstairs and I asked her if she could give it to her. Mum told me off when I was back in the car, but what did she know anyway. We drove for quite some time until Henk noticed a nice spot where we could have our lunch. Because Henk was doing the driving all the time I asked Tine why she didn't drive. 'She's still learning,' Henk said.

'Don't listen to him,' Tine replied. 'Ellie, dear, the reason why Uncle Henk is driving all the time is because he doesn't trust me behind the wheel.'

We all had to laugh about that.

I helped Mum and Tine unpack the lunch and put the blanket down. We had a great view of the lake from where we sat. Henk took out his camera and started taking pictures of the scenery around us. I was pulling faces when he wanted to take pictures of us.

'Don't do that, Ellie,' Tine said. 'That's not how we want to remember you.' So, I put on my nicest face. 'That's a sweet girl,' Tine then said, holding her own sweet face next to mine. I wondered why my mother couldn't be as funny as Tine was.

Mum and Tine were soon busy talking again and I wandered off with Henk who was looking for nice spots to take photos of. After a while, he asked me if I wanted to take a photograph. I was surprised that he trusted me with his camera, but when he said that he would show me how

I loved giving it a try. I took a few photos, one with Henk with the lake in the background.

After lunch, we drove on. Tine had changed places with me and was in the back with my mother. Being from the city Tine and Henk really enjoyed the natural surroundings here and Tine mentioned we were very lucky to have all that beautiful scenery so close to where we lived. Henk parked the car near a trail not far from the lake. He wanted to go on a walk but Mum wasn't wearing the right shoes. 'That's OK,' Henk said. 'This is an easy trail.'

'How would you know?' Tine said. 'You've never been here before.'

Mum backed her up; she didn't want to go on a walk. Henk jumped back in the car, saying he was just joking. 'Let's go for a swim,' he said. 'Such a big lake is hard to resist.' Tine, Mum and I weren't sure whether Henk was having us on or not but we went back in the car. Before long we were at the lake changing into our togs.

When we first came to this country I didn't know how to swim but Uncle Pieter had taught me. 'All Dutch kids should know how to swim,' he used to say.

I had a swimming race with Henk, but he won. Tine said it wasn't fair of Henk to take on a thirteen-year-old, but I didn't mind. I hadn't had so much fun for a long time. Later on, when we were relaxing in the sun, letting our bodies dry, Henk said he would really like to go for walks in the mountains. He loved the forests and mountains of New Zealand but they had never taken the time to see them properly.

'Next vacation we'll go on a camping trip,' Tine said. 'I'd love to see more of this country too.'

Henk thought that it was a great idea. 'No more windmills and tulips for me.' That was a funny thing to say I thought because there were no windmills and tulips here.

'Then you probably didn't have a good look in our garden when you were in Auckland that day,' Tine said with a laugh.

Mum said that she missed Holland still. I couldn't understand why. New Zealand was much nicer than Holland. But then, to my surprise, Tine said she sometimes had the feeling she would like to go back to Holland. 'There are just certain things in Holland you will never find here.'

'Like what?' I wanted to know.

'Clogs,' Henk said which left me in chuckles again.

'You know what I mean,' Tine then said. But Henk claimed he couldn't think of anything and challenged me to another race. Only, my mother said that I shouldn't get wet anymore. So I ran after Henk, back into the water, and we had another race, which he won again.

I got a nice tan that afternoon and Tine told Mum I probably inherited my father's skin tone for my mother always burned rather quickly in the sun. Henk suggested we could drive to Taupo and have a look around, but my mother said we should go back. 'By the time we get there everything will be closed.'

'What about the castle?' Henk asked.

'What castle?' We didn't know of a castle around here.

Tine said he meant the Chateau Tongariro.

'But that's a hotel,' Mum replied. Henk suggested we could still have something to drink there and it was on the way home. Mum started to grumble a bit and said we could never afford a drink there but Tine told her not to worry. 'It's not that expensive,' she said. 'Friends of ours stayed there last year and they could afford it. I think they paid about forty shillings, including meals.'

Mum was surprised; she thought it would be more expensive. Henk said that a room for that price was probably without a private bath.

We could smell the trees through the open car windows. I stuck my head outside the window and let the wind blow through my hair. It gave me a feeling of freedom, but my mother told me not to act so dangerously and to keep my head inside. I didn't want to, but then Henk said that there had been people who'd lost their head that way. I didn't believe him, but as not to scare the others I stopped putting my head out the window. Henk pulled up by the side of the road a couple of times because we passed by some beautiful water streams.

I will never forget the first view of the Chateau. I'd never seen anything so impressive. I asked Tine if all chateaux were like that. She said she was in France once, years ago, with her parents just before the war. She'd seen a few castles there and they were beautiful also. Henk parked the car in front and we went in. There weren't many people around, because of low season Henk said. We sat down at a table in the posh restaurant and a waiter came to take our order. Mum didn't want anything at first but Tine told her they would pay. 'For your birthday, Rita. Enjoy yourself for once,' Tine said.

Henk told my mother she should let go of her Dutch frugality. Mum became a bit more relaxed; she didn't mean to spoil the fun. We had a really nice tea. Mum, Tine and Henk shared a bottle of wine. I couldn't have any but was pleased with the cola I could have.

I enjoyed our time at the Chateau with its lovely atmosphere, very much. It seemed too soon when we had to leave, but it was getting late and we still had to drive home. There was still enough daylight outside for Henk to take a picture of us standing in front of the car with the Chateau in the background.

On Sunday morning I wasn't the only one up early. Tine also wanted to surprise Mum and decorate the living room. In a way, I was glad she did because I couldn't reach up high to attach the paper chain.

'A few more years and you'll be tall enough to do it all by yourself,' Tine told me in a soft voice. We had to be quiet so as not to wake Mum. We made some paper flowers too and then the room looked ready for the party. It had never looked so nice on my mother's birthday before, but then on other birthdays, we didn't have Henk and Tine staying. After the decorating, we prepared the table for a nice breakfast, but, of course, we put Mum's breakfast on a tray and took it to her. She was really surprised and pleased, that for once she didn't need to be the first one up to make preparations for breakfast. I bought Mum a nice blouse for her birthday. I couldn't afford it all myself but Uncle Pieter had chipped in too. She really liked the blouse. There was also a gift from Tine and Henk. 'But, what about the expensive dinner last night?' my mother asked. But when she opened the present, all she could say was that they shouldn't have done. It was a beautiful Dutch embroidered table-cover, with matching napkins. Tine had made it herself. Mum almost cried when she thanked them.

'Now, don't let your tea get cold,' Tine said. 'We'll see you in a moment.'

A while later Mum came into the kitchen. She was wearing the blouse I had given her and she had found a skirt to match it. She looked lovely and Henk got up and made a little dance with her around the table. Mum looked so happy, and she was amazed by the decorations.

'You're not going to strain yourself today,' Tine said when Mum wanted to get up and clear the table after we were finished. 'We will look after that.'

Mum went outside to relax on the veranda. Henk joined her while we were cleaning up and making everything ready for coffee with the surprise birthday cake. Well, that wasn't such a surprise anymore for Mum knew we were baking the cake Friday evening. Tine is very creative and she managed to write "34" and "Happy Birthday" with cream on the cake. Mum loved it and the cake was delicious. I asked for another piece but Mum said to save some for the others. 'And please,' my mother asked of Henk, 'no German jokes when Pieter gets here.'

Around lunchtime, he arrived with little Ursula. Grace wasn't able to come he said, but he gave Mum 'a little something' from her. I straight away took Uschi from Uncle Pieter as he was introduced to Tine and Henk. Uschi looked so cute. I bet the pretty dress she was wearing was Grace's idea.

Uncle Pieter carried a rather large parcel into the house and put it on the kitchen table. 'Your birthday present,' he said. Mum was a bit confused and didn't know what to say. We all gathered around and I said to her to open it. I was so excited. Mum reacted a bit nervous when she opened the box and couldn't believe her eyes when she saw what was inside. 'A radio? Oh, Pieter.' She gave him a big hug and a kiss.

'Now I can have that old one back that I lent you,' Uncle Pieter said.

We were all very excited and Henk suggested trying it straight away. It was the latest model he said. Uncle Pieter took the radio out of the box and plugged it in. Together with Henk, he searched for the channels and we could all hear it was working well. Uschi was more interested in the wrapping paper. She tore it all to pieces and was screeching with laughter, it was so funny. Henk picked up his camera and took some photographs of Uschi and Mum with her new radio. Tine lifted Uschi from the floor. 'She is so lovely,' Tine said.

'She just had a birthday herself,' I said. 'She's four now.'

'Did you?' Tine said to Uschi. 'And you're so pretty.' Uschi smiled but that's what she does a lot. 'She's a happy little girl,' Grace always said.

Mum poured Uncle Pieter a cup of coffee and cut another piece of cake. We went outside again to enjoy the nice weather on the veranda. Uschi was given a glass of lemonade and Uncle Pieter gave her some of his cake. Tine asked Uncle Pieter if he was the same Pieter that wanted to move to the South Island and of course he was, but Uncle Pieter said that it had been a bad idea. 'Couldn't get a good enough price for my property,' he claimed. But I think he just didn't want to be so far away from all of us.

Tine and I prepared lunch on this day. She had an idea to make things only the Dutch way, and she had brought some Dutch biscuits that she made before. 'Dutch things for the Dutch,' she said. I asked her if she really liked Holland better than New Zealand and she replied she did, sometimes. 'Sometimes I'd rather be in Holland, then, at other times I feel we are better off here,' she admitted. I could imagine how she felt for I had moments that I would want to be away from New Zealand so I told Tine that I would like to go to Holland one day.

'I suppose you would,' she replied. 'But we should be happy with what we have,' she said before we carried the trays with food outside. I took Uschi on my lap and we shared a plate of sandwiches. Uncle Pieter was happily talking to Henk and I heard Tine ask my mother why she moved to a place so far from where Pieter lived. 'Why didn't you buy something in Raetihi?' Tine wanted to know. Mum seemed a bit reluctant to reply. I sometimes wondered myself why we had to move away a lot farther. Tine mentioned she could tell what the situation was between her and Pieter but Mum hushed her.

Tine was right, we had always been close to Uncle Pieter ever since we first arrived here and he came to visit often. Mum said she hadn't been able to find a house in Raetihi that suited her budget.

We had such a nice afternoon. Me playing with Uschi and the others having laughs while they were drinking drinks on the veranda. I was sorry Uncle Pieter and Uschi had to leave again. And I was even more sorry I had to go to school the next day while my mother was going on day trips with Henk and Tine, who were going to stay with us for the rest of the week. I begged Mum, asking her if I could just have a few days off from school but she was unrelenting. I hated that, for it meant that that was the end of it. 'You can't always have it the way you want it,' she said, which left me running to my bedroom, crying.

My mother thought I was having her on when I told her I wasn't feeling well the next day. 'If this is one of your tricks to be able to stay home from school, you're wrong Ellie,' she said. I really felt a bit tired and my tummy ached. Mum said it might've been the excitement of last weekend, but Tine thought I did look a bit pale. 'You don't think she's coming down with that flu granddad MacIntosh had, do you?' she asked Mum. My mother took a good look at me and then decided it would pass and I was sent to school. I hadn't been in class long when the tummy-ache became worse. The teacher said I was lucky that the nurse was on duty today and she sent me to her.

The nurse asked me if I had eaten something wrong and I told her that it had been my mother's birthday.

'Always the same,' she said. 'People always overeat on days like that,'

I said to her I'd never been sick after someone's birthday. 'But we did visit Granddad and he had influenza,' I told her. She looked shocked when I said that. 'Why didn't you say so straight away, and your mother sends you to school?!' She scared me and I asked her if it was a bad disease. She looked at me and said it was very contagious. I mentioned that I kissed Granddad on his cheek and that I held his hand.

'You see? There you have it,' she said. She asked if she should contact my mother to come and collect me, but I told her I'd be all right, that I didn't live far from the school.

'You have your mother contact the doctor when your illness becomes worse,' she said before I left her office.

I walked home slowly and I wished I would have had the nurse contact my mother then at least Henk could've come to get me in his car. I felt tired when I walked up the steps and called for my mother. It was then I noticed the car was gone. They had left already.

I had a drink of water and lay down on the couch with a pillow under my head. At least that way the tummy-ache wasn't so bad. I must've dozed off and woke up because I felt a bit sick. I wondered whether I should ask the neighbour to contact the doctor or just go to bed. I had another drink of water and decided to go to bed because I wasn't too fond of the doctor. I didn't really sleep, just rested and thought it wasn't such a bad way to spend a school day. After a while, the pain became less and when I stood up to get a book from the shelf above my bed I was drawn to a red stain on my bed cover. I was puzzled as to where it had come from. Then I noticed my school uniform also had a red stain on it. I touched it with my fingers and realised it was blood. Quickly I took off the skirt to see where the blood was coming from. Panic seized me; my panties also had a bloodstain. I didn't know what to do. I went to the bathroom and tried to see if I had an injury somewhere but couldn't find anything. Fear overcame me. Granddad also had influenza but they hadn't mentioned he was bleeding. Maybe I had something much more serious. Panicked, I grabbed a towel and put it around me. I ran out of the house and to the neighbour. I called her name but there was no answer. I yelled until she finally appeared from behind the house. 'What's with you?' she asked.

I told her to call a doctor. 'I'm bleeding!' I cried.

She annoyed me by asking where I was bleeding. 'Get a doctor!' I yelled, crying. I felt a warm trickle going down my leg and Mrs Evans must have noticed because she took me by my arm and told me to be calm and come into the house. I tried to explain to her that the nurse at school had said to send for a doctor.

'Calm down first,' she said and took me to her house. She looked at me and once more asked me where I was bleeding and maybe she could do something about it. I was embarrassed but told her where I thought the blood was coming from. She just looked at me and asked me to sit down but I didn't want to get her chair full of blood.

'I take it your mother never had a talk with you?'

She confused me with that question, for Mum and I talk about a lot of things.

'About what it means to become a woman,' she went on.

I just stood there and thought about the time my mother had mentioned something about me getting a boyfriend.

'Do you know anything about it?' she asked. I told her that all I knew was that the nurse at school had said I might have influenza and that it now caused the bleeding. She didn't say much but took me into her bathroom and told me to remove the towel. She got a cloth and started cleaning the blood from my leg. I felt like a small child with her cleaning me up but she seemed to take me seriously and I was pleased about that.

'You know, I've seen people with influenza and you don't look like one of them,' she said. 'I'd say you're just having your first period.'

'My ... what?' I asked.

She shook her head and took some pieces of towelling from a cupboard. I recognised these pieces of cloth; my mother had the same ones. I once had asked Mum about those things but she had said she would explain about it when I was a woman myself. Mrs Evans handed the towel back to me and motioned me out of the bathroom. 'Let's go over to your house and I'll explain,' she said.

With the towel around me, I followed her to our house. She was irritated with my mother. She said it was not right for a stranger to tell her daughter those things. 'She must've noticed something,' Mrs Evans said, 'but still she goes off and leaves you to it. It's just not right,' she said once more.

I felt some kind of relief now that I had the impression that the situation wasn't as bad as it seemed at first. Mrs Evans told me to get a clean pair of panties and explained to me how to wear the pads, as she called them. When I was clean and dressed Mrs Evans told me I would have the period once a month and that it would last for a couple of days. There was nothing abnormal about it.

'Every woman gets it. That's what allows us women to have babies,' she added with a smile, 'something to be proud of. And now, let's have a cup of tea.'

After she had made us a nice cup of tea I felt better. The ache in my belly wasn't completely gone, but Mrs Evans said I would get used to that unpleasant feeling once a month. I told her I felt rather embarrassed about it all, but she said it wasn't my fault for I wasn't to know if no one had ever bothered to explain it to me. 'Keep track of the date when you get your period and you won't have any surprises,' she said before she went back to her own house.

I put my school uniform in some water, hoping the stain would come out. I didn't know what to do with the bedcover so I threw it in the washhouse and took a clean one from Mum's room. I then lay down and had a rest, trying to get used to the idea of becoming a woman. I felt the two small bumps on my chest, wondering if they would grow any bigger. I supposed they would; all women I knew had bigger ones.

My mother, Tine and Henk came home around three that afternoon. Their laughter told me they had enjoyed their day. Mum looked a bit surprised when she saw me walking into the kitchen.

'Home already, dear?' she asked.

She didn't even ask if I was feeling better. She had probably completely forgotten about that incident. 'The nurse at school sent me home,' I said to her.

'Oh? Did she?' is all my mother could say. 'Are you alright now?' She just continued making a pot of tea.

I told her I was all right, now that Mrs Evans had taken care of me.

'Who's Mrs Evans?' Tine asked.

Mum wanted to know if it was that serious, she said I didn't look that ill.

'She at least was there to explain about my menstruation!' I said in a loud voice. 'Something you failed to do!'

Mum looked shocked and told me to hush it with Henk being there, but I yelled at her not to be such a hypocrite. '*You* should have told me!' I cried.

My mother said not to make a scene and that we should go and talk things over quietly.

'You should have thought of that before!' I yelled at her. Tine intervened and put an arm around me. She took me outside and told me not to be so upset about it. 'I'll talk to your mother,' she said.

I felt a slight triumph when I sat down on one of the veranda chairs. Henk came out too and walked into the garden. I heard Tine's voice coming from the kitchen saying to my mother she couldn't believe that she never told her daughter anything about it. Mum just said she never wanted to give me any ideas if there was no reason. Tine's voice became lower and I leant back to be able to hear better. She said something about she could tell my breasts were growing when we were swimming at the lake and found it strange Mum didn't see a reason. 'She swims with boys her age too. Do you think they don't notice?' Tine said in a soft voice.

I looked down at my chest and straightened my blouse. I wondered what boys did think of my breasts. Mum said she had heard enough and a door closed. A moment later Tine came outside and I let her know that I hoped my mother wasn't angry with her. Tine assured me it would be all right. 'Don't worry about it.'

Now, that Tine and Henk were there, Mum slept in my room and that evening before we went to sleep, she apologised for what had happened. She gave me a book to read which explained a lot about the problems of becoming a woman, as she put it.

I was allowed to stay home from school for a few more days. Mum went to see our neighbour to thank her and had a talk to the nurse at school so they wouldn't be alarmed about my 'influenza'. Tine and I went for a walk one evening. She was fun to be with and I wished my mother could be more like her. Mum can be such a thickhead at times.

<< >>

When Marty pulls up the car in front of their house there's an uncanny silence around it. He peers through the windscreen and looks out in the street.

'Something wrong?' Chrissie asks. Marty shakes his head. He takes her crutches from the backseat and opens the door to help his wife out.

'I'll be alright,' Chrissie says. With the crutches supporting her, she walks through the garden towards the house with Marty beside her.

All of a sudden the front door flies open and the family comes out with Ellie yelling: 'Surprise!'

Chrissie starts laughing when she sees her mother and brother with Ellie and Bob, welcoming her home. 'And I was just saying to Marty we could have a quiet day in.'

'Not today, love,' Grace says. 'How are you?' She hugs her daughter carefully.

'I won't break, Mum,' Chrissie says and submits to the attention of the others. 'Hello, Jody,' she says. 'Good to see you. Did they let you off?'

'Not for a while yet,' Grace says, a bit displeased. 'He has signed up for the Air Force now.'

Chrissie looks at her brother surprised. 'Did you? What made you do that?'

'I want to become a pilot,' Jody replies.

Ellie ushers everybody inside. She rushes to get Chrissie a chair and tells her not to stand on her leg too long. 'Remember what that doctor said,' she tells her.

Chrissie gets another surprise when she sees the large cake on the table. 'Welcome home,' she reads laughingly.

'Here,' Grace says and hands Chrissie a knife. 'You slice that, it's your party.'

With Ellie holding the plates, Chrissie puts the pieces of cake on them. 'Dig in everybody,' Bob says. 'Ellie's been baking all day yesterday.'

The look Ellie gives him tells the rest he was exaggerating with that remark.

'We're all so pleased you're home again,' Grace says. 'Your dad tells me you have to go back to that hospital. Is that true?'

'No, Mum. He probably misunderstood. I only have to go to the local GP for check-ups,' Chrissie replies.

Marty tells her to be very careful for the next few months. 'It's also my child you're carrying,' he says. Grace assures him she will be there to help Chrissie as much as she can. 'And me too,' Ellie says.

Bob touches her arm. 'What about me?' he asks her quietly.

'You can help as well,' Ellie replies in a soft tone.

'That's not what I mean,' Bob says. 'We've hardly had any time to ourselves with you running off to the hospital all the time.' Ellie looks at him. 'Do you feel deprived or something?' she says under her breath.

Bob glances down at his half-eaten slice of cake. 'Forget about it,' he mutters.

Chrissie wants her brother to tell her all about his

plans with the Air Force when Grace takes Ellie aside, wanting to know whether she has talked with her mother lately. Ellie looks a bit puzzled. 'What do you mean?'

'You know what I mean, Ellie. I finally had a chance to talk to Pieter a couple of days ago. He wasn't willing, but he told me just the same.'

Ellie is getting slightly uncomfortable.

'Well, you said yourself I should ask him,' Grace continues. 'And I tell you, I was highly surprised ... but, at least a lot has become clear to me now.'

'I'm sorry, Grace,' Ellie says.

'It's not your fault, child.'

Ellie wonders if they can continue their talk in the kitchen. 'Do you think Uncle Pieter will marry Mum?' she asks, closing the door behind her.

'Well, that's why I asked you just now, if you had spoken to your mother,' Grace replies, 'for the impression I got was that there isn't going to be a wedding.'

Ellie stamps her foot. 'I ... I just don't understand!'

'That's why! That's why I think you'd better talk to your mother and listen to what she has to say for herself,' Grace says.

Ellie glances at Grace with a surprised look on her face. 'You don't think that it's my mother who doesn't want to marry, do you?'

'Well, that is a possibility.'

With a sigh, Ellie sits down at the table. 'And I thought it was Uncle Pieter. Him taking advantage of Mum.' She shakes her head. 'I don't understand it. Do you think ... they don't love each other?'

'That's what I asked Pieter,' Grace replies. 'But, he told me not to interfere.'

'Did Uncle Pieter mention at all how long they've had this affair?' Ellie asks.

Grace shakes her head. 'Frankly, it's just not the proper way.'

'I know that,' Ellie says somewhat irritated. 'Oh, I'm sorry, Grace. It's just that ... I love them both, but what can I do?'

'It's all right,' Grace reassures her. 'You cannot make the decisions for them.'

When Grace wants to go further into the matter the door opens and Marty enters. He takes a few beers from the refrigerator. 'Why are you locking yourselves in here?' he asks. 'Don't spoil the fun.'

'You're right,' Grace says and suggests they could do with a fresh cup of tea. She takes the kettle and puts it on the stove while Ellie joins the others. When she observes their busy talking, she goes outside, where she finds Jody who has made himself comfortable on the porch, his feet resting on the railing.

'Escaping civilian life already, are you?' Ellie questions.

Jody turns his head. 'Not really,' he replies.

Ellie takes a seat next to him.

'I don't know about them,' he says and makes a subtle movement with his head towards the open door, 'but I never thanked you for what you did for my sister.'

Ellie looks at him. 'You don't have to thank me. I couldn't have dreamt of leaving her behind.'

'Yes, well. If it hadn't been for you, she might've perished there.'

'Don't say that, Jody,' Ellie softly says.

He glances at her briefly and takes a sip from his beer.

'So, uh, I bet your father wasn't pleased when he heard you were joining the military,' Ellie mentions.

'It's not his life,' Jody says. 'He has his farm.'

'Yes, but, I thought you liked the farm.'

Jody takes the last few sips of his beer. 'I never hated it,' he says, 'but I never had the intention of taking over. And now, I've decided I want to be in the Air Force.'

Ellie has another look at his smooth, attractive face.

'I would never have pictured you in a military job,' she says.

'But you did picture me as a muddy looking farmer, I suppose, with a weathered face at forty,' he says half smiling.'

'Oh, I don't know,' Ellie replies.

A silence sets in until Grace appears in the doorway. 'More tea, children?' she asks. Ellie looks up and takes a cup from the tray. Jody declines. He nods in the direction of a figure approaching in the street. 'There's Rita,' he says.

'Oh, it is too,' Grace states. 'About time we met up again.'

Wearing a floral dress, Rita blends in nicely with the borders in the garden as she makes her way to the house. 'Sorry, I'm a bit late,' she says, 'it was very busy at the shop all of a sudden.'

'That's alright, Rita,' Grace says and hugs her. 'How have you been?'

'Can't complain. Oh, hello Jody. How are you?'

Rita follows Grace inside to welcome Chrissie home from the hospital. She hands her a gift and says it is still a bit early but one can never start early enough getting the layette together. Curiosity drives Ellie into the house as well to see what gift her mother brought for Chrissie who is delighted to find an exquisite, hand-knitted baby outfit in the wrapping paper.

'Thank you, Rita,' she says with a happy smile. 'It's so lovely. Look Mum,' and hands it to Grace. 'Isn't it beautiful?'

Even the men can't help but admire the tiny pieces of clothing.

'Mum, cuppa tea?' Ellie asks her mother. 'Have some cake too.'

When the quietness of the evening sets in, Grace decides on accompanying Rita home. Jody offers to drive them, but his mother feels that won't be necessary. 'It's a lovely evening for a walk,' she says. 'You have fun amongst yourselves.' Grace takes her shawl from the spare room and wraps it around her shoulders. Together with Rita, she strolls through the garden and onto the street. 'A bit nippy tonight,' Rita remarks.

'It is, still, this time of year,' Grace replies, greeting a neighbour who is arriving home. Rita seems somewhat ill at ease as she strolls beside Grace along the darkening streets.

All of a sudden she halts. 'Grace, I don't know what you think about it, but Pieter and I will never get married,' she says out of the blue.

Grace stops, too, and turns to face her. 'Why?' she asks, slightly surprised. 'Have you ever discussed it with Pieter?'

'Not in exact terms,' Rita replies.

'Rita, you know I don't like to be kept in the dark,' Grace pronounces. 'I've known you both now for many years and I think that all that secretive behaviour is rather distressing. Now, you either marry him or you let him go.'

An astounded expression appears on Rita's face. 'I'm sorry Grace,' she says dismayed, 'but I think I'm old and wise enough to rule my own life.'

'Old, yes, but wise?' Grace wonders. 'Do you have any idea how Ellie has been feeling about this situation?

And as for little Ursula, well! I tried talking to Pieter about this but ... ' She makes a vague gesture.

'I don't know about Uschi,' Rita says, 'but you know yourself how dramatic Ellie can react to certain situations.'

'And this time she has good reason,' Grace goes on. 'I'm advising you, Rita. Do something about it.' She gives Rita one more look and then continues on her way. Rita vacillates, only to follow a moment later.

'The thing is, Grace ... ' she becomes somewhat irresolute, 'I have a feeling Pieter doesn't love me enough to marry me.'

Grace turns and looks at her searchingly. 'Well. So it is true, Pieter is just using you. I don't see how – '

'Grace!' Rita interrupts her. 'Grace, I – '

'Don't let yourself be used, Rita,' Grace urges.

Rita appears to be lost for words as they silently follow the way to her house.

'I'll catch up with you later,' Grace says when they've reached Rita's garden fence. 'I'm going to be in town for a couple of days.' Rita gives her an appreciative look before she enters through the garden gate.

'And remember what I said,' Grace says before she walks off.

Ellie takes a suitcase from the storage and goes to her room where she opens her closet. After an examining look, she takes out most of her clothes and lays them out on her bed. A few dresses, skirts, shorts and slacks. Indecisive she looks at the pile of clothes. Next, she starts folding them and tries to fit them all in the suitcase. When the clothes are crammed into the case she pushes with all her might to close it. To no avail. While taking out most of the clothes her attention is drawn by a soft rustle. She turns to see Pieter standing in the doorway. In silence, she continues unpacking.

'Are you ... leaving, or coming back?' Pieter asks. Ellie sorts out her clothes and tries to fit the favourite pieces back into the suitcase.

'So ... you're leaving,' he concludes.

'Mum's not here,' Ellie says.

'I know. She's at work, she told me.'

Without saying a word, Ellie looks at him and continues packing the suitcase. With the chosen clothes fitted in the suitcase, there is still room for a few more pieces.

'It's you I wanted to see,' Pieter says. 'That is, if you can find the time.'

'What do you want, Pieter?' Ellie demands.

'Pieter, aye? What happened to *uncle*?'

'What do you want, *Uncle* Pieter.'

He makes a slight movement with his hand and wonders if they can't sit down to talk things over.

'Talk things over?' Ellie asks. 'Since when are you one for talking things over.'

'Don't you think it's about time we had a chat?' Pieter offers. Without saying a word Ellie walks to the door and passes him by to go to the living room. Pieter follows her close behind.

'OK,' she says and sits down. 'Chat.'

Pieter looks at her searchingly. 'Well. I know your mother and I haven't been really fair to you – '

'Or to Uschi,' Ellie interjects.

'OK, OK, but she's too young to understand.'

'You know, Uncle,' Ellie goes on, 'I've been doing a lot of thinking lately and sorted this whole situation out for myself. So, I don't really see why we're having this conversation.' She looks at him in an accusatory manner. 'All I have to say is that I'm happy. That finally, after all these years, you've decided to "talk things over".'

Pieter sighs and sits down across from her. 'I just want this ... hostility that's between us now out of the way,' he says calmly. 'It's been going on for weeks. How much longer do I have to put up with it?'

Ellie shrugs her shoulders as if it matters nothing to her.

'Rita hardly wants to see me anymore,' Pieter resumes, 'Grace has been giving me the cold shoulder, and as for you ... I thought we were a family, that we meant something to each other?'

He shakes his head, while Ellie keeps silent. She merely looks at his despairing face.

'It takes two to tango, you know,' Pieter says. 'Rita was just as willing. I never forced her.'

'You should've married,' Ellie reproaches.

Pieter rises from the chair and starts walking about the room. 'I was married once,' he then says. His voice sounds sad. 'Or have you forgotten?' The indifference in Ellie's attitude amends to a more compassionate manner as she asks him whether he loved Birgit.

'Of course,' he says.

'Well ... considering it was a shotgun marriage,' Ellie continues, 'one could ask oneself.'

'What? What do you mean, Ellie?'

'Uschi was born a perfectly healthy child,' Ellie replies, 'scarcely seven months after the wedding.' She looks up at him and adds that she does know how to calculate. Pieter is dumbstruck for a moment. He sits down again and says that that's not what he came to talk about.

'Why didn't you marry Mum?' Ellie demands. There's a brief silence while Pieter looks at her. 'Well – '

'And don't say it's because you've been married

before, Pieter,' she interrupts his attempts to explain.

Pieter falls quiet. Then he gets up and walks to the door. 'You don't have any idea what I went through back then, do you?' he says before he leaves. With force, he closes the door behind him. The slamming makes Ellie shrink back. For seconds she gazes at the shut door. Then, she jumps up and runs towards it. 'Uncle Pieter!' she calls out as she pulls to open the door. 'Uncle Pieter!'

Pieter doesn't take any notice of her calling and starts the engine of his car. Ellie runs to grab the car door. 'Please,' she implores. 'Don't go!'

When Pieter doesn't make any attempts to stop the car Ellie begs him not to leave. 'Please, Uncle Pieter. Don't go away angry.'

He hesitates. A moment later, however, he stops the engine. 'I'm not angry,' he says calmly. 'Just disappointed.'

Ellie gives him a compassionate look when she notices his eyes moist with tears.

'Could you please let go of my car, so I can leave?' Pieter asks.

'Uncle Pieter, I'm sorry, I really am. Please!'

Pieter seems reluctant but then steps out of the car. 'Anything else you need to get off your chest?' he wants to know. 'Or is this behaviour yet another trick to have things your way.'

Only, Ellie is serious when she tells him it is not a trick. She slides her hands around his neck and in a gentle voice apologises for being so ignorant. Pieter takes her wrists and removes her arms from his shoulders. He looks at her, trying to determine whether she meant what she just said.

'I never thought about ... what you and Birgit had together,' Ellie says with remorse. 'Gosh, I hardly knew her.'

'I'm glad you finally realise,' Pieter ascertains. He opens the car door and wants to get in.

'Why don't you believe me?' Ellie utters disheartened.

'Ellie,' Pieter says as he leans on his car door, 'I do believe you.'

'Well, won't you ... stay for a while?' Ellie asks. 'Have a cup of coffee or something?'

Pieter pauses for a moment but then gives in. He closes his car door and together they stroll back to the house with Pieter wondering what's with the packing business. 'Are you off somewhere?'

'Not yet,' Ellie replies, 'I was just trying to see what I could take with me to Wellington.'

'When are you going?'

'Next month, still have to find a room,' she says.

'Do you need a ride there?' asks Pieter. 'I could take you if you want.'

'Thanks, but Jody offered to take me.'

Pieter is surprised. 'Jody?' He holds the door open so they can enter the house. 'Is Bob too busy?' he asks as he takes the kettle from the stove to fill it with water. A faint uncertainty shows in Ellie's posture. She takes out two cups and puts them on the table. 'Jody had to be there anyway,' she replies. Pieter gives her a quick glance before shaking the coffee into the filter. When the water boils, he pours it over the ground coffee and soon the smell of the freshly percolated brew fills the kitchen.

« »

It's strange how certain situations can trigger one's memory. I hadn't thought about my father for a long time.

Life with him in Holland seemed so long ago, in a faraway past. Until the day I was walking along a busy street in Auckland. Uncle Pieter, who was dropping Uschi off at her aunt's, had given me a ride.

I heard a few men talking to each other in Dutch when one said he had to be at the ferry to meet his friend Godfried. I had never heard that name mentioned, not since my dad had said to my mother once, he had to meet his friend Godfried. It could possibly not be the same person. I looked again at the men and tried to determine their ages, but they looked much older than my father would have been. He would have been thirty-six now, the same age as Mum.

The reason why I wanted to go to Auckland was to see if I could find some nice Christmas presents. I had saved up my pocket money and didn't want to spend it on the same old things again. It had taken some persuading, but Uncle Pieter was the one who had convinced my mother. 'You can't keep her on a leash forever,' he had said to her.

But instead of going through the shops, I found myself on a bench in a park, watching a young couple playing with their small children. I wondered what having a father around could have been like all these years. I wondered what it would be like if I would've had my father with me right there and then. I thought of what I would say to him if he had been sitting next to me. About the play I was in at school? About the good grades I had this year after last year's bad grades? I wondered if I should tell him about the boy who lives a few streets away from us. I had a big crush on him and he liked me. But I wouldn't dream of telling my mother, she would have a fit. She was always warning me about boys. I wondered if fathers were the same. Maybe I should ask Uncle Pieter about it, but then what did he know? His daughter was only six now.

I thought of the time when I last saw my father. It was on a chilly day at the end of summer. It must have been in September for the seasons are different in Holland. He hadn't been nice to me that day and I didn't know why because I hadn't done anything bad. When he wanted to leave the house I wanted to go with him. It was Mum who had convinced him to take me. 'What ever happened, you have no reason to take it out on her,' something like that she had said. So, she dressed me in a warm coat and I went with him. He took me by my hand and walked on. I had to take quick steps to keep up with him. He didn't say much, just that it wouldn't be long now before we would go to this new country. I remember asking him if we really had to go. He said it was for the best. 'We have to start over again,' he said. I didn't understand what he meant then, but for him it would never become reality.

We stopped at the grocery shop to buy some things Mum needed. The man in the shop asked my father if all was arranged. 'My son is going away too,' he had said. But his son was going to another country. I was given a sweet as my father took the money from his pocket to pay for the groceries. When we were outside he decided not to go home yet. Instead, he wanted to go and see this friend who lived a bit further on, in another street. The friend had a little son whom I played with while my father and his friend talked. I remember them having quite a few laughs. For some reason, we had to leave when the friend's wife came back. My father laughed about it when he told me the wife didn't like him very much.

We walked quite a long way until we came to a river. Dad said that the Germans had bombed a bridge to pieces there. I asked him what that was "bombed" but he became very sad. He sat down on a bench with his head in his hands. To cheer him up, I put my hand on his shoulder and told him he shouldn't feel bad because they were already building a new bridge. But he jumped up and yelled at me. He yelled not to ever say something stupid like that again. It still makes me frightened today when I think about that sudden outburst of rage. He walked off and I ran after him trying to keep up. I remember becoming very fearful because I lost sight of him. But all of a sudden he was there again. He didn't say a word but took my hand and we walked the long way back home.

Mum was complaining a bit because we had been gone so long but my father just sat there in his chair. I wanted to cheer him up because he looked so unhappy, but was afraid he would become angry again. When he noticed me looking at him he beckoned me to come forward. He took me on his lap and whispered something.

I can't recall what it was.

He held me in his arms until Mum asked about the groceries. Daddy said he probably left them with his friend. He looked at me and gave me a kiss on my cheek before he got up to put his coat back on. I looked out the window and watched him leaving through the low garden gate, and that was the last time I ever saw him.

A couple of days later I was sent to a friend of my mother's and not long after we went to go on the boat. I never saw our house again. Mum had said there was nothing out there anymore. Most of the furniture had been sold and the rest was packed to go.

Sitting on that bench in the park I tried to remember the last thing my dad had said to me but I couldn't recall. People looked at me strangely because I had started to cry. Quickly I got up and ran out of the park and into the street. I didn't feel like buying presents anymore. I walked along the streets and finally stopped at a shop where I bought something to drink. I wanted to talk to Uncle Pieter but I didn't exactly know where his sister-in-law lived. It's funny, Uncle Pieter doesn't at all remind me of my father, although they were brothers. Maybe it was because Uncle Pieter had never been in a war. Although we had had some history lessons in school about the wars, I realised that there must be something I'd missed out on. There were things I could not comprehend.

After a while, I went to Tine and Henk's house for that's where I was staying the night. Tine was surprised that I hadn't done any shopping. A while later I decided to tell her about my memories of my father. She understood.

When Uncle Pieter came to collect me in the morning, he asked if I hadn't been willing to part with my money. I told him that was not the reason and I regretted not buying the presents I wanted to get. I wondered if we could stop in Hamilton on the way home, but Uncle Pieter had no time for that. He had to get back to his farm. After we had driven for a while I asked him if he could tell me about my father. Uncle Pieter never talked about him.

'Why do you want to talk about your father all of sudden?'

I told him I just wanted to. 'You knew him a lot longer than I did,' I said. 'You must remember something.'

Uncle Pieter tried to recall but couldn't think of anything, except that his brother used to steal his toys.

'Please Uncle Pieter, you must know more than that,' I pleaded. 'What was he like?'

He said he didn't spend a lot of time with his brother when they were growing up. 'Klaas was always off with his father, helping on the farm, going places.'

I asked him, with his brother being away all the time, who he played with. He was quiet for a moment and then said that he used to play with his sister, who is less than a year younger than he is.

'And I had a good friend at school. I used to sneak off and get into all sorts of mischief with him.' Uncle Pieter said all of that changed when the war began because the friend he had was Jewish and one day he had disappeared. They never saw him again. 'Partly because of that I decided not to wait around until the Germans came for me. I left home and after a couple of weeks I found myself in London.'

Driving on through the warm weather, squinting my eyes against the sun that shone into the car, he didn't say much for a while until I asked him if my father was in London, too, during the war, but that was not the case. He was rounded up by the Germans and sent to a labour camp. 'That had hit him hard, that time in the camp,' Uncle Pieter said.

I wondered if he ever wanted to fight against the Germans, but that had never entered his mind. He wanted to get away from Europe, that's why he went to England.

'Why did you go there then?' I asked him and he replied he wanted to go to America. In England, he had signed on to a freight ship that went to America. 'Little did I know it was South America. I signed on to another ship when we ended up in Panama and that one went on to Australia.'

He had mentioned a couple of times that he'd been out at sea but I never thought that he had been out there to escape a war. I looked at him and couldn't help thinking that he must have been quite an adventure when he was young. That had never crossed my mind before. I've always known Uncle Pieter as a hard-working farmer. I asked him why he had wanted to go to Australia then, and he said he had heard a lot about it. 'But when we arrived in Auckland to get some supplies, I decided I wouldn't mind giving this country a try first. And here's where I am still.' He looked at me and smiled.

'Dad should've been here too,' I mentioned after a while but Uncle Pieter said to put that out of my head. 'That was a long time ago and he was a troubled man.'

I asked him what he meant by that but he didn't give me a straight answer.

'Let it rest, Ellie. No use dragging that old stuff up.'

When we arrived in Hamilton Uncle Pieter pulled up and parked the car in a street. He suggested we could stop for a little while and have something to eat. We sat down at a small table in a milk-bar after we had bought what we wanted. At a given moment Uncle Pieter said that Klaas had been a good man and that I shouldn't forget that. 'The suffering he had been through was not his fault,' he said.

When we had finished our food and walked back to the car he said that if I wanted I could still get some gifts.

'I thought we didn't have enough time for that,' I said.

'Just be quick about it,' he replied.

We passed by a store that attracted my attention because it had some foreign items in the window. I found a handcrafted music box from Kashmir that was rather expensive, but I bought it just the same, as it would make a perfect gift for Nana and Granddad. I told Uncle Pieter that all the rest of them just had to do without a present.

'Maybe not entirely,' he said, 'Father Christmas might still come.'

He asked if I shouldn't get anything for my mother but I told him that Mum likes the small things. 'She'd be just as happy with a tin of biscuits.'

Uncle Pieter had to agree, but he stopped at a shop just the same and bought her a really nice silk scarf.

Since we were passing not far from Rangataua I asked Uncle Pieter if we could pay Nana and Granddad a short visit so that I could take them their present and he agreed to it.

Granddad hadn't been well for a while now and when we came to the house his daughter was just helping him to bed; it was only just past three pm. Nana said he usually became tired around this time and wanted to go to bed. She looked worried but she was very happy that we had come. She was delighted with the present and said she probably couldn't wait until Christmas to open it but she would try.

We sat outside and it felt a bit strange because Granddad wasn't there with us. Uncle Pieter seemed happy talking to Gwen while I sat with Nana in the gazebo. We spoke about my writing activities and how Mum was doing. I felt I could confide in her about my experience the day before, what it was that made me think of my father and I told her about the last time I saw him. She said to write it down. 'You know how it will help you to overcome things like that.'

Before we left, Uncle Pieter asked if he could use the phone. He wanted to let his farm-hand know he'd be a little late. 'I should've been back hours ago.'

I said to him that it was he who wanted to stop in Hamilton. 'Yes, but you were glad we did, weren't you?' and pointed at the present that was on the table. When he put the phone down he said that instead of taking me home, maybe he should put me on the train so he could save some time. Nana suggested that I could stay with them and then Gwen could take me home the following day. Uncle Pieter thought that was fine and we said goodbye.

I was sorry to find Granddad asleep when I had gone up to see him but he was awake when Gwen went up to give him his tea. It was a sad sight to see him being helped with his food while he was sitting, propped up in his pillows. He looked so old and needy. Even the twinkle in his eyes was gone, but he smiled at me when I came to greet him.

Later on, I asked Gwen if Granddad would be well again. I was worried about him. She said that her father's health had been going up and down. 'It's hard to tell when people reach this age whether they'll be well again.'

I could tell by Nana's face that even she wasn't certain if Granddad would ever be healthy again. The evening just wasn't the same knowing that Granddad was up there while we were having nice cups of tea downstairs.

« »

Jody has just entered the city of Wellington and is now driving his car up a street until they reach the university entrance, where he stops the car near a building.

'I think I have to drop my bags off at the student hostel,' Ellie says. Jody wonders where that might be. 'Have a look at the map.'

It doesn't take long for them to find the street where the hostel is situated. They remove the bags from the car and walk into the building, which Ellie finds rather stuffy smelling.

'You'll get used to it,' Jody says. 'Where is your room?'

Ellie looks at the piece of paper that came with the

instructions. 'According to this I have to go up the stairs, room nineteen.'

They ask a passing student whether they're going in the right direction. Soon they find the room and go in. At first sight, the cluttered corners here and there are a bit of a nuisance to Ellie. She puts her bags on the one bed that is still free and has another look around. 'I think I will like it here,' she then says with a contented look on her face and sits down on the bed.

'I think you will too,' Jody observes.

Ellie decides to unpack later and suggests they should have a look around the city. 'That is, if you still have time,' she says.

'No worries,' Jody replies, 'I could show you a thing or two.'

Ellie puts one of the bags in the wardrobe and sticks a note with her name on the door. 'That they know this one's mine,' she says. On leaving the room, they almost bump into someone entering.

'Oh, hello,' Ellie says, 'are you in this room as well?'

'No, no. I just came to return this book. Are you new here?'

'Yes,' Ellie replies.

'Me too, arrived yesterday. I'm in ten.' The girl puts the book down on the table. 'Well, probably see more of you,' she says and walks out the room, followed by Ellie and Jody.

'I wonder if I should lock the door,' Ellie says. 'They gave me those keys.'

'I think it'll be alright,' Jody replies. 'It wasn't locked when we came in.'

'Yeah, I suppose you're right.'

'Just don't forget the one for the outside door,' Jody says.

They go down the stairs and walk into the street as they decide to go in the direction of the harbour. Ellie reveals she doesn't remember much about Wellington. 'We went here last year to pick Opa and Oma Visser up from the boat,' she explains, 'but we never had a look around the city.'

'Oh, you mean your grandparents from Holland?' Jody replies. 'I heard they didn't stay long.'

'No, Opa Visser was causing problems with Uncle Pieter, so they went. I think they stayed with friends in Auckland. Oma did send us a letter though. She had seen the Queen and she was totally thrilled about that.'

'I was there too,' Jody says. 'We had to stand guard. Saw the Queen up *that* close,' and he holds his hands one foot apart. 'She wore a lovely hat,' he adds.

'Since when are you interested in the Queen's hats?'

'Well,' he replies, ' … since I'm not interested in her.'

Ellie laughs about Jody's reasoning when they pass a tea-shop and Jody suggests a drink. 'This one is lovely,' he says. 'Very popular place, remember the name, "The Earl on Grey".'

'Appropriate,' Ellie replies.

They sit down near the window at Jody's suggestion. 'People watching, very interesting pastime,' he says.

There are quite a few young people in the establishment and Ellie wonders if they're all students.

'Probably, most of them,' Jody says. 'Apart from those,' and he points at a few sailors. They finish their drink and when they are about to move on, Ellie notices a sign in the window. 'Look,' she says. 'Hold on.' She goes back into the tea-shop and asks if she could speak to the manager but he is not in. 'I'm interested in that job you have advertised in the window,' she tells the young man who attended to her. He reaches for his pen and gives Ellie a piece of paper. 'Just write down your name and where you can be reached. My boss will get back to you. Do you have any experience serving?'

Ellie replies she has. 'I've worked in a shop for a few months.' Ellie hands the paper and pen back to the young man and they leave the tea-shop.

'I didn't know you had been a waitress,' Jody says when they're outside again.

'Well, it wasn't really a waitressing job, just some work in a dairy,' Ellie replies. 'But I was still serving people. Wouldn't you say?'

'Clever,' Jody says.

They carry on through a small side street that takes them to the harbour. Jody points into the distance. 'That's where I saw dolphins once,' he mentions.

'Did you?' Ellie responds. 'That must have been quite a sight,' regretting not having seen any dolphins yet. 'I had hoped to maybe see some when we went on that camping trip last year, around Egmont, but, as you know that was cut short.'

Jody sits down on a bench. 'Well, what you need to do, that is, if you can find time, is to sit down here and keep your eyes on the water and one day you'll see them.'

Ellie sits down next to him and squints at the specular surface of the water. The sun creates a blanket of glittering stars on the surface and after a while, she has to give up.

'Here's where I first set foot in this country.' Ellie says pointing at the international terminal. 'If they'd told me then that dolphins lived in these waters, I probably wouldn't have felt so bad about coming here.'

'You didn't like it here at first, did you?' Jody says. 'I can still see you, standing all lost near that fence. Wanting your father to come get you.'

Ellie is silent for a moment. 'Well, I suppose, then I still thought we had left him behind. I still expected him to show up one day.'

She closes her eyes and lets the sun shine on her face. 'Lovely today,' she sighs, 'and so calm.'

'It is for now, but you'll get your share of windy days yet,' Jody assures her. He stands up. 'Shall we go on?

Ellie turns her head to see who just called her by her name. An elderly woman approaches her. 'Elisabeth Visser?' she asks once more.

'Yes?'

'There was a phone call for you while you were attending lectures. Kindly call back at this number.' The lady hands her a piece of paper.

'Thank you,' Ellie says. 'Where can I use a telephone?'

'There's one in the office, down the hall.'

Ellie walks in the direction the lady pointed out and soon finds the room. 'I was asked to call back at this number,' Ellie explains and hands the office attendant the piece of paper.

'You're on,' he says and sits down. He motions Ellie to take a seat and a few moments later hands her the telephone.

'Hello?' Ellie asks. 'Ellie Visser speaking.'

'*Hello dear,*' Rita's voice sounds at the other end of the line. '*It's me, your mother.*'

'Hi, Mum, how are you?' she asks, surprised.

'*Fine. Is everything going well with you there?*'

'Sure, couldn't be better. I already have a job and classes are going well. It's great down here, Mum.'

'*I'm glad to hear that,*' Rita replies. '*I was worried a bit after that bad storm there a couple of days ago.*'

'Oh, Mum,' Ellie says, 'don't be silly. It wasn't that bad.'

'*Well, it's hard to tell from this distance.*'

'Where did you call from anyway. I don't know this number,' Ellie goes on.

'*Oh, yes. That's what I wanted to tell you. I had a telephone installed, so we can talk more often.*'

'You did what?' is Ellie's reply. 'Wasn't that expensive?'

'*Not too bad and I just felt it would be better. Now you can always reach me at home,*' Rita says.

'Good idea Mum,' Ellie says as she watches the office attendant putting some files away. 'How is everybody by the way?'

'*Everybody is doing fine,*' Rita answers. '*Uncle Pieter and little Ursula say hello. They came by for a visit today.*'

'Oh yeah?' is the reply. 'Well Mum, I should go now. Say hello to everyone from me.'

'*I will, dear. And please, don't lose that number.*'

'I won't Mum. Bye.'

'*Bye, dear.*'

Ellie hands the phone back to the man and asks how much she owes for the call and hands him some change.

'That's fine,' he says and takes a sixpence from her. Ellie thanks him and walks along the hall to go to the library. At the desk, she inquires where she can find books on European history. In the sedate silence of the room, she makes her way through the aisles to find the books she wants. She sits down at one of the tables, takes a notebook and a pen from her bag and starts reading about the information she needs. Rather concentrated on her work, she doesn't notice the time passing by and when she looks at the clock some time later, she is alarmed. 'Christ!' she mumbles. With swift movements, she pulls her things together and puts the books back on the shelves. Hurriedly she makes her way out of the building, runs across the lawn and down the street to the hostel where she bumps into one of her fellow students.

'Oh, John. Sorry 'bout that,' she says.

'No worries,' is the reply. Ellie is on her way again when she stops and asks John about his car. 'I'm late for work you see, I thought maybe ... '

'I'm sorry, Ellie. My car's in the repair shop.'

She doesn't take the time to drop off her bag with college books and rapidly makes her way down to the tea-shop on Grey Street. Her boss isn't too pleased that she is almost three-quarters of an hour late for work. 'A full house and you don't show up.'

Ellie apologises and quickly ties an apron around her waist. 'I was at the library, forgot all about the time.'

But her boss is not interested in her excuses. 'Quick, get on with it,' he says. Trying to make up for it, she works even harder than usual to do a good job.

~ ~

A warm breeze plays around the house as Grace carries the tray with the drinks out. She puts them on the small table on the veranda and sits down. 'Lovely day today,' she says. 'We have been lucky with the weather.'

'We sure have,' Rita replies. One of the cats chases a few dry leaves that flutter by, but they drop to the ground before he can catch them. Chrissie smiles about the silly sight. She adjusts the pillow in her back and rests a hand on her expanding belly. 'Finally had a letter from Ellie yesterday,' she says. 'I started to think she'd forgotten about us.'

Grace hands her a glass of juice. 'Well, I think she's been rather good with keeping in touch.'

'It seems she's enjoying herself,' Rita says. 'I had only hoped she would phone more often, but it's usually me that's doing the phoning.'

'Of course,' Chrissie says, 'that way it doesn't cost her anything.'

'I think she is just too busy,' Grace affirms.

Rita picks up her crochet and spreads it out on her lap. 'I wish she was less busy and more considerate.'

'Oh, please, Rita,' Grace says. 'You should be glad she's trying so hard.'

'I know,' Rita replies, 'but, it would be nice for me to know what she's up to.'

'Ellie won't tell you anything that can't bear the light of day, Rita,' Chrissie stresses.

Rita observes her handiwork. 'You could be right.'

'Oh, stop you two,' Grace says. 'You make it sound as if Ellie doesn't look before she leaps,' when in the distance a young girl comes hopping and skipping towards the house.

'Hello,' Ursula greets them. 'Can I *please* have some lemonade, Grace?'

'Your father forgot to get you some?' Chrissie asks.

Grace promises her lemonade and goes in to get it while Ursula sits down on the steps and watches her aunt being busy with her crochet.

'I'm trying for potholders, Uschi,' Rita explains. 'But I think I've messed up.' She has another look at the pattern.

'Can't be that difficult,' Chrissie says. 'Just a square piece of cloth.'

With a serious expression on her face, Ursula tells Chrissie that it is very difficult to make potholders. 'Aunt

Rita always makes really nice ones.'

Chrissie smiles at Ursula. 'You're right, Rita does make the nicest things.'

Grace comes out of the house and hands Ursula her drink asking her if her father isn't home. 'Yes, he is,' the girl replies. 'He's with his cows and he forgot to buy lemonade.'

'No good,' Chrissie says. 'He should be punished for that.'

'Shouldn't you be doing some homework?' Rita asks Ursula.

'Yes, but I can do that later. Then I can ask Dad to help me,' is Ursula's answer.

'Right you are,' Chrissie says.

'Well, I think I have to go now,' Ursula says when she has finished her drink. 'Thank you for the lemonade, Grace.'

'You're welcome, child,' Grace replies. They watch as the nine-year-old skips along the dirt road and back to her own home.

When Ursula's cheerful chattering has been replaced by the tranquillity of the late summer once more, Grace casts a somewhat worried look at her daughter. 'You're not having one of those headaches again, darling?' she asks.

Chrissie puts both her hands around her belly. 'No, it's just the baby, Mum, it moved,' she says. 'He's been playing up quite a bit lately.'

'Thought of any names yet?' Rita wants to know.

'Well, yeah, we have. Or that is to say, I have,' Chrissie replies. 'I made a list of boys' names but Marty says that's not being realistic. He wants a girl you see.'

'Let him make a list with girls' names then,' Rita suggests. 'What if it is a girl?'

'I know you should be happy with what the good Lord gives you,' Grace has to admit. 'But, to be honest, we could do with another boy around here.'

'Hear, hear,' is Chrissie's reply.

~ ~

'Room warming tonight at nine,' Kate reads the announcement on the board. 'B.Y.O.'

'A room warming? Halfway through term?' Ellie wonders. 'Who moved?'

'Don't have a clue,' her roommate replies. They carry their bags with groceries to the kitchen and take the pots and pans out. Ellie fills one of them with water and places it on the stove. She rummages through her things and takes out a packet of rice.

'Cup a tea is in order, I'd say,' Kate says and puts the kettle on. 'Now where is that tea?' She empties her bag but can't find the tea she bought at the shop. 'Where on earth is my tea? I did take it with me, didn't I?'

Ellie holds up a packet. 'Here you are,' she says.

'How did it end up between your stuff?' Kate wonders. She takes the teapot from a shelf, but the handle breaks. 'Shit, teapot broke. Tea strainer gone missing. Well, I suppose we'll have to strain the tea with our teeth.'

Ellie pours the rice into the boiling water while Kate shakes some tea leaves into the cups.

'Are you going to that party tonight?' Ellie asks and starts cutting the vegetables.

'I wouldn't mind if I did,' Kate replies. 'We still have some of that beer from last time. Saves us money on buying new.'

'No,' Ellie says, 'I don't think so. We drank that the other night.'

Kate looks disappointed. 'Oh, we did too. Crap.'

She gathers the vegetables, Ellie has just cut, from the plate and puts them in the frying pan.

'Do you think they'd mind if we come empty-handed?'

'Nah,' Ellie replies, 'all we need is glasses. Someone will fill them up.'

'Yeah, you're right.'

Kate starts stirring vigorously in the pan to stop the vegetables from burning. 'These pans are no good,' she mumbles.

'Add some more butter,' Ellie says.

'You better keep the rice from burning,' Kate says when the pan starts making frightful noises. Ellie checks it and determines the rice is cooked.

'Already? Let's have a look.' After a close inspection from Kate, they conclude it could cook a while longer. In the meantime they enjoy their cup of tea, minding they don't swallow the leaves when they reach the bottom of their cups. A little later they dish up their meal. When trying it out, Ellie and Kate agree that they have once again surpassed their cooking skills. 'Marvellous food,' Kate says. 'Now, what room was that party in?'

'Don't know,' Ellie replies. 'It didn't say.'

Another student enters the kitchen. 'What's that smell?' she asks.

'What smell?'

'Oh, you're having your tea,' Clarisse states.

'Yes, have some too,' Kate says. 'There's still some in the pan.'

Clarisse declines and casts her eyes over the shelves. 'Where is that ... vessel with a spout, in which one can make tea?'

'Broke and gone to heaven,' Kate says.

'Who broke it? The one who broke it should buy a new one,' Clarisse says.

'No one broke it. It just gave up,' Kate replies. 'You know, like having a heart attack.'

Clarisse spots the teapot with its handle missing and after a closer inspection determines that it is the flowerpot she always wanted.

When they have finished their plates Ellie gets up to wash them. 'Do you know what room that party is in tonight?' she asks.

'Are we having a party?' is Clarisse's reaction.

'Yes, a room warming,' Kate replies.

'Oh, that's probably in five,' Clarisse says. 'Barb moved out of there last week. Found herself a nice flat. Lucky critter.'

'She can afford it too, probably,' Ellie says. 'Well, I should be off. Still want to get some information at the library.'

'Come on Ellie. Have the evening off for once,' Kate expresses. 'You are working too hard.'

With an uncomfortable smile, Ellie says that that's what she is here for. 'I'll see you at the party.'

When Ellie nears the hostel almost two hours later, squalls of Rock 'n Roll music meet her when she crosses the dusky street. A few of her fellow students hang about the front door. She makes her excuses so she can get through. When going up the steps a young man winks at her, but Ellie doesn't take any notice. She goes into her room and drops her bag on her bed only to drop herself on the bed a moment later. With a sigh, she closes her eyes. She doesn't hear the door being opened and doesn't notice someone coming in. It isn't until the person says "knock-knock" that she slowly opens her eyes. Baffled she looks at the young man standing at the foot of her bed. 'Who are you?' Ellie demands.

'Sorry to barge in like this, but I did knock,' he says.

Ellie sits up and asks if he is a friend of Kate's.

'Kate?'

'My roommate.'

'No, I don't know any Kate.'

'So … What are you doing here then?'

'Well, uh, I saw you pass by and I thought … No, let me rephrase that. I've seen you around the grounds, several times, and I thought it was about time for us to be introduced.'

Ellie looks surprised. 'Do you? Well, I'm Ellie,' she says. 'And will you please leave now? You might've "knocked" but I never invited you in.'

'Well, uh, sorry.' He acts somewhat undecided. 'Will you be coming down?' he asks.

'I'll go when I feel like it,' Ellie replies.

'Well, see you later then,' and he walks to the door. 'Oh, by the way, my name is Paul.'

Still a bit bewildered Ellie lies back down to try and catch another wink. She tosses over, but then with a sigh, she gets up. She casts a look in the mirror and straightens her hair. The noise of the music increases as she opens the door. It becomes louder as she goes down to the kitchen trying to avoid the good many people in the hall.

'Ellie! There you are.'

Ellie turns but doesn't see Kate straight away. 'Come meet my friend!' Kate's loud voice sounds. 'This is … uh.'

'Travis,' the young man replies.

'Travis.' She pulls Ellie by her arm. 'And this is Ellie … Isn't he cute?' she whispers in Ellie's ear. Ellie casts Travis a quick smile.

'Where is your glass, El? We need to fill you up.' She turns to Travis. 'She is so diligent, she needs to unwind.'

'I was just getting a glass, but I suppose we're all out,' Ellie justifies herself. Kate rushes off and comes back with a cup, filled with Cold Duck. 'Here you are.'

'Thanks, Kate. Great music, whose is the gramophone?'

'Don't know. But who cares? As long as it's playing the records,' Kate replies. She pulls Travis by his arm. 'Come along, let's find a spot where we can dance.'

'Nice meeting you,' Travis says before being whisked off.

'Same here,' Ellie responds. She makes her way outside and leans against the railing that lines the steps. Sipping the cheap wine she watches the small groups of people, chatting and laughing in the sparsely lit garden. A sudden breeze makes her shiver. She turns to go inside when someone taps her on the shoulder. 'Slept well?' Paul asks.

'No,' Ellie replies. 'Some person woke me up.'

'I'm sorry. Can I get you another drink?'

'You're full of apologies, aren't you,' Ellie says.

Paul is vaguely bewildered. 'What do you mean?' he asks.

'We've hardly talked and you've already apologised three times.'

'Have I? Well ... I lost count. Now, what about another drink.' He takes her cup and goes in to find a bottle that still contains some alcoholic fluid. A few minutes later he is back with a bottle that is still half full. He fills Ellie's cup and toasts her before taking a swallow from the bottle.

'Now that we know each other a bit better,' Paul says, 'how about telling me something about yourself?'

'How about you telling me something about *your*self?' Ellie replies.

There's a sparkle in his dark eyes when he looks at her. 'OK, but, I won't bore you with my previous life. So, I'm a second year, taking English and Maths.'

'Fascinating,' Ellie says dryly. 'And, that's all?'

'Yes. I must admit, not all that thrilling. And what about you?' He moves closer to her. 'I can tell you are a fascinating person.'

Ellie glances at him with an amused look on her face. 'Well, I'm a first year and I'm taking History, mainly European, and English Literature.'

'European History? How come European, what's wrong with the rest of the world?'

Ellie smiles. 'Nothing. It's just that Europe interests me. I uh ... I was born in Europe, you see.'

'Yes, who wasn't?' is Paul's reply.

Ellie looks surprised. 'You're also from – '

'No, I'm just a plain old Kiwi, second generation.'

A few students staggeringly make their way down the steps and bump against Paul who cannot help colliding with Ellie. 'Sorry 'bout that,' he mumbles close to her ear.

'It's OK,' Ellie says. 'It wasn't your fault.'

Paul smiles at her. 'Where was I,' he goes on. 'Oh yes, my grandparents came here from Europe.'

'See?' Ellie says. 'Of European descent after all. What country?'

'Britain. Where else. And what about you?'

'Holland.'

'A Dutch descendant,' Paul states. 'I knew there was some familiarity when I spotted you.'

'You think so?' Ellie replies. 'Do you know any Dutch people?'

'No. But, come to think of it, we're practically

neighbours.'

'You're being silly,' Ellie smiles.

Another couple passes, causing an infinitesimal space between Ellie and Paul. 'What would you say if we went somewhere less crowded?' Paul whispers close to her face.

'I'd say that's not such a bad idea,' Ellie replies and puts her cup down.

With a chivalrous arm movement, Paul makes way for Ellie and they walk down the steps. The music fades behind them and Ellie asks Paul what it is that's so boring about his "previous life" that it is not worth mentioning.

'Well, maybe *boring* is not the right word,' he admits. 'I was orphaned at a rather young age, brought up by an aunt and uncle. Great people, but, it was a tough life. No, let me rephrase that, an interesting life.'

Ellie looks at him. 'Interesting?'

'Yes. There were three more children in the family and we all had to work hard. But I suppose that gave me this strong urge to survive.'

'And are you?' Ellie wants to know. 'Surviving, I mean?'

Paul stands in front of her and spreads his arms. 'Here's the living proof,' he says. In the dim street, they stand silent for a moment.

'My father died when I was six,' Ellie then says.

'That must have been hard on you,' Paul responds as they walk on. 'Did he die here?'

'No, that was in Holland still,' Ellie replies. 'Mind you, I never knew he had died until we'd been in New Zealand for a couple of months.'

'We?'

'My mother and I.'

'Strange,' Paul says. 'I mean, that you weren't told.'

'Oh, well. That's just my mother. She thought at the time that it would be too hard on me to know the truth.'

A soft rustling sounds as the wind plays with the treetops above them. 'Parents do the strangest things,' Paul says. 'God! Listen to us!' he quite suddenly cries out. 'We've become all serious!'

He grabs Ellie by her shoulders. 'We should go somewhere and party.'

'Go back to the hostel?'

'No, maybe go somewhere else.'

'There's not much going on at this hour.'

Paul has to admit she's right. 'We could go to my place, there are usually less crowded parties going on.'

'You mean ... parties for two.'

'If you don't mind,' he says.

'And where is your place?'

He motions with his head. 'We're standing in front of it.'

Ellie lets her eyes slide past Paul to the house behind him. There is a light on in some of the rooms.

'I share it with a few others,' he explains.

Ellie gives it some thought, then decides that a cup of coffee won't hurt. Paul leads the way as they walk up the narrow garden path and into the house. He introduces her to the couple that is occupying the couch in the lounge room. Ellie gazes in amazement when she notices the television set that they are watching. 'Gosh! You have a television!' she calls out. 'May I?'

'Be our guest,' one of the friends says.

Ellie slides onto a chair and looks at the black and white screen asking about the programme that is on.

'We don't really know,' is the reply. 'These are just the commercials, extremely boring.'

When Paul comes in with two cups of coffee, Ellie

still has her eyes fixed on the small screen that seems to dominate the room.

'Shall we go to my room, or do you want to watch this trash?' he says.

She glances at him for a second. 'Sure,' she says.

'Sure, what?'

Ellie drags her eyes away from the screen. 'We can go to your room.' She gets up and follows Paul to one of the rooms in the hall. 'It's just, that you don't see those things very often,' she justifies herself.

'Broadcast will be finished soon anyway,' he says and offers her a seat on his bed, handing her the coffee.

'Thanks.' She briefly looks at him as he sits down next to her. Ellie holds her cup with both hands and cautiously takes small sips from the hot liquid, while Paul starts playing with her hair.

'Do you have a girlfriend?' Ellie asks him.

'What?'

'I asked you if you had a girlfriend.'

'Would I invite you over here if I had a girlfriend?'

'I don't know what you'd do.'

Paul sighs and puts his coffee down. 'No, I don't have a girlfriend.'

Silence sets in with Ellie finishing her coffee. 'That was nice,' she says. 'Good coffee.'

'Thank you,' Paul replies.

'So, how old were you when your parents died?' Ellie asks.

'Do we have to talk about that now?'

'No, but I thought maybe you wanted to.'

'Not really.' Rather abruptly he gets up. 'You know, I didn't bring you here under false pretences. I did lose my parents and I hate to talk about it!'

'You're the one that started that conversation,' Ellie

defends herself.

Paul looks downwards. 'Yeah, well. I thought ... it was all right to mention it to you.'

'Why?' Ellie asks in a soft tone.

'Don't ask me why,' he says defensively. 'Are you always so full of questions?'

'Sorry I asked,' Ellie replies and gets up. 'I think I should go. Thanks for the coffee,' she adds and walks to the door. 'Good night,' she says before she closes the door behind her.

This time Paul lifts his head. 'Yes, see you around.'

Shortly after Ellie's leaving through the garden gate, the front door opens and Paul comes out of the house. 'Ellie! Wait a moment.' He is quick to approach her. 'I ... am sorry to say, I have to apologise yet again. I didn't mean to chase you off like this.'

'You didn't chase me off,' Ellie replies. 'I just thought it was time for me to go.'

'You know what I mean. You wouldn't have left if I hadn't bored you with my past.'

'Oh, Paul, that's not the reason,' Ellie says. 'It's getting late, I should go.'

'Shall I walk with you?' Paul suggests.

Ellie shakes her head. 'It's alright, it's just around the corner. Bye.'

Paul watches her as she walks away. He then turns and goes back inside.

With the music of the party still playing in the background, Ellie slides her naked body into the comforting warmth of the water in the bathtub. A relaxed expression passes over her face when she leans her head back. Hardly a few minutes in the calming atmosphere and someone is trying to open the door. 'Hurry up in there,' a voice calls out.

'Christ,' mutters Ellie.

Again the person on the other side of the door rattles the doorknob.

'Go away!' Ellie yells. 'I'm having a bath.'

'And I need to go to the loo!' is the answer.

'There are more toilets downstairs,' Ellie replies.

'They're all taken! Can't you just hurry? How long does it take to have a bath anyway?'

Ellie leaves the person to her complaining and leans her head back once more. The rattling sounds again.

'Please open up, I'm bursting!'

Ellie closes her eyes and sinks down until the water reaches her lips.

'What am I to do?' The girl sounds desperate.

'Wet yourself,' Ellie replies.

Despairing sounds are heard on the other side as footsteps move away from the door. Without further interruptions, Ellie finishes her bath and wraps a towel around her to walk back to her room. On entering she sees her roommate in intimate entanglement on the bed with Travis. For a moment she looks shocked but then quickly moves to her corner of the room and hides behind the door of the closet. Amidst the amorous sounds of kissing and sighing, Ellie puts on her panties and shirt for the night and throws the towel on the chair. Just a tad too noisily, she closes her wardrobe door. The sound makes Travis look up but he doesn't notice Ellie swiftly crawling between the covers of her bed.

'What's the matter?' Kate's sighing voice sounds.

'I thought I heard a door,' Travis replies.

'Oh, there are so many doors in this building,' Kate mumbles. She turns his face towards hers and continues where they left off. But when Ellie turns to lie on her other side, a light creaking of the bed again draws Travis's attention. They both look over their shoulders and see the bump on Ellie's bed.

'Ellie?' Kate asks. A soft moan sounds and Ellie moves the covers from her face.

'How long have you been there?' Kate wants to know.

'Just got in,' is the diffident reply.

'Well ... why didn't you knock?'

'Why would I knock when I'm entering my own room?'

'*Our* room,' Kate states.

'Maybe it's best I go now,' Travis says.

'No,' Kate demands and pulls his sleeve. 'Stay.'

'Yes, stay,' Ellie says, 'don't mind me.'

'Ellie!'

'I'm really sorry,' Ellie says. 'But I didn't know that you were in here? You weren't here before I went to have a bath.'

'You could at least have made some more noise when you came in,' Kate says accusingly.

'I am sorry, but I didn't want to disturb you. OK? And can I now have some sleep?'

Travis gets up and suggests they can go to his place. Although Kate is reluctant she agrees and they leave Ellie to catch up on her sleep.

5

I don't think I've ever felt so confused in my life. Paul asked me to marry him. We'd been seeing each other for a year but marriage had never entered my mind. We were friends, lovers, but as far as I was concerned, that was it. If it would've been Bob asking me at this stage I would have considered accepting. I never thought of Paul as my husband. Paul is a nice guy, but he has so many unsolved problems from his past. More than once I found him in his room, suffering from his depressive moods, caused by his unhappy childhood. And more than once I told him to go and talk to someone about it, but he never did. Next day he would be sweet and considerate as ever, acting as if nothing had happened. Paul would probably be the last to admit it but his "previous life" definitely reflected in his present one. His conflicting moods bewildered me more and more. They had started to affect my own life, and while I had concluded that we should put an end to our relationship, Paul, out of the blue, proposed to me.

I didn't want to be yet another person in his life adding to his unhappiness by bluntly declining. It frightened me to think what could happen. I began to think of excuses, like telling him that we didn't need to be married to live happily ever after. After all, that's what my mother and dear uncle had been doing for years.

But when the time came, all I could say to Paul was that I was not ready for commitment, that I felt that at this time there were more important things I needed to do. The expression that showed in his eyes then was one I'll probably never forget. And I started to realise that he always must have thought of me as his future wife. To him, it must have sounded as if I was offering him a divorce, to a marriage that never was. I tried to cheer him up and said that it was not the end of the world; we could still be friends and see each other. There were still a few years of studying ahead of us. But he just shook his head and told me to leave him alone. He turned and walked away and my calling of his name could not make him change his mind and come back.

In my heart, I knew I had made the right decision but I felt the need to talk to someone. Only, there weren't that many people on the premises I would confide in. In fact, there weren't any. It crossed my mind to call Nan on the phone but decided against it for I didn't want to worry her. So, in the end, there was just my dear roommate Kate, even though she never seemed to be serious about anything but she, at least, would lend a sympathetic ear.

I found her as she spend one of her rare moments in the library. I pulled her away from her favourite section, as she put it, science and technology. Kate knew what the situation was between me and Paul. She also knew about my decision, which made it easier to share with her how I felt.

'Don't take it to heart, Ellie,' she said. 'You can't help it if he's like that?'

I explained to her that I felt bad about the situation because I still cared about him and I couldn't bear seeing him walk away like that. It almost had me in tears.

Kate assured me he would come around.

'It's just the initial blow. Once he's over it, he'll be on your doorstep, showering you with goodies.'

For some reason, I knew that that was not going to be the case. I was almost convinced I had spoiled the friendship I had with Paul. Kate must have detected my state of mind. 'Don't be so awfully serious about this,' she said. 'Take me, I never come away from a relationship hurt to pieces.'

'You are never in a relationship long enough to be hurt to pieces,' I replied.

She had to admit I was right and suggested I should do the same. 'Shop around a bit. There are a lot more studs in the paddock than you might care to admit.'

Kate always has her way of cheering people up.

Not long after, we found ourselves at The Earl laughing about things I don't even remember. I do remember my employer being more than kind to me when we were there. I had given him my notice a few days earlier and he asked me if I would consider staying on a while longer.

'Don't give in,' Kate said to me. 'Think about your priorities.'

And my priorities were my studies. I had found it too hard to be a full-time student and work on the side. Most of the money I had earned the first year was in a bank account and my mother occasionally sent me some money to live on.

I assumed that when studying would become simpler, I could always get another job.

Rather suddenly Kate nudged me with her elbow and said that because of all my complications she completely forgot to tell me about the flat we could have. 'Remember that place where Barb moved into last year? Two more have moved out and now they want replacements. I told them to look no further.'

After that account from Kate, it was not up to me to be apprehensive, but I did have my doubts. It would be more expensive. When I subtly dropped that complaint Kate's answer was to worry about that when the time came.

Almost a week went by and I had not heard from Paul; something that even had Kate wondering. That Saturday morning I could not wait any longer and walked over to his house. One of his housemates opened the door and told me Paul was not home, they hadn't seen him for a couple of days. I became worried and asked if he knew where Paul could have gone. He had said that he needed some time off and had left.

'We don't know where he's gone, but he did pay his rent so that's good enough for us.'

Before I left, he promised to let me know if they heard anything. As I walked back, I became aware that apart from what he had told me, I knew very little about Paul. There were no relatives I could phone for the simple reason I didn't know anything about them. It crossed my mind to ask at the office, they would very likely have an address of a relative.

But, why didn't Paul leave me a message? Maybe he just didn't want to be found and after I had consulted Kate, I decided to leave it alone for the time being. 'He'll show his face again,' Kate assured me. 'You said he'd left money for his rent, so, why worry any longer?'

With the new housing facilities on the way and therefore more expenses, I told my boss I wouldn't mind keeping the job if I only could work fewer hours. He agreed, even though he was reluctant at first, but he would wait and see how things would progress and if necessary hire an extra person.

Kate had managed to rope in some people to help us move our things to the house that we were going to share with Barb and her boyfriend Daniel. The rooms we were going to have, looked badly in need of almost everything and I suggested we should paint them.

'Paint them? That costs, Ellie. We'll just throw a few drapes against the walls,' was Kate's reaction. But the thought of having to study and sleep in a room that looked like something out of a Charles Dickens novel did not appeal to me at all. So I went out and bought some paint, a considerable expenditure, but when I saw my room transformed by my hands into a pleasant and bright shelter, I knew it had been worth it. And it must have been contagious for the others started to decorate their rooms as well. When we looked over the end result we concluded that our landlord should give us one month's rent for free, but we knew that that was not likely to happen. To celebrate our new "Villa Flamboyant", we went to the pub to party. Normally I was rather careful with consuming alcohol, but somehow this time I didn't care much. I drank the beers I had purchased and the rounds that others had paid for. We had so many laughs that my face felt sore at one stage. I don't remember much of what happened after that. I have a vague recollection of us stumbling out the door and I think I was the one that fell in the street or maybe it was this bloke who came with us. Someone was on top, either he or I was, it was hard to tell in the darkness. I think it was Kate who pulled me by my arm and on my feet again.

When I opened my eyes the following morning I didn't know where I was at first. I was lying at the end of a bed, staring at this spot on the floor. There was an appalling smell of stale beer. I tried to get up but my whole body was sore, and I felt sick. Cold and sick. Trying to remember what had happened, I slowly came to my senses.

I lay there for a while, staring at the ceiling, before scrambling to my feet. It seemed like things were moving about in the room and before I knew it, I was back on the bed. The second time I was more careful with rising from my bed. I slowly made my way to the bathroom, where I got rid of this nauseating feeling in my stomach. I had a shock when I saw my face in the mirror. It made me slowly become aware of what state I was in. I ran the tub full of warm water and took off my stained and smelly clothes. Immersed in the warm water, fragranced by the fresh-smelling soap, I soon started to feel better.

When I was making a cup of tea a while later, Barb walked into the kitchen. For some reason, a hangover seemed to have passed her by. She asked if that bloke had gone home but I didn't know what she was talking about.

'Well, he probably did,' she said. 'We dumped him in the lounge room and he's not there anymore.'

We sat outside on the steps drinking our tea when Kate came back. She looked a bit worn out, complaining about this place that did not even have a proper bathroom. 'That's the last time I'm going with that oaf,' she moaned. Barb and I wanted to know who the *oaf* was but she didn't remember his name. 'He probably didn't even have the decency to tell me,' she said.

'Did you ask?' was our reaction. But she went in and took something to drink from the kitchen. When she joined us a moment later she enquired how I was and I told her I had survived. 'That's not what I thought when I saw you leave that pub last night,' she said. Barb told me that it was better to leave the hard liquor if I could not hold it. I thought we had been having beers and wondered what they were talking about.

'Never mind, Ellie,' Kate said. 'As long as you're having fun,' and she got up to have a bath.

It's not easy to fit in pieces of a puzzle when most of them are missing so I thought it best to forget about that unclear episode of the night before. I went to my room to clean the vomit from the carpet. It still left a stain even after I had been scrubbing for ten minutes. I must have scrubbed so loudly that Daniel came in to ask if I could be a bit quieter, I had disturbed him. He was still sleeping off his debauchery.

After a trying morning class, followed by a rather intense lecture, I was pleased to walk off the university grounds and towards the way home. The professor's voice still lingered in my head. His explanation about the unfinished business of the First World War leading to the Second World War had held my attention all the way through. I should have worked that afternoon but as I still wanted to do some studying at the library, I phoned The Earl and told my boss I could not make it. It was not easy for me to call off work for I needed the money and I started to doubt if my first priority shouldn't be my second, but I soon brushed that thought aside. Better to live on a shoestring for now, to have the benefits later. I had promised my boss that I would work all through next semester break, to keep him happy. Once in my room, I made myself comfortable with a sandwich in one hand and my notes in the other, when Kate knocked and barged in.

'Someone to see you,' she said, rather secretively. Immediately Paul's name came to mind.

'He's a hunk,' Kate swooned.

Somehow that didn't describe Paul, even though he was nice looking.

'He claims he's your uncle.'

Instantly, I felt a warm feeling come over me and asked Kate where he was. I went down to meet him and gave him such a big hug it even surprised Uncle Pieter. I was so happy to see him.

'I had some business here, so I thought I'd pay you a visit,' he said. 'I was at your other address but they told me you had moved.'

I explained how Kate and I were given the opportunity to move into this house and that I had sent Mum the new address.

'I haven't seen Rita for a while,' was his reply. That was something I did not want to hear. I had come to terms with the affair they had had, but secretly I still hoped that they would get married one day. They all had been disappointed that I hadn't been home during the last semester break. I explained that I was trying to save as much money as I could, although I was sorry to have missed Chrissie and Marty's little boy's birthday.

'Why don't you come back with me now?' he suggested. 'No classes at the weekend.'

He had me in doubt by asking that. I really wanted to go home and see everybody. 'My studies, Uncle Pieter,' was all I could say.

'Take your books with you. Come home with me and we'll have you back here on Monday. I'll treat you to the train fare.'

For a few seconds, I didn't know what to say, but then I threw my arms around him and assured him that he was the sweetest uncle in the world. I ran to my room to pack some clothes and my books. When I came down I found Kate in animated conversation with Uncle Pieter, which I broke up by saying we should go.

'Nice meeting you,' Kate said to him. 'Come again.'

Uncle Pieter probably felt flattered, but I wasn't pleased. 'Leave my uncle alone,' is all I had to say to Kate before I left the house.

'Nice girl,' Uncle Pieter said when we were on our way. I had to agree he was right but told him that we never knew with whom she was doing it and when. 'She goes through a lot of boyfriends,' I explained, but I wished I hadn't brought it up, for Uncle Pieter then asked about my boyfriend and I was not inclined to talk about Paul. I said it was over. Luckily Uncle Pieter is one who then leaves it at that and does not continue asking all sorts of questions like my mother always does. I asked him about his women situation. 'How come you haven't seen Mum for a while?'

He told me not to go into that unless I wanted to hitch-hike the rest of the way. I knew he wouldn't put me out of the car but I saw what he meant, remembering the outbursts I had with him about this issue before. He started telling me about Uschi's achievements at school. She had been doing very well. It was a joy listening to Uncle Pieter being so proud of her. He had promised her a trip to the South Island during winter break. I was sure Uschi would enjoy that very much.

It was dark by the time Uncle Pieter pulled up in front of our house. I asked if he wanted to come in but he had to go home. 'Just for a cuppa, it has been a long drive,' I tried again.

'Better not, Ellie,' he said, so I took my things and said goodbye to him.

He left me standing on the pavement rather bemused. There had to be something going on between my mother and Uncle Pieter that I failed to comprehend. I walked up the garden path when the door opened. 'Ellie!' Mum called out. 'I thought I heard something. What a surprise!'

She asked me how I got here. When I told her Uncle Pieter had given me a ride her reaction was coolish, only to switch to her former delight a moment later and she started making tea.

'Have you eaten? Shall I make you something?'

Although I said that was not necessary she made some sandwiches. Before I touched any of the food I needed to know what was happening between her and Uncle Pieter. She replied nothing was happening and that nothing would ever happen again. 'Pieter is seeing another woman.'

I couldn't believe my ears.

'Better get used to the idea, Ellie. They're very serious about each other.'

I didn't know what to say, or to think. What did other women have that my mother hadn't? 'And I thought he never wanted to be married again after Birgit's death!' I cried. Mum didn't say anything; she just sat there. I asked her if she had any idea how Uschi felt about this new "stepmother".

'You know Ursula, she is not one to stand in the way of her father's happiness. Although she did mention the other day that she didn't feel like going anywhere if that woman came too.'

That sounded more like Uschi to me. Now that I had come home I was looking forward to visiting Grace and William as well, not to mention Uschi, but after what Mum just told me, I was uncertain whether I should. I didn't think I would be able to keep my calm when the likelihood of running into Uncle Pieter occurred. In all the years that I had known him, I thought I had come to understand him well, but now, I began to doubt that. My appetite was gone and I told Mum I was too tired to eat and wanted to go to bed. Mum was highly surprised. 'Since when are you too tired to eat?' And she complained that I had lost weight and wanted to know if I ate at all, besides the studying I did. I assured her that I was as healthy as ever. Unwillingly she put the sandwiches in the fridge and we both had an early night.

« »

Remnants of a cold spell that has fallen upon the area during the night, can still be seen. A still, white veil covers the surrounding hills while in the streets of the town, cars have turned the icy flakes into an unattractive slush.

'Strange, that you cannot even buy something warm to drink here,' Ellie says while they await the train on the otherwise deserted platform of the small train station.

'This is not the city,' Rita replies.

'We should have taken something.'

'Oh, it's only a short journey,' Rita says, 'and I did pack the sandwiches from last night.'

'A shame Chrissie and Marty weren't home,' Ellie says and blows some warm breath into her hands.

'Why don't you wear those gloves I made you?' Rita asks.

'Forgot to take them. Hopefully this train will arrive soon.'

Rita suggests they could wait inside the building but Ellie would rather stay outside. 'Fresh air will do me good,' she says.

'I do think you've lost weight, Ellie. If you need more money, just tell me. I don't want you to starve yourself.'

Ellie explains it is not caused by the lack of food, rather the hard work that she has been doing. 'I eat like a horse, Mum.'

The sound of a whistle draws their attention and soon the train pulls into the station. Rita tells the guard where they would like to get off before finding seats in one of the carriages. There aren't many people on the train and they sit down next to a window. With lunchtime approaching, Rita takes the sandwiches out of her bag together with a tea towel that she spreads on her lap. Ellie watches with amused curiosity at the snug scene her mother is creating and takes one of the sandwiches Rita hands her. 'And there's a bottle of water in my bag,' Rita says.

Nibbling their sandwiches, they enjoy the serene landscape that glides past the window. The frosty fields lie peacefully in front of the white peaks in the distance. Ellie looks thrilled when she sees Mount Ruapehu completely covered in snow. A few skiers have already found their way up the hills and make tracks down the white slopes. 'Would love to do that one day,' she says.

'You would have to learn first,' Rita replies.

'That's no problem,' Ellie says. 'Come sit on this side, so that you can have a better view.'

'Remember when we went to the Chateau that day with Tine and Henk?' Ellie goes on. 'I sent them a letter a while ago.'

'They're in Holland at the moment,' Rita says as she gazes at the mountain. 'Beautiful with all that snow. It does give the world a different feel.'

'It sure does,' Ellie agrees.

Sitting quietly, they enjoy the last part of their journey. When they reach their destination, Gwen is waiting for them at the station with Granddad's old car.

'Oh, Gwen, we could have walked that short distance,' Rita says.

'It's no problem at all,' Gwen replies. 'Get in. Mother can't wait to see you.'

When the car pulls up in the drive Kathleen MacIntosh is waiting behind the window. Ellie is the first to get out of the car and rushes to the door to meet her. Warmly she embraces the elderly lady. 'Good to see you, dear,' Nana says in a soft voice. Ellie brushes a tear from her cheek when she makes way for Rita to greet Nan.

'Oh, let's go inside,' Nana says. 'It's so cold out here.'

'I'm so happy to see you, Nana,' Ellie says as she hangs up her coat. 'I should've come sooner but, well, you know how it is.'

'Not really dear,' Nana replies. 'But I take it you are very busy.'

The fire in the lounge is lit when they enter, and on the small table, a tray with cakes and biscuits is placed beside a pot of hot tea. They make themselves comfortable while Gwen pours them all a cup. 'Quite unexpected, this cold spell,' she says.

'Yes,' Rita responds. 'But the children seem to love it. We saw them going up and down the hills this morning.'

Ellie reaches to take a piece of cake from the platter. After they've made themselves comfortable, Nana takes Ellie's hand. 'Now tell me, how have you been? You do look a bit peaky. I hope you're not neglecting yourself.'

'No, not at all,' Ellie replies. 'But I need to work hard, with the studies and the job I have. Although I've cut down on that a bit.'

'Your job?' Nana asks. 'Is that worth it, isn't that too much?'

Ellie says she doesn't mind the hard work. 'And I can make almost five pounds a week when I work every day.'

'And that's after classes?'

'Yes, of course. But, it was becoming a bit difficult, because I also have to study. That's why I'm working less now.'

'And you're right too,' Nana says. 'You are wearing yourself out, dear.'

'That's what I told her,' Rita states.

Ellie assures them they needn't worry.

'Gwen, could you please put some more wood on the fire?' Nana asks her daughter.

'Mother likes it hot,' Gwen says and gets up to give the fire a prod.

'Now, Rita what is this I hear about Pieter,' Nana enquires. 'Will he be married?'

Somewhat surprised Rita looks at her. 'Where did you hear that?'

'Do you mean I was informed wrongly?' Kathleen asks.

Rita becomes somewhat reserved. 'Not entirely,' she replies.

'I so hoped it was true,' Nana continues. 'It's about time that little girl has a mother. Not that you are not good to Ursula, of course, but you have your own life too.'

'Yes Nan,' Ellie replies. 'But, Uncle Pieter always does things his way.'

'I believe he would,' Nana says. 'Well, now that we have heard all about you, let me tell you something about me,' and she smiles with delight. 'In a couple of weeks Gwen will accompany me on a trip to India – '

'Oh, Nan. That's wonderful!' Ellie exclaims. 'How ... How did that come about?'

'Well,' Kathleen begins, 'you know how fond Henry and I always were of that country, and, it was one of his wishes that, if at all possible, I should make the effort to go there one more time.'

'That's so great,' Ellie says and puts her arm around Nana's shoulders. But Rita has her doubts.

'Are you sure about this?' She looks at Kathleen before casting a glance in Gwen's direction. 'India is ... well, it is not such a sanitary country.'

'Oh Mum,' Ellie sighs.

'Don't you think I don't know that?' Kathleen says.

'Really, Rita.'

'I'm sorry, that's not what I meant.'

'Mother knows the consequences,' Gwen says. 'Don't think I haven't tried to talk her out of it. But in the end all I could do was give my consent. Provided, I go with her.'

Ellie sits back and smiles about Nana who is finishing her tea with a gratified expression on her face. 'In fact, it is going to be a round the world journey,' Gwen continues. 'Mother has never been to America and I thought it was about time she spent some time with the family.'

'That is nice,' Rita says. 'When is the last time you saw your grandchildren, Kathleen?'

'That was at Henry's funeral, when they came,' she replies. 'Only, they didn't stay long. These children nowadays they all have obligations.'

'It will be awfully tiring for you,' Rita says. 'Such a long journey.'

Kathleen brushes that remark aside. 'Those aeroplanes go very fast and we will be stopping in Europe as well. What was the name of that city again, dear?'

'Zürich, Switzerland,' Gwen replies.

'That's right, Zürich. My sister lives in Switzerland, you see. And from there we will go to London.'

'It's a marvellous journey,' Ellie says.

'You will be gone for a while then,' Rita presumes.

'Yes, Rita. That's why I'm glad you came, so I could ask you personally,' Nana says. 'You see, we will be gone for six months and I wondered if you wouldn't mind looking in on the house for us occasionally.'

'Not at all,' Rita replies. 'I'm sure I could come over

here every now and then.'

'The neighbours will water the plants, and the garden, so that won't be a worry for you,' Kathleen continues, 'but there are a few things that need some looking after. I'll explain later.'

Rita tells her she would be pleased to help out. 'But don't forget to send us a nice postcard,' she says. 'You won't be going to Holland?'

'No, I'm afraid not.'

'When will you be leaving, Nan?' Ellie asks.

'We will leave in August,' is the reply but Kathleen leaves it to Gwen to give them the full details.

'Yes, August the fourth is when we leave,' Gwen answers. 'First, two months in India, then a month at Aunt Bronwyn's before we go to London and then we should be in Boston before Christmas, so we can spend the Holidays with the family.'

'This is so nice, Nana,' Ellie says. 'Spending Christmas with the whole family. And in winter at that.'

'Yes, it will be lovely,' Nana says with a happy face. 'Just like the old days when we still lived in England.'

'Actually, it looks a bit like Christmas now,' Rita says.

'We should light some candles,' Gwen suggests.

'Great idea!' Ellie says.

'Now, Ellie, how are you doing with your writing?' Nana asks. 'I haven't had the pleasure of reading your journals for quite some time now.'

'I'm sorry, Nan. I do write as often as I can, but maybe not as often as before. My studies have priority.'

'You should see it as part of your studies,' Nana says. 'A lot of people earn their living writing. I told you this before.'

'I know, Nana.'

'Well, then. Why don't you ask at one of the newspaper offices in Wellington if you can do some work for them?' Kathleen suggests.

'Me? Writing for a newspaper?' Ellie looks embarrassed. 'I couldn't do that!'

'Why not?'

'Yes, why not?' Rita backs Kathleen.

'You are spending all your energy on this serving job,' Nana says, 'while you could spend your energy on writing some odd bits for a paper.'

'Who would want to read what I have written, and who says I will earn money doing it?'

'Well, dear, if you don't ask you will never know.'

Ellie remains uncertain but promises she will see when she is back in Wellington. 'I do like the job I have now,' she says.

'I'm sure you do, dear,' Nana replies. 'But that is not what you want to do for the rest of your life, is it?'

'Nan is right, Ellie,' Rita says.

Gwen comes in with a few candles and the supplementary candlesticks. 'I had to search a bit for these,' she says, 'but here we are.' She places the candles in the holders and lights them. 'Isn't this lovely?' she says. 'Christmas in June.'

'I think another cup of tea is in order,' Kathleen says.

'All we need now are the presents,' Ellie says.

'You still have to be patient for another month, dear,' Rita says.

'Will you be coming home for your birthday?' Nana wonders. Ellie replies that it's not likely. 'I promised my boss I'd work through the winter break.'

Rita lets out a disappointing sigh. 'Again you're not coming home,' she says displeased. 'Can't you call it off?'

'Mum, I promised ... and, I could do with some extra

money as well.'

'I told you this morning, I can give you some more if you need it.'

Nana soothes the conversation. 'I think Ellie wants to earn her own money, Rita.'

Darkness has fallen when Ellie and Rita walk home from the train station, engaged in conversation about Nana's and Gwen's journey around the world. Their breath creates little clouds of vapour that are quickly dispersed by the cold winds. Shortly, they reach the small house and walk up the steps to the front door. On entering Rita notices an envelope on the floor. 'It's for you,' she says and hands it to Ellie.

'Mm, Uncle Pieter kept his word,' she says and removes the ticket from the envelope. 'He promised me the return fare.'

'Oh, that's nice,' Rita replies. She takes her coat off and hangs it on the coat-rack in the hall.

'Gosh, it's cold in here,' Ellie says and turns on the electric heater. 'We should have left it on.'

'I don't think so,' Rita reproaches. 'I'm the one having to pay the electricity bill.'

'We should have taken a woodburner,' Ellie utters as she looks around for her bag.

'Wood costs money too,' Rita says.

'Yeah, I suppose,' Ellie replies and spots her bag underneath a chair in the lounge area. 'What's for tea?'

'You won't believe it but I made pea-soup yesterday,' Rita replies.

'Pea-soup?!'

'Yes, 'snert'.'

'Oh Mum, you and your Dutch dishes. I think you should move back to Holland.'

'Maybe I will, one day,' Rita replies while she puts the soup from the refrigerator into a pan to heat it up. 'I'm eager to know how Tine and Henk are experiencing Holland at the moment.'

Ellie places some of her books on the table and sits down. 'Mum,' she says, 'I know I have never mentioned this in so many words, but when I've finished my studies I want to go to Holland. Actually, that's one of the reasons why I want to keep a job.' There is no reply from Rita as she silently stirs the soup to keep it from burning.

'You could come,' Ellie continues. 'We could go together.' Rita takes a few soup plates from the cupboard and puts them on the bench. 'Why ... would you want to go to Holland?' she asks.

'Because, I think I should. My roots lie there.'

'Yes, but, why now?' Rita questions as she ladles the soup onto the plates.

'I don't know exactly. It's just, I feel there's some unfinished business.'

'Unfinished business? What do you mean? You have your life here!'

'Well, Mum, as you never bothered to tell me that my father had died *before* we left Holland, I never had the chance to see his grave, let alone attend his funeral.'

Rita places the plates with steaming soup on the table and takes a few spoons from the drawer. 'Ellie, it's so long ago. And what's there to see about a grave?'

'It's my father's grave. Don't you ever want to go back and visit his grave? I mean, he *was* your husband.'

Rita sits down and inattentively stirs her spoon in the soup. 'Like I said, it's a long time ago.'

After blowing the heat off the soup Ellie carefully takes a spoonful.

'And where will you stay?' Rita asks. 'There's

nowhere for you to stay, and I don't think Oma and Opa's a good idea.'

'I can stay with Aunt Hetty and Uncle Geert,' Ellie says.

'You can't stay with them.' Rita sounds resolute. 'You don't even know them and besides, they don't have the space.'

'What do you know?' Ellie says agitatedly. 'You don't even know how they live!'

'Ellie, they have three children themselves. Where will they put you? On top of that, you don't have a passport.'

'So I'll get one!' Ellie cries out. 'What's the problem, Mother? Here I am making great plans, and you have to spoil it again.' She shoves her plate away from her.

'No need to get so upset,' Rita says. 'I just don't want you to get your hopes up. We don't have such a good relationship with the relatives in Holland.'

'What do you mean? You've been writing to Aunt Hetty for years!'

Rita is quiet for a moment and then says she hasn't heard from her for a long time.

'You must still have her address,' Ellie says. 'I will write to her.'

'I don't have her address anymore,' Rita claims.

'Then I'll ask Uncle Pieter, he will know. She's his sister.'

She pulls the plate towards her to finish her soup. 'I will go,' she says resolutely. 'No matter how you feel about it.'

Ellie rolls up the blinds and opens her bedroom window. For a moment, she leans out and takes a deep breath in the crisp morning air. She watches a few icicles that, melted by the sun, fall from the eaves to the ground, creating tiny tinkling sounds.

Dilatorily Ellie gathers her things and makes her way to the bathroom to freshen up. When she enters the kitchen some time later, Rita is pleased to see her looking rested.

'Yeah,' Ellie replies, 'I slept almost ten hours.'

Rita pours her a cup of tea while Ellie makes some toast. 'I'm glad you didn't stay up all night to study,' Rita says.

'I could hardly do that with my eyes closing on me all the time,' is Ellie's reply. 'The fresh air here made me sleepy.'

'I don't think it's the air,' Rita says. 'More likely you were very tired.'

Ellie takes her piece of toast and tea and walks outside where the sun is warming the surroundings. When she has finished her breakfast, she puts her coat on and tells her mother she is going for a walk. 'Maybe Chris and Marty are home now.'

At her ease, Ellie walks along the quiet street. Nearby, the singing of hymns in the church can be heard. When she turns into the next street, the singing becomes louder. Ellie slackens her pace when she reaches the wooden building but passes by the open gate to continue on her way. With the church sounds fading behind her, she walks through the main street until she reaches her friends' house and knocks on the door. The crying of a baby sounds through the closed door and Chrissie can be heard yelling to open up.

'Ellie?' is Marty's reaction as he opens the door. 'This is a nice surprise. Come in.'

Ellie follows him inside. 'I hope I'm not calling at an inconvenient moment.'

'No, not at all. Chris! Look who's here!' He enlightens Ellie about little Charlie being hungry and that's the reason he's playing up.

'So uh, everything going well here?' Ellie asks.

'Oh yeah. Very well,' Marty replies.

Carrying the little one on her hip, Chrissie enters the room. 'El, hi.' With one free arm, she hugs her friend Ellie. 'Mum told me you were in town. Good to see you.'

But Ellie has her attention fixed on Charlie. 'Look at you,' she says to the still sobbing child. 'Gosh Chris, he has grown.'

'Yes,' a proud Chrissie replies, 'almost fourteen months now.'

The toddler's face clouds over again. 'Oops, better get this one some lunch before he starts again.'

'I'm sorry I missed his birthday,' Ellie says with regret. 'But I seem to be so busy since I went to Wellington.'

'It's alright,' Chrissie replies and tries to mix some bread with milk in a bowl when Marty takes the child from her and puts him in the high chair.

'By the way, thanks for the present you sent,' Chrissie says. She hands the bowl with the mixture to Marty, who begins to help Charlie with his food.

'Can I get you something?' Chrissie asks. 'Cuppa tea?'

'Whatever you're having is fine with me,' Ellie replies.

Chrissie puts the kettle on and takes a plate from the cabinet.

'I wanted to come by yesterday but you weren't in. So Mum and I went to see Nan.'

'Oh? How is she?'

'Good, very good. In fact, she's going on a journey

around the world with Gwen.'

'You're joking!' Chrissie calls out.

'Is she?' Marty asks.

'Yes. For six months,' Ellie says, 'this August.'

'Well, good for her,' Chrissie replies. 'Marty wat ...'

But the warning comes too late. The bowl with Charlie's food ends up on the floor. 'He always does that,' Chrissie says. 'If you don't pay attention he just shoves his plate over the edge.'

Marty tries to discipline the little boy, but to no avail. The toddler looks at him as if he is not conscious of having done any wrong, which leaves not much for Marty to do but to clean up the mess and make his son another bowl of food. With the sound of Charlie hammering with his little spoon on the tray, Chrissie finishes making the sandwiches and prepares the tea. A while later the little boy is happily eating his newly made lunch under the watchful eye of his father. Chrissie and Ellie make themselves comfortable in the lounge.

'You're doing well, I hear?' Chrissie says.

'Yes,' Ellie replies. 'It seems all the latest news has already trickled through.'

'Yeah, well. Word gets around quickly here.'

Ellie reaches and takes a sandwich from the plate.

'Cucumber and cheese that one,' Chrissie says. 'Your favourite.'

'These days anything is my favourite, Chris,' Ellie replies. 'You can't be too choosy when you're a poor student.' She takes a bite and determines she hasn't had such a nice sandwich for a long time.

'I ran into Bob the other day,' Chrissie says. 'He asked after you.'

'Did he?' Ellie sounds surprised. She changes the subject by asking what Chrissie might know about her uncle's new lady friend.

'Not much. I know Uschi isn't too fond of her,' Chrissie says. 'Last week when I was at Mum's she spent most of the day at our house because Pieter had his girlfriend visiting.'

Ellie shakes her head. 'I find it strange. Do you think he's serious about her?'

'Oh, I don't know, Ellie. I'm not going to worry about what Pieter is doing,' Chris replies. 'Actually, I thought she was rather nice.'

'Do you? What does she look like?'

'Blonde hair, rather friendly,' Chrissie replies. 'I think they met in a pub in Hamilton.'

'Good lord,' Ellie says. 'I wonder how long it will last.'

'Just forget about it, Ellie. It's not your problem.' Chrissie grabs Ellie's arm. 'Guess what? Marty will take over his dad's business.'

Ellie looks surprised. 'You mean, take over? Not just work there?'

'No. He will be the boss. His father wants to go back to England and offered Marty the business.'

'Oh, that's wonderful!' Ellie replies and calls over to Marty: 'How did that come about?'

Marty lifts Charlie from his high chair and goes over to the lounge. 'Well, Dad always was a bit homesick for England and now they've finally cut the knot.' He sits down and takes the last sandwich from the plate.

'And your mother?'

'She goes with him,' Marty replies.

'One should hope so,' Ellie says, 'but I thought she liked New Zealand.'

'Compared to Holland, yes. But she doesn't mind giving England a try.'

'I wonder how long she'll last though,' Chrissie says. 'She is so fond of little Charlie here, I don't think she could be away long.'

Charlie toddles around the coffee table to bury his face in his mother's lap a moment later.

'But that will be hard with half a world between,' Ellie says.

'Well,' Marty says. 'She can also keep herself busy with my sister's kids in England.'

'So, when is this going to take place?' Ellie asks.

'Couple of months,' Chrissie replies as she gently strokes the child's hair. 'What about us going for a walk? Some fresh air will do this one good.'

'What about me going?' Marty suggests. 'Then you can catch up with Ellie.'

'No, it's all right, we can talk on the way. I thought you needed to do those calculations for your dad?'

With a reluctant sigh, Marty gets up. 'That is true,' he says.

Chrissie picks Charlie up off the floor and hands him to Ellie. 'You sit with your aunty,' she says. 'I'll get his jacket.' Ellie gladly has the little one on her lap and starts singing a song to him, about the goblin sitting on a toadstool until Chrissie comes back with Charlie's jacket and hat. 'Look, Rita made this one for him,' she says. 'Doesn't he look adorable?'

'Handsome is the word,' Ellie replies. 'Better keep an eye on him when he grows up.'

'Not for some time,' Chrissie says and cuddles the little boy. 'He will be my little angel for a while yet.' Charlie is not very thrilled about the attention and pulls a funny face.

'That's not what he has in mind,' Ellie says laughingly. She puts her coat on as well and opens the front door. 'We won't be long,' Chrissie calls over to Marty before they walk into the crisp sunshine outside and onto the street.

Ellie watches attentively as the man across from her reads her story.

'*I stared in amazement, as I walked along the deck of the huge ship, my mother beside me holding my little hand tightly. 'That,' she said, 'is amidships. Always stay on that side, don't ever go over to that railing. Do you hear me?'*

'*Why can't I go over to the other side?' I asked my mother.*

'*Because then you will fall into the big ocean and you will never see mama again.'*

That's how my mother made me familiar with the ship that carried us to the new country many years ago. At the time I never thought we would go to this new country to stay. I thought we were going on a great journey across the sea. A sea that could be seen from the Dutch coast and where on its beaches I had enjoyed playing. Shortly after we embarked I found a friend, another six-year-old girl by the name of Annie. She was moving to this new country as well, with both her parents. One of the first things we did together was to climb onto some obstacles and peek over the forbidden railing to watch the waves passing by. We had done this several times before we were finally caught by my mother.'

The man sitting behind his desk lowers the sheet of paper.

'Your experiences?'

'Yes Sir,' Ellie replies.

'Mm,' the man mutters and continues reading.

'*My mother was upset, but Annie stood up for me and said it had been her idea. We both must have looked like the most innocent angels on earth, or on the ocean, for my mother could not find it in her heart to punish me. Instead she agreed to let me near the ship's pool as long as there was always a parent present, either my mother or Annie's parents. Both Annie and I could not swim but lying on our bellies on the edge of the pool we sailed our little wooden ships in the water. One time Annie's boat moved away too far from 'shore' and she leaned over to grab it. She almost slid into the water. I was just in time to grab her dress and pull her back. We furtively looked over, but luckily our parents had not noticed. They were busy talking and laughing. We only hoped that the sleeves of Annie's dress would dry before her mother found out. Another time we were sitting in the middle of the deck playing with our dolls when a boy came and grab ...'*

The sound of the man's voice gradually slides into mere silence. Ellie has her eyes focused on his serious face. For a while, only the dull, nervous sound of Ellie's drumming fingers can be heard. 'If you don't like it, Sir ... I could just ... '

With his eyes focused on the sheet of paper, he motions her to be quiet.

'It has potential,' he says after a while and reads on. *'We swore to be friends for life but it was never to be. Not only did I lose my friend Annie as soon as we disembarked the ship, but months later my mother finally told me that Daddy would never join us in the new country, for he had died before we left Holland.'*

He lowers the paper. 'Well,' he says, 'a nice read. All your own experiences?'

'Yes Sir,' Ellie replies.

'I think we can use it,' he continues. 'We are having a series of articles about immigrants to New Zealand and their new lives here. This might fit in nicely.'

'So ... You're not sure whether – '

'Like I said, it has potential. Do you think you could write a follow up to this? I take it you have been living here all these years?'

'Yes Sir.' Ellie looks at him with anticipation.

'And do you think you could write more about how you felt when you came here?' he questions. 'Like it says here for instance, your father died without you knowing it. That could be an interesting topic. Drama always goes down well.'

'What do you mean, Sir?'

'Nothing in particular, just write what you felt back then and I'm sure we can work something out,' he assures her.

'So, you keep my story?' Ellie asks.

'Sure. You want it printed, don't you?' he replies. 'Oh, you mean the pay. Bring in the follow up, by that time I will have consulted my colleagues. Just leave an address where you can be reached.'

He stands up and shakes Ellie's hand. 'I'm sure we'll see more of you.'

'Thank you, Sir,' Ellie says before she leaves the office.

With a happy expression on her face, Ellie walks down the stairs to the ground floor. After leaving the newspaper office she makes a little twirl on the pavement before she goes on her way. The windy, chilly day doesn't seem to bother her and she gaily goes on her way home. When she passes the post office, she stops in her tracks and then goes in. At the window, she asks if she can make a telephone call.

'You can go over there, in that booth,' is the reply.

When the telephone rings Ellie picks up the receiver.

'Nan?' she asks.

'*Ellie? No, this is Gwen. How are you?*'

'Fine, couldn't be better,' Ellie replies, 'and what about you? Are you all packed to go?'

'*Getting there. I'm afraid Mother is better at this sort of thing than I am. She keeps telling me not to take so much.*'

'I suppose Nana is quite excited by now.'

'*Oh, I wouldn't say that. She acts as if travelling round the world is a daily thing for her.*'

'She would, would she,' Ellie smiles. 'Well, she has seen quite a bit of the world already.'

'*Yes, that's right. Do you want to talk to her? Here she is.*'

A moment later Kathleen's voice sounds through the telephone. '*Ellie, dear? Is that you gossiping about me to my daughter?*'

'No gossip Nan, just plain facts,' is Ellie's reply. 'Nana listen, you'll never guess where I just came from.'

'*No, and I will miss the aeroplane if you don't tell me now.*'

'Well, I went to a newspaper office and they are interested in printing one of my stories. Isn't that wonderful?'

'*I'm not surprised, dear,*' Nana says. '*I never doubted your abilities. Do you know when it will be in the newspaper?*'

'I'm not sure yet,' Ellie replies. 'This nice man, Mr Reynolds, wants me to write a follow up to what I gave him today and he said that they might publish it with a series of articles or something.'

'*That sounds promising, dear. I would be so proud if your stories would be in a newspaper.*'

'Thank you, Nan. I will keep a copy for you if they publish it.'

'That would be lovely, dear. It was so nice of you to phone.'

'I just wanted to let you know before you left on your journey. And I hope everything will go well for you in all these far away countries.'

'I'm sure it will, take care of yourself, dear,' Nana replies, *'and don't forget to let those newspaper people pay you for your efforts.'*

'I won't, Nan. Keep well, both of you.'

'Thank you. Bye dear.'

When the engaged signal sounds at the other end, Ellie hangs up the horn.

There's a quietness in the house now that all the others have gone out. Ellie clears the lounge and straightens the cover over the worn-out couch before she makes herself comfortable with the books she collected from the library. Not for long, she is so concentrated on the book she is reading, she doesn't hear the faint knock on the kitchen door. When she gets up a while later and walks into the kitchen she is startled when she finds Paul there, sitting at the kitchen table.

'Paul. What are you doing here?'

'Came by to see you. But I saw you were busy, so I thought I'd wait here.'

'Don't you ever knock?' Ellie says, rather annoyed.

'I did kno – '

'I don't want you to sneak up on me like that!' Ellie says in a loud voice. 'If you're here, make yourself known!'

'I did. Oh, what's the point,' Paul says. 'How have you been?'

'How have I been, he asks? I have been well, thank you. Anything else?'

'Look, I'm sorry I walked out like I did but – '

'Oh, he still remembers,' Ellie says. 'That was more than two months ago, Paul. You don't only ever knock, but you don't bother letting people know where you are either.' A strange silence descends as a threatening expression appears on Paul's face. 'I am sorry,' he says in a slow voice. 'Don't you ever let people finish!?'

Ellie is taken aback by Paul's outburst of anger and she asks him, cautiously, to leave.

'Not until you have listened to what I have to say,' he continues menacingly, but Ellie has no intention of letting him explain.

'I am not interested, Paul,' she says. 'You just disappear off the face of the earth and now you come back as if nothing has happened? That's not how it works, Paul.'

The sudden blow on the table makes her shrink back.

'Listen to me,' he says, as he keeps his mad eyes fixed on her.

'Paul … I … there's no need to get angry,' she says with a trembling voice. She swiftly jumps aside as Paul moves towards her.

'Please … Leave … '

This time she is not quick enough and his fist hits her face. She stumbles and falls against the kitchen cabinet. With Paul coming towards her again, she quickly moves away and scrambles to her feet. The chair that she knocks over behind her makes him almost lose his balance, but it gives Ellie enough time to run for the door and out onto the street.

'He attacked me!' she cries at a passer-by. 'He attacked me!'

The man watches her run off, when at the same time Paul approaches. 'Hey you!' he yells. He grabs Paul by his sleeve and slaps him in his face. 'Attacking women, aye,' and he hits him again. Paul pulls himself loose and with a perplexed look on his face makes himself scarce.

Blood runs down from her face when Ellie staggers to hide behind a bush. A passing woman asks her what has happened. Ellie trembles all over her body and tries to explain, but words won't come. The man who came to her rescue comes nearer as well.

'Did you see what happened?' the woman asks.

'Yes,' the man says. 'Are you all right, love? Come, let us help you.' He takes Ellie by her arm and leads her away from the bush. 'Some idiot attacked her,' he explains.

'Poor thing,' the woman says. 'We should call for the police.'

'Yes. Would you, please?' the man asks and walks Ellie back to her house. 'She lives over there.' He nods in the direction where he had seen Ellie being chased from the house. 'Now let us help you,' he says to Ellie. 'Everything will be all right.' Ellie tries to say something, but instead, tears start streaming down her face.

'It's all right, love,' the man says. 'We'll first get you cleaned up and then you'll feel better.'

In the kitchen, he takes a towel from the bench and pours some water over it from the tap. 'Now, you sit down over there so I can clean your face,' he tells Ellie, who is still shaken by the incident. Noticing the fallen chair he stands it upright. 'Come sit here,' he says and then gently wipes the blood from her face. 'It always looks worse than it is,' he observes.

'He just hit me,' Ellie utters. 'Just like that.'

'Don't worry about it anymore,' the man says. 'This needs a bandage. Do you have something in the house?'

Ellie shrugs. 'I … I'm not sure.'

'Well, blood still seeps through this cut here. We need to put something on it.' He rummages through a drawer and finds a clean tea towel. He carefully presses it against the cut and tells her to hold it there tightly, when Kate walks in. She looks a bit surprised to see a stranger in the kitchen, bent over her housemate. 'Have we met?' she asks the man.

'Not that I know of, but, I'm Colin.'

Kate looks at him and then notices Ellie's tear-stained face. 'What happened to you?'

'She was attacked,' Colin explains. 'I'm just here to help her.'

'Attacked? Who would want to attack you?! And what's this with your face?'

'Paul came back,' Ellie softly replies.

'Paul?'

Kate gently removes the tea towel from Ellie's face. 'Let me see. He did *that* to you?'

'I'm afraid so,' Colin answers.

'The bastard! I knew he was weird. But ... We have to tell the police,' Kate says. 'This is an offence.'

'Yes, this lady was going to call for the police,' Colin replies.

Kate sits down next to Ellie. 'Forget that Paul, he's not worth it.'

Ellie sighs. 'I was trying to, Kate. And then ... all of a sudden he was sitting here in the kitchen.'

'What do you mean? Was he waiting for you?'

'Sort of. I did ask him to leave, but ... he ... he didn't want to go.'

'And so he bashed your brains in,' Kate says. 'I will tell the police a thing or two,' she adds, outraged. 'Just comes into our house and starts bashing things about! It's unheard of!'

'Kate,' Ellie says quietly, 'it wasn't like that.'

'You were attacked in your own home, Ellie. It *was* like that.'

'Let's not get all excited,' Colin says. 'Let's wait 'n see what the police have to say.'

'I'm sorry, Sir,' Ellie says, 'she gets carried away sometimes.'

There's a knock on the door and a constable can be seen through the window. Colin, who stands leaning against the bench, walks towards the door and opens it.

'Afternoon,' the constable says. 'We had a call that someone was brutally attacked. Are we at the right address?'

'You sure are,' Colin replies. 'Please, come in.'

With his colleague close behind, the policeman enters the kitchen.

'This young woman here was beaten by a man, right here in this kitchen.'

'And you are?' the constable questions.

'I just walked by when she came running out of the house,' Colin replies.

The other policeman takes out a pen and notebook and has a look at Ellie. 'Would you care to explain to me what happened?' he asks. Before Ellie can tell him, Kate stresses not to leave anything out. 'That'll teach him.'

'Were you here when it happened?' the officer asks her.

'No,' Kate replies, 'but – '

'Then we don't need to hear your interpretation.' He turns his attention to Ellie. 'Please, Miss, your name?'

The remaining constable approaches Colin in an interrogative manner. 'Did you see what happened?'

'No Sir, I wasn't inside,' Colin replies, 'but this young lady here came running out of the house, blood all over her face, yelling that she was attacked. And she just ran when this bloke came after her. So uh, I grabbed him, to stop him, you see.'

'He attacked you as well?'

'No Sir. That is to say, I didn't give him a chance. No, he just looked all confused and then he took off.'

'Confused? Do you have any idea about what?'

'Well, I did slap him in his face. To keep him away from her of course, and that must've scared him off.'

'I see. Are you in any way acquainted with this young lady?'

'No, not at all. Never seen her before. I was just on my way to a mate. He lives here, in this street. He'll be wondering where I am by now.'

'Right. Could you please state your name and address?'

'But, I haven't done anything wrong,' Colin says. 'I just helped her out.'

'I am sure you did all you could,' the constable replies. 'But I take it you want us to catch this man? For the record, we might need your help again.'

'Well,' his colleague says, after he has listened to Ellie's side of the story, 'you will have to tell me his name and address, so we can take him in.'

'Will you arrest him?' Ellie wonders. 'I don't want him to go to prison.'

'Ellie?! He'll come back if the police don't catch him!' Kate tries to convince her.

'Miss, please,' the constable addresses Kate before turning his attention to Ellie again. 'You are pressing charges, aren't you?'

Ellie nods and then gives him Paul's name and address. The cut in her eyebrow starts trickling blood again.

'Thank you. We'll see what we can do. In the meantime I would advise you to keep your door locked, until we catch him.'

Kate pours some water on the tea towel and wipes the blood from Ellie's cheek. 'Christ! What confusion in this quiet old town,' she says.

'If I were you, I'd have a doctor look at that. It might need a stitch,' the constable says and gets up. 'Well, I think we have all the information we need. You'll be hearing from us.'

« »

It wasn't until two days later that Paul was found. He had not been at his house for more than two months and now he showed up at the wrong moment. For us, those two days were rather nerve-racking as we expected him to be back and maybe cause more damage. Kate was convinced he would be just the type to do such a thing. We didn't go anywhere on our own. For safety, we went out in twos or all four of us together, which was a comfort to me, for my black eye seemed to draw more attention than I cared for. The cut needed a stitch to let the split skin heal quicker. Mentally it took me a while longer to heal. I had never been hit before, even though in the past, there had been more reasons than one for grown-ups around me to give a child, with a temper like mine, a thrashing. But they never did.

It wasn't the mere fact of the fist splitting my eyebrow, rather the realisation that Paul was a lot sicker in his head than I had ever thought and that was what made the whole experience a terrifying one. For weeks I could not walk on the streets without looking over my shoulder, afraid he would be there again. I talked about this with

Kate but she said not to worry about it, he was incarcerated for a while yet. But we both knew he would not be locked up long for a minor offence.

Weeks went by and I never went out after dark by myself. I always made sure I could be with fellow students. One evening it was Colin who offered to walk with me to one of the buildings on campus. He turned out to be a very considerate neighbour, even though he did live in another street.

The whole situation with Paul kept my mind occupied a lot longer than I had imagined. I started reading about how a bad upbringing can affect a person in later life. A better understanding of this helped me with my own problem and gradually my fear was overcome. My strength was reinforced by the fact that the newspaper printed both my stories in two consecutive Saturday issues. Mr Reynolds asked me if I had any plans of writing more stories and I told him I was seriously thinking about it.

'You do that and we will seriously consider giving you some steady work,' were his exact words.

I decided to use my latest experiences and put them down on paper. When I presented the result to Mr Reynolds, he looked rather serious after he had read it, and for a moment I thought I had pushed my luck too far.

'Heavy stuff,' he said. 'Your own experience?'

I told him it was the result of an experience and what had caused me to write it. 'People should be much more aware of how they treat their children.'

'I agree, but you make it sound as if the whole world mistreats their children,' he replied.

I explained that the article was not about the good parents of the world.

'Well, make that clear at the start and we have

another story,' and he handed it back to me. I told him I would. 'That's the spirit,' he said and he asked if it could be ready by next Wednesday.

My studies had suffered these last few weeks and as soon as the article was finished and handed in, I was back at the library and went to every lecture that aroused my interest. Although I had made a little extra money with writing, it was not enough and so I had to plan my spare moments around the waitressing apron once more. I was so busy that I almost forgot Uschi's birthday. I wasn't reminded of it until I noticed the comment in one of my notebooks. Knowing she would be disappointed if she did not hear from me on her birthday, my first thought was to phone her. Her father, however, had never bothered having a telephone installed; he still relied on Grace and William's telephone.

I went out to buy her a small gift. It wouldn't arrive on time, but I was certain she would be pleased just the same. Her eleventh birthday already, time goes by so fast. She would be in her teens before we knew it. I tried to remember being eleven myself, still living with Nan and Granddad. I suppose that was the one birthday just before Uschi was nearly taken to the South Island by her father. I never really knew why he did not make the move. Maybe another love affair that had gone sour.

It was around the same time Mum had to go to the hospital for a few days. She managed to convince me it was not serious. 'Just a normal procedure that women go through.' It never made me worry about her. Now, I wonder what it could have been. And the upset Jody had caused one day, being caught in the shed with one of his friends. William had whacked him so hard he had passed out for a few minutes. I didn't understand anything of it and I felt awfully sorry for Jody. I suppose William was the first person in my life who had made me feel what hate was. Thinking back on that incident only gave me additional confirmation, that what I had written in my latest article was correct. After that occurrence there always remained some friction between Jody and his father.

Arriving home one evening after work, a strange, cloying smell entered my nostrils. First I thought my housemates were burning incense but the smell was more intense. I found them in the lounge area, snugly sitting on the floor, Daniel, Barb and Kate with her new boyfriend Richard. Smoking, something that was normally not done in our house. Barb asked me to close the door and asked if I wanted to join them. I told her I did not smoke.

'You will like this, El,' Barb said and handed me the cigarette. I was a bit hesitant but when Kate told me not to be a dowdy twit about it, I joined in. The first drag went down with huffs and puffs and I wasn't sure whether I was going to like this, but after I had tried it again and the smoke circulated in my lungs, it wasn't so bad.

'Leave it there for a while and then blow it out,' Richard said. And that is what I did. The cigarette made the rounds and I don't know what it did to the others but it made me feel relaxed in a peculiar way. A feeling I had never experienced before, but then, I had never smoked dope before. At the time I found it a nicer way to unwind than having beers and I wondered how they had come by it, for marijuana is not widely available in the stores. In a curious, slow voice Kate explained that Richard had his connections. He had met this bloke at the Beatles concert last year who grew his own.

'How ... fascinating,' I managed to say. By that time it seemed like our meagre furnishings started to look like waves in the ocean. 'The Beatles ... ' I said at one stage, 'let's play the Beatles,' and someone got up to put the record on, but for some reason, they didn't sound like they usually did.

I don't recall how many drags I had but the smoking made me feel very drowsy in the end and I lay down on the couch, which I'm sure had a blue cover when I last saw it, but maybe the others had bought a new one.

It was pitch dark when I woke up. I didn't know where to go at first when I saw a tiny streak of light coming from underneath somewhere. I crawled to my feet and went towards it. Opening the door, I noticed it was a street lamp sending a faint light into the kitchen, but it was adequate for finding the light switch. When I turned around I was looking at Kate's bare bum as she was lying on the floor, snuggled up against Richard. She at least could have had the decency to pull her knickers back up. I took the cover from the couch, that by this time had turned to blue again, and threw it over them. With a funny feeling in my head still, I sought my bed where I slept until late in the morning.

It was too late to join an English lecture I had planned to go to, so I took a book and a cup of tea and sat outside on the steps in the noon sun to catch up on an issue I wanted to know more about. I liked reading the work of the Brontë sisters. I wondered why they had to die so young. Bad conditions in those days I suppose but then, others did make it to a ripe old age.

Kate finally made it to the land of the living and joined me a while later. Richard had left early, he worked at the docks. She too was late for a class, but for her, that was the rule rather than the exception. I sometimes asked myself whether she spent time at the university grounds at all. Usually not the one who is worried about what state the house was in, or what it smelt like, Kate mentioned she had opened all the windows and left the door open to air the place because the smell of marijuana still lingered. 'You never know when police might show up,' she said.

I asked her if she was involved in anything that made her worry about the police calling. She claimed not to be. 'But I still remember that thing with what's-his-name. Before you know it they're in your house.'

I hoped we never would have to go through something like that again. And then she asked if I had heard about Paul being replaced. 'His room has a new tenant.'

I wish she hadn't mentioned that name but it was good to know he wouldn't be living there anymore. I asked her if she knew whether he would be back at college at all. She said she could find out. 'But it's not likely he'll be back for this term though.' That was comforting, for now.

As we both felt we could do with some time free from obligations, we went to the harbour. We bought lunch and sat down on a bench at the waterfront to enjoy life passing by around us. Kate appeared a bit downhearted. I thought perhaps that was caused by last night's joint party, but after a while, she said she was pregnant. Although I told her I was not surprised, in a way I was. She claimed always to be very careful and didn't really understand how it could have happened. She sounded rather desperate and didn't know what to do. 'I don't think it's Richard's, Ellie, and I don't want anyone else's baby.'

I didn't know what I could possibly do to help her, apart from babysitting after it was born and wanted to know if she was certain about having a baby. 'Have you seen a doctor at all?'

She had and said she was three months gone. I wondered if that meant she would leave university and go back to her hometown. 'No, I want to stay here and finish what I have started. And I want to be with Richard,' she added. In my opinion, she could do just that, until the baby was born.

'You don't understand, Ellie,' she said. 'It's not Richard's.'

She hadn't told him and I suggested she should. He could not blame her for what she had done before they got together. Only, she did not want a baby by a stranger, now that she had planned to stay with Richard.

'What will you do then?' I asked. 'Have it adopted?' A strange feeling came over me when she shook her head. 'There are other ways, Ellie.'

I had heard of those other ways and if Kate had started this conversation to seek my approval for that, she had come to the wrong person. Normally she always seemed so sure of herself, ready to take on the world, but that attitude appeared to have been washed away with the knowledge that she carried a new life inside of her. She tried to explain something about a doctor who could help her, while I tried to convince her not to do anything foolish. Then, it doesn't matter who the father is, what matters is the one who raises you. I told her how I grew up without my father but that there were always people around, ready to help me.

'Yeah, like who?' She was a bit sarcastic about it.

I mentioned my uncle. I suppose he had always been the next best thing to what my father could have been. 'You've met him,' I said.

'You mean the bloke who came for you that day?'

'That's the one. And of course I had Nan and

Granddad, who weren't even my own grandparents.'

'Yes, well, I suppose you've had a lovely childhood, but that doesn't solve my problem.' Kate could not picture Richard playing happy daddy to someone else's child. I made another effort to try and change her perception and said she should at least talk to him to be sure how he felt about it. 'Maybe he's very pleased.' But even that remark did not go down well. She remained uncertain about the situation and I wondered if she was at all certain about her relationship with Richard if she could not even talk to him about it.

I never understood why people don't feel like talking matters through. If issues weigh too heavily on my patience I just belt it out. Apparently, that did not apply to Kate. She became subdued and said she could just pretend it was Richard's. 'By the time it's born, he won't recall when we first slept together.' For now, that sounded like a good solution, it at least drew the attention away from destroying the tiny life. She made me promise not to let anyone know what she just told me and I was happy to give her my word.

The fact that she was with child could not be disguised in the months to come, but the father's identity could.

《 》

'Message from the paper,' Barb tells Ellie and hands her a note. Ellie puts her bag on the chair while she reads what it says. She frowns and says she had better go and see them. 'But first, something to eat.' She makes a sandwich and puts the kettle on for tea. 'D'you care for a cuppa as well?' she asks Barb.

'Sure.'

A while later they sit at the kitchen table having a mid-afternoon snack, which for Ellie is lunch.

'We don't see much of you lately,' Barb says.

'I have a lot to do,' Ellie justifies herself. 'I'm seriously thinking of giving up that job, I hardly have time to write my papers, or to read books.' She takes a bite from her sandwich and with her mouth still half full, she asks Barb if she is interested.

'In your job?'

'Yes. Pay is not too bad.'

'OK, I'll give it a thought. Who could not do with some extra money?' But she wonders about Ellie's. 'How will you manage? Your ticket to Europe is still a long way off.'

'I could always find work later again, when studying won't take up so much of my time.'

'Don't expect that to happen,' Barb replies.

'I could always put Europe off till later,' Ellie says. 'I don't really *have* to go in a year's time.'

She finishes her tea and gets up. 'Got to go, see what *they* want,' and she waves the piece of paper. When she steps outside it has started to rain and she asks Barb if she can borrow her umbrella.

'No worries. I put it in the hall.'

Barely a few yards from home and rain gushes down the umbrella to the ground. Ellie holds it close to her, so as not to let the wind slap the rainwater against her body. It blocks her view and she has to mind not to bump into people.

Shivering, she enters the newspaper building and goes up the stairs to Mr Reynolds' office where an unknown man approaches her when she enters.

'I'm looking for Mr Reynolds,' Ellie explains.

'He's not here today, but he asked me to talk to you,'

the man replies. 'I'm Dean Jones. How are you?'

Ellie shakes his hand and, slightly uncertain, takes the offered seat. 'Where – ' but he doesn't let her finish. 'Yes, we've been discussing your articles as they've caused quite some reaction. Specially the latest one. Don't get me wrong,' he is quick to add when he sees the worried look appear on her face, 'mainly positive. So, we wondered whether you would consider doing some more work for us. We'll give you a contract of course, and you supply us with anything you would like to write about … ' He pauses for a second. 'Well, not anything but … What do you say?'

'I … I don't know,' Ellie replies. 'I mean, I'm not a journalist, I'm still studying and – '

'Don't worry about that,' Mr Jones interjects. 'We like what you've written, the people out there like it.' He moves his head in the direction of the window. 'And it's the readers that count. They buy the newspapers.'

'I'm very busy, Sir. I'm even thinking of giving up the job I've done so far.'

'What do you do?'

'I was, still am, working in a tea-shop. Fun, but too many hours.'

'You earn good money there?'

'Enough, about five pounds a week, when I work every day.'

'We can give you six, if you supply us with a few stories every week.'

'Every week?! What will I write about?'

'You'll think of something,' he replies.

Ellie shakes her head. 'No, I can't do that. What's more, it will take up too much of my time. I do want to pass my exams, Sir.'

Dean ponders on that for a few seconds. 'What about

one story a week? You think you can manage that?'

Ellie is still not certain. 'I don't like to make promises I can't keep.'

'OK,' Dean says, 'we'll try it for a month. One story a week, if you can't manage, we can always change our minds.' He stands up. 'Deal?'

Ellie smiles and shakes his proffered hand. 'I'll try,' she replies.

'Right then. We thought perhaps you could write about subjects that keep you busy. Our boys in Vietnam, the situation of the young people in our country, whatever. You belong to the generation that will take over when the time comes, so it would be interesting to know how your generation feels about world issues.' Ellie looks at Mr Jones who cannot be more than thirty-five himself. 'OK,' she says. 'Same pay as for the stories I wrote before?'

'For now,' he replies. 'We can always negotiate a raise later.' With a satisfied smile, Ellie gets up. 'Next Wednesday early enough for the first story?'

'Fine. Hope to see you then.'

Ellie is about to leave the office when Dean calls her back and hands her a few letters. 'I'm sorry they've been opened, but they were addressed to the paper. Reactions to your stories and I think you should read them.'

Ellie thanks him and puts the letters in her bag. Through the subsiding rain, she makes her way to Grey Street, shaking the drops off the umbrella before she walks in the door of the tea-shop. Her boss is glad to see her and asks if she would mind working today as one of her co-workers has called in sick.

'I'm sorry, Andre. That's not why I came,' Ellie replies. 'I just wanted to let you know that ... I'm giving up the job.'

His disappointment is hardly noticeable when he asks

her to reconsider. 'I'd hate to see you leave,' he says, 'you know that.'

'Yes, Andre, but, it's all too much,' Ellie replies, 'I told you before,' and she puts forward that one of her friends might be interested in the job.

'That's not the issue, Ellie. I will have a replacement in no time. The fact is that you are a good worker, I'd hate to lose you.'

Ellie shrugs her shoulders. 'There will be more people who know the ropes,' she says.

'Yes, I will have to see about that though,' Andre questions. 'You will work until the end of this month, I hope?'

'Of course. I'll be in tomorrow. Oh, what the heck. I'll work today as well.'

She walks to the back and takes an apron from the kitchen. A few minutes later she's taking orders to the tables of the late afternoon customers.

With a tired look on her face, Ellie finally sits down a couple of hours later. Andre puts a cup of tea in front of her and places a plate with leftover sandwiches on the table.

'Done that,' he says. 'I'm very glad you helped out, I don't know how I would have managed by myself.'

'It's all right,' Ellie replies. 'Honestly, I don't see why you don't hire a few more people. You can afford it.'

'I already have five on the payroll,' Andre says, 'but if they don't show when they're supposed to work? And as for today, normally a quiet day.'

'Mm,' Ellie mutters with her mouth full.

'I hope Jude will be back tomorrow,' Andre goes on. 'So, you will bury yourself in the books from now on?'

Ellie nods. 'Well, not all the time. I suppose I should

not tell you this, but the paper made me an offer as well.

'So that's why you're going to be too busy.'

Ellie washes down her sandwich with the tea. 'It's not what you think, Andre. I will only do one story a week for them. But that shouldn't be too strenuous. Not like running around here for a couple of hours almost every day.'

Andre says she might be right. 'But I know of a friend of mine who works as a journalist, the man is never home.'

'I'm not a journalist,' Ellie replies. 'I'll just do some, what do they call it? Free-lancing?'

She suddenly remembers the letters Dean Jones gave her and takes them from her bag. 'Look,' she says. 'Comments on the last stories I wrote.'

While she starts reading a letter, Andre reaches and takes another one. He lets his eyes run over the lines.

'Here, this one wants to know what ship you were on when you came here. He claims to know you.'

'What?' Ellie mumbles. 'This one's not very nice, wants to know how I came by such nonsense. It must be about the last thing that was printed.'

' … *I was whacked all the time when I was young and it never made me a bad person*,' Ellie quotes.

'They probably whacked all sense out of him,' Andre says and takes the next letter.

'Here's another one who claims to know you,' he says a couple of minutes later. 'A woman by the name of Anne Nickols.'

'Anne Nickols? I don't know any Anne Nickols.'

'Hold on,' Andre continues and reads: '*you probably remember me as Annie van Worden.*'

'Annie van Worden?' Ellie bends over and reads the words Andre uttered before her.

'Annie van Woerden. Annie!' She takes the letter from his hands. 'We were on the same ship when we came out here,' Ellie says excitedly. 'Christ!'

'Was he there too?' Andre wonders.

Ellie shakes her head in disbelief. 'Who'd have thought?' She continues reading the rest of the letter. 'She says ... she moved to Christchurch when she got married ... Her mother sent her the articles.'

'It's a small world,' Andre says. 'Well, it's getting late. I'm closing up.'

Ellie takes the letters and puts them back in her bag, wondering if she should write back to someone she hasn't seen for so long.

'Get your things,' Andre says as he locks the front door. 'I'll give you a ride home.'

'Oh, thanks,' Ellie replies.

A stern wind is blowing when Ellie leaves the house. She shivers and pulls the collar of her coat up to her cheeks. Bent against the wind, she starts walking down the street, when her attention is drawn to a woman walking up the street towards her. An expression of disbelief starts emerging in her face. A few yards away from her the woman looks up, strain showing in her face.

'Grace?' Ellie utters, astounded.

'Oh, Ellie. There you are,' Grace says, trying to get her breath back. 'Phew, that storm, and walking uphill! I'm getting too old for this.'

'But, Grace! What brings you here?'

'Maybe I should have called,' Grace replies. 'I think we have to have a talk.'

'Of course,' Ellie says and ushers Grace back to the house. 'But let's get out of this wind.' They walk back up the steps to the kitchen door and quickly go inside. 'How on earth did you get here?' Ellie still cannot believe Grace made all the effort.

'So, here's where you live,' Grace says and has a look around the kitchen. 'Nice.'

'Have a seat,' Ellie says.

'I came to see Jody. He's here, in Wellington for a few days,' Grace explains, 'thought it was a nice opportunity to fill you in, Ellie.'

'Fill me in about what? Is something wrong?'

Grace takes her coat off and sits down. 'It's Pieter and Ursula.'

Ellie looks worried. 'Something is wrong,' she determines. 'Are they ill?'

Grace shakes her head. 'It's Pieter. He got drunk a couple of nights ago and upset the little girl. She came over to our house for help.'

The worried look on Ellie's face intensifies. 'Drunk? But, how's Uschi now?'

'She's alright now, but she doesn't want to stay at home with her father.'

Ellie shakes her head and sits down across from Grace. 'I can't imagine Uncle Pieter being drunk,' she says. 'Does Mum know?'

'Yes, she's aware,' Grace says.

'Poor Uschi. How can Uncle Pieter be so irresponsible!' Ellie exclaims. 'I feel like going over there and slap his face!' At the same time, slapping her hand on the table.

'I don't think that's the answer, Ellie. Although I felt like doing that myself,' Grace assures her. 'It's just that, he hasn't been himself since that lady friend walked out on him.'

'What? She walked out on him?'

'Yes, a couple of weeks ago.'

'And now he takes it out on Uschi?'

'I don't think he's doing it intentionally – '

'The bastard!' Ellie calls out.

'Hush, hush, Ellie,' Grace calms her down. 'Like I said, it's not his intention to hurt his daughter, but it's certainly not fair on her.'

'You could say that,' Ellie says. 'I've never seen him drunk. I can't imagine – '

'He's been drunk before, Ellie, but then the child was well out of his way.'

Ellie shakes her head.

'Ursula has been asking for you,' Grace continues. 'Maybe you can give her a call, tonight?'

'Yes, I will, I definitely will. Is she staying at your house?'

Grace nods. 'Yes. Until Pieter comes to his senses.'

'What a worry, Grace,' Ellie says.

'I'm sorry about all this, Ellie,' is Grace's reply, 'but I thought I'd better let you know.'

'Thanks. I'm glad you told me, and I am glad that Uschi has someone like you she can rely on. Thank you, Grace,' Ellie says. She bends over and gives Grace a kiss on her cheek.

Grace smiles. 'Well, it's the least I can do. Now, didn't you mention something about a hot chocolate? Would be lovely with this wintry weather.'

With a serious look on her face, Ellie makes her way out into the corridor. Still preoccupied with the latest knowledge, she walks into the lecture-hall and finds herself a seat. After some ten minutes, Ellie's face has turned to amazement. ' ... Sexual reproduction the two alleles are distinctly divided ... '

Ellie becomes more astonished when the lecturer

starts drawing a formula on the blackboard. She turns to the person next to her. 'What is he talking about?' she whispers.

'Genetics,' is the surprised answer.

'Isn't this the lecture on philology?' Ellie asks.

' ... No.'

Whispering excuses Ellie swiftly moves to the door and into the corridor where she soon finds out that the lecture she wanted to attend is in another building. Whispering more excuses, she finds a different seat in the right hall a while later.

' ... thus we can presume that Esperanto is an official language ... ' the professor's voice sounds. 'And thank you for joining us, young lady.'

Slightly embarrassed Ellie looks down and quietly takes her notebook from her bag.

' ... Although not confined to one particular country or culture, and perhaps therefore best suitable to become the World's First language ... '

A few potatoes mixed with carrots are boiling in a pan. Ellie shakes a bit of salt into the dish and takes out another pot for the eggs. She cuts some onion and mixes it with the eggs in the frying pan.

'Are you going healthy tonight?' Daniel asks her.

'What do you mean? I always eat healthily.'

'Sorry I mentioned it. Listen, we're going to see a movie tonight,' Daniel says. 'Care to join us?'

'Sure,' Ellie replies. 'What's on?'

'Bond, James Bond.'

'Oh really? I think I've seen that one.'

'From Russia with Love?'

'No, haven't seen that one,' Ellie responds. 'What time?'

Daniel looks at his watch. 'In half an hour. We're meeting some more people at the theatre.'

'Oh. I'd better be quick then,' Ellie says. She flips the egg over and a moment later piles the food on her plate.

'Are we driving?' Ellie asks.

'Yes, we might as well,' Daniel replies as he leaves the kitchen. 'Barb? ... Barbara!'

'What!'

'Are you going to be much longer?' he asks.

'Almost finished,' is the muffled reply.

Ellie puts the plate in the sink and goes to the bathroom to tidy her hair a bit. 'Have you been painting the bathroom?' she asks Barb.

'No, I dyed my hair,' Barb replies. 'What do you think?' She shakes her henna-coloured locks around her shoulders.

'Nice, very nice,' Ellie says in admiration. 'Different but, nice colour.'

'Yes. I like it too. Sorry for the mess, but I'll clean it up later.'

'Is Kate coming too?' Ellie wonders.

'No, she went home today,' Barb replies. 'She hadn't been feeling well.'

'Oh. I hope she's doing all right,' Ellie says.

Daniel is outside waiting for them by the car. He gets in when the two finally appear. It's only a short drive to the movie theatre but when they arrive there are hardly any people waiting. 'Looks like the others have gone inside already,' Barb says.

'I'm not surprised,' is Daniel's reply. 'The movie has started.'

'Alright, you park the car while we get the tickets,' Barb suggests.

Ellie and Barb get out and cross the street to the

theatre where Barb puts a few shillings down at the window to pay for the tickets.

'Ellie!'

Ellie turns to find Dean Jones walking towards her.

'Hi, how are you?'

'Good,' he replies. 'We had expected your article on New Zealand culture today.'

'I'm sorry, something came up. I'll bring it by tomorrow.'

'That's OK. Going to see the movie?'

'Yes,' Ellie replies, 'or is there something else to see in a movie theatre besides movies?'

'Depends on what you're after,' Dean says. 'These friends of yours?'

'Yes, Barb and her fiancé, Daniel.'

'Well, better go in,' Daniel says, 'if we don't want to miss the rest too.'

The flickering of the band of light that projects the movie on the screen lights their path as they make their way to a few seats that are not taken. Barb sits down beside Daniel and Dean takes the empty seat next to Ellie.

~ ~

With rapid steps, Rita walks through the dreary hospital hallway, an unhappy-looking Ursula right behind her.

'Why don't you say anything, Aunt Rita? Are you angry?'

'No,' Rita says, without slowing her pace. Ursula tries to keep up. 'Are you angry with Dad? You shouldn't be angry with him now.'

Rita eases her pace and turns to face the girl.

'Ursula ... ' she commences, but then walks on.

When they reach the right room on the men's ward, Rita tells Ursula that she had better wait outside as she wants to talk to her father first.

Ursula is unsure. 'Aunt Rita? I don't want you to upset my dad,' Ursula says and looks at Rita with a serious face.

'I won't upset him, sweetie,' Rita says calmly. 'I won't say anything that will upset him.'

Ursula appears to be pleased with the answer and sits down on a bench outside the room when Rita opens the door and goes in. She looks around and spots the bed where Pieter lies. He smiles when he notices her. Some purple coloured skin shows from under the bandage around his head.

'I hope you're satisfied with yourself now, Pieter,' Rita says sharply while keeping her voice down.

Judging by his face, it is not the greeting he'd expected.

'Don't you have any sense of responsibility?' Rita questions. 'All that drinking that you do and now, driving your car into a tree.'

His eyes show discomfiture when he tells Rita that it hadn't exactly been his intention to crash into a tree.

'Oh, shut up Pieter!'

Rita restrains herself. 'What else had you expected, the way you've been behaving. It's about time you started thinking about your daughter again.'

'Rita, don't tell me I'm neglecting my daughter. She's always been my first priority.'

'She always *was* your first priority,' Rita corrects him. 'You've become a selfish bastard, Pieter.'

'Now, hold on, Rita – '

'No, you hold on. That child has been worried sick about you these past months, but you never even noticed. You were more than happy to have her out of your way. Sent her over to Grace, or to stay with me.'

'She likes it at Grace's,' Pieter defends himself, 'and at your place.'

'Listen to yourself, Pieter,' Rita expresses in a deprecatory manner. 'Why don't you put Ursula in an orphanage right now? So you can kill yourself with a clear conscience.'

Pieter becomes impatient with Rita's patronising behaviour. 'Now I know where that daughter of yours gets her dramatic skills from,' he says.

Rita looks at his battered face with a conflicting expression. 'I'm not here to discuss Ellie with you. I'm here to try and make you see that Ursula needs her father. And I don't mean one that's drunk half the time. But, you're obviously not willing to face up to your responsibilities.'

'I know my responsibilities,' Pieter says. 'I wonder about yours,' he adds scornfully.

For a moment Rita seems bewildered by his remark, but then she turns to walk to the door.

'Ursula is waiting outside,' she merely mentions, 'but I suppose you have no desire to see her.'

'Send her in, Rita,' Pieter demands in a soft tone as his glance follows her out the door.

When Rita closes the door of the room behind her, Ursula gets up from the bench. 'How is he, Aunt Rita? Is he all right?' the girl asks.

'He's fine, Uschi,' Rita replies, 'but he is very tired, and now he's sleeping. You can see him tomorrow.'

Rita puts her hands on Ursula's shoulders and directs her back to the exit. 'We'll be back to see how he is.'

'Was he still drunk?' Ursula asks.

'No,' Rita says. 'That has worn off by now, but he has a bit of a bump on his head which means he has to rest a lot.'

'A concussion,' the girl says.

'Yes, that's right,' Rita replies.

'The doctor told me,' Ursula explains. They leave the hospital behind them as they make their way back to the bus station.

'Aunt Rita?'

'Yes dear?'

'Why is Dad so strange all the time? Is it because of that lady friend he had?'

'I think that might have something to do with it,' Rita says.

'I don't like him when he's like that,' Ursula says with a sad look on her face.

'Yes, well, he certainly hasn't made himself very popular lately.' She puts her arm around Ursula's shoulder as they continue.

'And he broke the car,' Ursula goes on. 'William says it cannot be fixed anymore.'

'Then he will just have to buy a new one,' Rita responds.

6

Although I passed my driving test I couldn't afford to buy a car. Or, that is to say, I didn't want to spend the money I was saving on a car. Dean refused to lend me his and I tried to explain to him how I would never get any practice if I never drove myself. In the end, he had someone fill in for him - he should have reported on a political event - and we both went home to my mother. Part of the way Dean let me drive, but only because he was right there with me in the car. Once I was behind the wheel I honestly didn't know what the fuss had been about, for it is rather easy, driving on the main road, perhaps even easier than within the city with its many motorists, all trying to get somewhere.

I had told Mum about Dean but she still seemed a bit surprised when she saw him. Uschi liked him instantly. As her father was still recovering, she was staying with Mum for a few days until she had to go back to school. Then Grace was the one looking after her. At first, my mother had wanted to live at Pieter's house and look after Uschi there for the time being, but she had not been willing to give up her job, so Grace and she had come to this resolution.

When the news of Uncle Pieter's accident was told to me, I was in shock, but at the same time, I was worried about my cousin Uschi, although she seemed to be taking it well, knowing her father would be all right and would be coming home soon. Mum and I had had long conversations over the phone about Uncle Pieter's drinking habits. I was almost certain they were caused by the dent his pride was given when his girlfriend had dumped him last year. Mum seemed to think it wasn't just that. Although I had been angry with him, I could not have borne the pain if he had not survived the car crash.

I was slightly nervous when we set out to visit Uncle Pieter. Afraid he wouldn't be the same person I'd always known. Uschi went with us to the hospital to visit her dad. Uncle Pieter was up and walking the corridors when we arrived. His face lit up when he noticed us, saying he couldn't wait to get out of the place. He still looked pale with a large plaster taped over his forehead, but he assured us he was feeling a lot better. It was a joy, and a relief, to see how caring he was about Uschi. She stayed by his side the whole visit. He had no opinion about Dean and seemed to approve of him although Dean is almost fifteen years older than I am.

On the way home Uschi mentioned that she really wanted her father home again. She hoped that everything would be normal once more very soon. I couldn't agree more. I wished for Uschi what I never really had, my own dad. We paid a short visit to Chrissie and Marty before we drove back to Wellington. Chrissie was two months pregnant with her second baby, so I had to go and see for myself how she was. Marty was still at the coffee bar that he was running now.

Driving on to Wellington I asked Dean, who had taken the wheel again, if I should write something for the paper about alcohol abuse. I had been thinking about it but thought it might not be appropriate. 'Write what you think you should,' he said. 'If it's not suitable it can always be rejected.'

I was in doubt at first when Dean suggested I could go with him to his place instead of going home to mine. But as I didn't feel like being by myself, I went to spend the night at his flat. Dean and I had known each other for a few months now and had been on dates. Perhaps he is not the one I would have chosen, but I had grown very fond of him. The relationships I had before with Bob, whom I thought I was in love with, and that other bloke never went anywhere. After tea Dean offered me some wine but I didn't feel like any. I hadn't felt like drinking since Uncle Pieter had his accident, so Dean made me a cup of tea and we sat on his couch. I huddled against his shoulder, talking journalist talk. The more he told me about the profession the more I liked it. A newspaper could send you overseas to work for them. I liked the sound of that.

A few more glasses of wine and another cup of tea later, Dean became rather loving. He caressed my cheek and started kissing me. Bob used to do that. But this felt different. Dean seemed gentler and I got to taste the wine after all. He pulled me so close I could feel his heartbeat and before I was aware, my clothes were on the floor and Dean's heated body on top of me. It was not at all like the nervous fumbling the bloke before him had put me through. Dean's ways made me tingle and warmth flooded my whole body.

He kissed my face before he got up. He came back with a blanket and put it around me. 'It's late,' he said. 'I think we should go to bed.'

About a week after Uncle Pieter was released from the hospital I phoned Grace hoping to find Uschi there, but she wasn't. Fortunately, Pieter was doing well and according to Grace, he hadn't touched anything else but his coffee. 'It looks like he has started taking life seriously again,' she said, which made me put the phone down with a happy feeling in my heart.

I spent an increasing amount of time in Dean's

company. It probably had been the age difference at first that had made me think of him as being just another acquaintance instead of a lover, but he was so caring and considerate that my feelings for him had changed rapidly. His flat had become more of a home to me than my own and Dean didn't seem to mind that I did my studying at his place. He was very supportive, also, when it came to writing the weekly article for the paper. They were almost ready to go to print after Dean had looked them over.

Kate had gone to her mother's to await the birth of her baby; by then Richard had disappeared off the scene. One day he just stopped coming over, which made me believe she might have told him the truth after all, but according to Kate he never wanted the baby in the first place. Barb and Daniel were mostly the only ones occupying the house. It made them wonder if they could have the house to themselves after they were married. At one stage they asked me if I had any plans of moving in with Dean, but that had not crossed my mind. Besides, Dean's place was too far away from the university.

One day after English Literature I came to the house and found a slimmer Kate there. Sooner than we had expected she had returned. The plan was to have her mother raise the baby so she could finish her studies and Kate intended to nurse the child for the first few weeks at least.

Kate was rather matter-of-fact when she said she had given the child up for adoption. I was quite surprised about that for she had given us the impression she wanted to keep the baby. After a while, she entrusted me with the real reason. The child had coloured skin. 'I never thought it could've been from that Maori chap. We were only out for one night,' she said. Her mother had told her it didn't make any difference but Kate did not want a coloured child being raised in a mainly white community. 'What would people have thought? It was a scandal to begin with, and now a black child at that.' And so she had left it at the hospital. I didn't want to ask Kate about it, she had been through enough, but I could not understand why the skin colour of the baby should be the cause of depriving it of the care of its own mother. Maybe I should not have told her that it's the one who raises a child that matters.

In the evening I tried to talk about it with Dean, but he had no opinion about raising children or adoptions. He claimed he didn't know the first thing about children. And I had to admit, I didn't know a lot about it either. One could hardly say that doting on my little cousin had anything to do with raising a child.

Life took its pace again. A more serious Kate focusing hard on what she had come to do in Wellington to begin with. Barb and Daniel took a few friends with them to church one day and came back as husband and wife. Kate and I had prepared a happy marriage party in our small back garden. It was a party with just a few friends and some relatives but it was a success anyway. After work Dean showed up, and in the evening we danced a few waltzes. I had not expected him to be a dancer, but it was he who taught me, as I knew no dance whatsoever. Apart from the silly jiggling, we exhibited at regular parties. It was hard to tell whether it was Dean's courteous manner or the slow music, which made us move over the grassy patches, but quietly a sense of utter devotion had crept up on me. As he held me in his arms and led the way I wished we would be together always.

《 》

Ellie stares through the window as she sits on the train, watching the green, hilly landscape gradually pass by. The announcement that they are approaching Taihape makes her sit up in her seat. She has a look at the familiar setting as the train stops at the platform but she doesn't attempt to disembark. A few minutes later the train slowly leaves the station and continues on its way. An elderly couple, who boarded the train in the town, are making their way to their seats, minding not to fall as the train jerkily finds the right track. They give Ellie a friendly nod and sit down in the seats across the aisle.

Some time elapses before Ellie reaches her destination. She gets off at the tiny railway station. Following the road, she arrives at Kathleen MacIntosh's house a while later. After a knock on the front door, it's Nana herself who opens up.

'Ellie!' she calls out. 'Why didn't you let me know you were coming?'

'I wanted to surprise you,' Ellie replies as she hugs her nan.

'Well, you certainly succeeded. Come in.'

Ellie follows Kathleen through the hall and into the kitchen. 'Is Gwen not here?'

'No, she went back to America last week, to be with her children,' Nana says and puts the kettle on.

'Oh, let me help you,' Ellie offers.

'No, it's all right. I may be old but I'm not an invalid. I take it you've heard about my plans?' Kathleen continues.

'Yes, Mum told me. That's one of the reasons why I came.'

'What do you think?' Kathleen wants to know while she puts a few cups on a tray. 'Don't you think it's a good resolution?'

'Yes. I suppose you gave it some thought, before you made the final decision.'

'I think it's for the best,' Nana says. 'Gwen never really wanted to be away from her children and I cannot ask of her to pass her days with me all the time. So ... ' She pours the boiling water into the teapot.

'It's a bit of a shame about this house though,' Ellie says. 'We had so many happy times here.'

'Yes, but one cannot dwell in the past. As I said, I may be old but that doesn't mean I don't have some future left.'

'Oh, Nan,' Ellie says delighted. 'You never cease to be an inspiration.'

'Thank you, dear. Now let's have some tea. Could you take those cakes with you?'

Ellie follows Kathleen to the lounge room. 'But Nan, don't you think it's a pity about this house?' Ellie expresses once more. 'It's such a ... fantastic home.'

'The house I've seen in Boston is fantastic too,' Kathleen replies. 'Different, but it's a real nice home.' She places the tray on the coffee table. 'The biggest problem will probably be to find the right buyer,' Nana continues. 'I don't want this home to go to just anybody.'

'Yeah, you're right,' Ellie agrees. 'Have you had people looking at it already?'

Nana nods. 'I have, and one couple is particularly interested. Rather young people with small children, it would be ideal for them.'

'I hope it works out well,' Ellie says, but Kathleen can't help but notice something is bothering Ellie.

'What is it, dear?' she wants to know.

'Granddad ... he's here.'

'Oh, Ellie. The things that are on your mind. His grave will be looked after, and you can visit as many times as you want.'

'That's not really what I mean, Nana.'

Kathleen looks at her. 'I thought I told you this before,' and she takes Ellie's hand to enforce the words she is about to say. 'It's just his body in the grave, I will take his spirit with me wher*ever* I go.' The expression on Ellie's face softens.

'Mark my words,' Nana adds. 'And now, tell me, what is this I hear about Dean? Is he a nice man?'

Ellie's face lights up and it doesn't take much to make Kathleen understand that she is head over heels in love. 'I'm happy to hear that,' Nana says with a smile. 'It's good to know you have someone to look after you. I have been worried about you, all alone in that big city.'

'There's no need for that, Nan,' Ellie says convincingly. 'I have made some really nice friends.'

'I'm sure you have, dear. But be aware just the same.'

Ellie pours them another cup of tea and asks when the big move will take place.

'Thank you, dear,' Nana says and takes the cup from Ellie. 'Gwen will come back to help me with that. It could take a few more months, but once the house is sold I will leave this country.'

She allows her thoughts to drift for a spell. 'Almost seventeen years, we've lived here.'

'Was that the longest you have lived in a country?' Ellie wonders. Kathleen gives it a brief thought. 'No, no I don't think so. I think with all the travelling we've done, it's still England where we've lived the longest. Of course, I was raised there as well.'

'Well, Nana, if you need any help with packing, just let me know,' Ellie offers.

'That's kind of you, dear. Rita has offered her services as well. We will manage, I'm sure.'

Nana hesitates for a moment before she asks Ellie about the situation her uncle has gone through. 'Don't misunderstand me, dear, I don't mean to pry, but it had me worried. And I'm sure Rita wouldn't have told me if she didn't want me to know.'

'He's doing fine now, Nana, he's back on his feet. I suppose he has learned a lesson.'

Kathleen is not so sure. 'It's a bad thing, that drinking. What will become of little Ursula?'

'Don't worry, Nana, they'll be fine,' Ellie says. 'Actually, I wanted to visit Uncle Pieter and Uschi while I was up here. I haven't been to their house for a few years now.'

'You haven't?'

'Well, I did see them of course. Nana, do you know if there's a bus going that way? From here, I mean.'

'No bus, not that I know of,' Kathleen replies. 'But, why not take Henry's car? You have a driving licence, don't you?'

'Yes.'

'Take the car. I know it's an oldie, but it works perfectly. Gwen uses it all the time.'

Ellie admits she could. 'It never really crossed my mind, actually,' she says and checks the time. 'I suppose if I go now I'll have the car back before dark.'

'Oh, don't worry about that, dear. It also works in the dark,' Kathleen adds with a smile. 'I'll get the keys.'

Not long after, Ellie is in the car-shed attempting her skills on the vehicle. After she has tried a few times the engine starts purring and Ellie drives the car out of the garage. Nana claps her hands. 'See, it works fine,' she says. 'Is there enough petrol?'

'Yes,' Ellie replies when she has checked the meter. 'I'm off! Thank you, Nana. See you later!'

When she reaches the gate Ellie stops the car for a moment and glances at the house at the end of the dirt road. It lies there peacefully with the somewhat neglected garden around it. Ellie pushes the pedal down, turns into the path and parks the car in the shade of a tree. When she steps out, Pieter opens the door to the veranda. He looks surprised to find it's Ellie who drove the car up.

'Hello, Uncle Pieter,' Ellie says as she walks towards the house. 'How are you?'

'Alright, what about yourself?'

'Fine,' Ellie replies and embraces him. 'Place hasn't changed much, I notice.'

'No, no it's still the same as always. Won't you come in?'

'Sure.'

Pieter lets Ellie proceed before entering the house himself. 'So, uh, whose is the car?' he asks.

'Granddad's. Nana lent it to me. She's very kind.'

'She did, did she?' Pieter has another look at the car before he closes the door. 'Can I get you something to drink?'

'Whatever, tea will be fine,' Ellie replies and sits down at the kitchen table. She watches Pieter fill the kettle and put it on the stove. The thin, pinkish line on his forehead is still a silent reminder of his unfortunate situation.

'How have you been feeling?' she asks.

'Good,' Pieter replies. 'Completely recovered.'

'Completely?' Ellie questions.

'I take it you're talking about the accident,' Pieter says.

'Yes, what else?'

Pieter gives her a brief look before he puts some tea in a mug.

'Look,' he begins, 'I know I had a drink or two too many back then, but that's behind me now, so don't give me any doubtful looks. OK?'

With her eyes cast downwards, Ellie enquires about Uschi.

'She's at school, doing well,' Pieter replies. 'And what about you? How are you going at that university?'

'Couldn't be better,' Ellie asserts. 'And I'm making some extra money with articles I write for a newspaper.'

'Your mother told me about that,' he says and pours out the boiling water. 'A shame we don't get that paper here, I wouldn't mind reading what you've written.'

'That's no excuse, Uncle Pieter. You can always get a subscription.'

Pieter raises his eyebrows and admits she is right. 'So, you've earned quite a bit since you've been there?'

Ellie seems a bit indifferent. 'I'm trying to save, but I also need money to live on.'

'I thought your mother had been giving you money,' he says and puts the mug of tea in front of her.

'She has done, but not that much. I want to make it on my own, Uncle Pieter. I don't want to rely too much on her.'

Pieter sits down on the side of the table. 'Have you saved enough for your trip to Holland yet? I thought you were quite keen on going there.'

'Yes, but now there's all this talk about the changing of the currency,' Ellie replies. 'How will I know if I have enough money by the time I want to go? All the prices will change, what will a flight cost by then?'

'That currency change won't mean that our money devaluates,' Pieter reassures her. 'I should hope not, everybody will lose money. We'll get an uproar in this country.'

Ellie glances up at him. 'So, you think, prices of flights to Europe will be about the same?'

'I'd say so, Ellie,' he says. 'And I bet that, if you find you haven't saved enough, there will be people around who will slip you some extra cash.'

'I don't want hand-outs,' Ellie says.

'Don't be silly, girl,' is Pieter's reply. 'We all would love to see you go on this trip, you've worked hard for it.'

'All? All but Mum,' Ellie states.

'Rita? Rita doesn't want to go to Holland, but that's no reason to keep you from going.'

'Every time I want to talk to her about it she tells me it's not a good idea. And I hate that.'

'Well, leave it to Rita to spoil the fun,' Pieter replies.

'That's how I feel!' Ellie says annoyed. 'She always does that.'

Ellie falls quiet for a moment and then asks Pieter if it was her mother.

'What?'

'Was it Mum's fault that you didn't marry?'

' … You could say that,' Pieter replies. 'But let's not go into that, shall we?' He gets up and says he wouldn't mind a cup of coffee himself.

'Could I have one as well?' Ellie asks. 'The tea is nice but I already had tea at Nan's too.'

She rises from her chair and asks Pieter if he has any bread in the house. 'I'm getting a bit hungry.'

'Help yourself,' Pieter replies and aims at the cabinet. 'Bread's right there, cheese and jam in the fridge.'

'Uncle Pieter?' Ellie asks while preparing the sandwich. 'Could you maybe give me the address of Aunt Hetty in Holland? Mum says she lost it.'

'She probably has. Do you intend to stay with them?'

'Well, not the whole time. But as they are family, I should at least visit them.'

Pieter gives her a brief look. 'Yeah, you should. Write first though.'

'Of course! I can't just show up.'

She puts the cheese back in the fridge. 'Do you think, I should send them a photo of myself? They probably don't even know what I look like anymore.'

'That might not be such a bad idea,' Pieter replies and takes the cups of coffee to put them on the table.

'Are you staying for dinner?' Pieter asks. 'Or do you have to go somewhere?'

'No, not particularly. But I don't want to return the car too late.' She sits down again and has a bite of the bread.

'Ursula would be pleased,' Pieter tries again.

'I never said I would not stay for dinner, Uncle Pieter,' Ellie says with her mouth full.

A quick smile passes over Pieter's face as he takes a seat at the table. 'Are you still seeing this man, Dean?'

'Yes. Of course,' Ellie replies as if it's a needless question.

'Don't you think he's a bit too old for you?'

'Sorry?' Ellie says, slightly bemused. 'I thought you approved of him.'

'Since when do you seek my approval?' Pieter wonders. 'Do you love the man, that's what counts.'

'Very much,' she answers.

'Good,' Pieter states. 'So, when's the wedding?'

Ellie, who has her sandwich halfway to her mouth to take another bite, looks up. 'What wedding? There's not going to be a wedding.'

'No? How come?'

'Well … just … we never talk about it. I suppose, we're quite satisfied with the situation as it is.'

'So in the meantime, you're living in sin,' Pieter says.

Ellie looks at Pieter as if she is trying to determine whether he's serious about the issue. 'What do you mean?' she asks.

'I mean what I say. How does it feel to be living in sin?'

'… …'

'Or don't you remember how angry you were, when you found out about your mother and me having it off,' Pieter states.

'Uncle Pieter – '

'It's exactly the same, Ellie,' he says. 'Admit it.'

'No. That was not the same!' she calls out. 'That was about you and Mum!'

'Don't,' Pieter warns, 'start raging. I just want you to think about it.'

'It's not the same,' Ellie says once more. 'Dean is … my boyfriend. Things happen, when two people get together.'

'Like they did with Rita and me.'

Ellie's attitude changes slightly. She looks at Pieter and asks him if their love for each other simply died.

'Yes, I suppose it did,' he replies. He gets up. 'Now, how about if I show you the new car, it's in the shed.'

When they step out on the veranda they see Ursula admiring Granddad's old vehicle. She looks up to find her father and cousin leaving the house. With a cheerful face, Ursula calls out Ellie's name and runs towards her. 'How are you?'

'Good,' Ellie replies and hugs her cousin.

'Is that your car?' Ursula asks. 'Hi Dad.'

'No, borrowed it from Nana,' Ellie replies. 'It used to

belong to Granddad.'

'Nice car,' Ursula finds.

'It's a nice museum piece,' Pieter says.

'Well, if you want it. Nana might sell it to you,' Ellie offers as they walk to the shed. 'I suppose she won't have any use for it now that she's leaving the country.'

'I don't think so. I just spent my savings on this one,' he says as they reach the shed.

'A Vauxhall,' Ellie says admiringly. 'It looks nice, is it a new one?'

'Almost. Not many miles on it yet and in perfect condition.' He strokes the hood as if to enforce his words.

'Dad's new baby,' Ursula tells Ellie.

Ellie smiles. 'Well, it is a nice car.'

'But not as nice as this one,' Pieter says and teasingly he puts his arms around his daughter.

'I'm not a car, Dad,' Ursula says and releases from his grip.

'I know that, sweets,' Pieter says.

'Ellie? Will you be staying for tea?' Ursula asks.

'Yes, she will,' Pieter replies. 'Shall we go? Too much admiring might take the shine off this car.'

Pieter asks Ursula to see what they have in the garden for dinner as they walk back to the house. Ursula throws her school bag on the veranda, and together with Ellie enters through the gate into the slightly overgrown vegetable garden. 'Oh, dad!' Ursula yells out to her father.

'What is it?'

'I had an A today for that science project. The paper is in my bag!'

'An A! Very good,' Pieter says. 'I'll have a look.' He picks up the bag and goes into the house to prepare for tea.

'Dean?' Ellie asks as she stands in the doorway of his

study. He mutters a reply as he keeps his eyes focused on the sheet of paper in his typewriter.

'Dean, could I ask you something?'

'Yes.'

'Have you ever thought about marriage?'

He looks over his shoulder, wondering: 'Is one of your friends getting married or something?'

'No, but I thought … We've been together for a year now. Shouldn't we at least, think about it?'

'I thought we had,' Dean replies and continues with his article.

'I'm serious, Dean. Won't you listen for a minute?'

He finishes the last line and then turns around in his chair.

'Do you want to be married?' he asks.

Ellie is slightly taken aback by his question. 'Well, I don't know. Do you?'

'To be honest, I don't see a reason,' Dean replies. 'We have a good relationship. Do we need a marriage certificate to prove that?'

Ellie is tentative. 'Well, don't you want us to live in the same house in the future?'

'You're here all the time,' Dean replies. 'We already live in the same house.'

'Dean,' Ellie says and approaches him, 'that's not what I mean. We are actually just living together, and we're not even married.'

'You mean, we're shacking up. So what? But, you don't agree,' he says as he sees the expression on her face. He takes her hand and asks if it bothers her.

'Well, what bothers me is,' Ellie says, 'that people seem to think it's not the proper way.'

'Excuse me? Since when do you care about people's opinions.'

'I do care,' Ellie defends herself, 'that's what I write about.'

'Not really,' Dean says. 'You write about the issues that people should pay more attention to. You don't do anything about the reactions you provoke once it's printed.'

'You said yourself that I shouldn't worry about that too much,' Ellie replies defensively. 'We're journalists, not psychiatrists, is what you said.'

'True.' He gets up from his chair. 'Look. What's the real reason for your problem with this shacking up business.'

Ellie shrugs her shoulders.

'I ... Do you want to get married, or not?' she demands.

'What if I say no? Will you run out on me?'

'Dean!' Ellie punches him on his arm. 'Why do you always have to make things so complicated?'

'You haven't answered my question yet,' he says.

Ellie stamps her foot and walks out of the room.

'Ellie ... '

As the bedroom door slams, Dean resumes his seat at his desk. He hits a few more keys on the typewriter before he takes the sheet of paper out. After he has read the finished product and made a few annotations with his pen he puts it down. He walks over to the bedroom to find Ellie at the foot of the bed, staring at the ceiling. 'Ellie, let's not fight about this.' He sits down and glances at her face. 'What do you say.'

'I'm sorry, Dean. I suppose I was preoccupied with things from the past.'

'What do you mean?'

'Personally, I don't care that we're living together, but ... ' She straightens up and sits down next to him on the bed. 'I told you about my mother and my uncle – '

'Yes, you did.'

'Well, I guess I always wanted them to be married because, I thought, we could live as a family, like all the kids at school who had a father at home. Rather selfish, aye.'

'That's not selfish, El. That's normal for a kid to want a father and a mother around the place.'

'Yeah, but there were always people around when I was growing up. I was never neglected in any way, it wasn't like that.'

'So, why worry?'

'I've had a few awful fights with both my uncle and my mother,' Ellie continues, 'because I thought it was scandalous thing what they did.'

'But what you actually wanted, was to be part of a nice little family unit,' Dean says. 'And it never happened.'

'No,' Ellie says with a quick smile. 'It's like Uncle Pieter always says, it takes two to tango.'

'Your uncle,' Dean says and moves closer, 'is a very wise man.' He strokes her cheek and tenderly starts kissing her face.

《 》

Maybe we should not have passed Nana's house, but it was my idea. I wanted to show Dean where I had spent happy times when I was younger. Now, the sight of the house, made me feel distressed, as it stood there, a large deserted building, with windows gaping back at us like meaningless eyes. I told Dean we should go because there were still a few friends we needed to visit. I watched the house as it slowly disappeared behind the trees. I felt sad, but at the same time, I felt a sense of happiness, knowing that Nana was building a new life that very moment; be it somewhere far away from here. It had crossed my mind to send her my journal as she is always interested in reading them, but somehow I found the last one, not all that appropriate for her to read. Then again, one could never know with Nana.

We drove back to Taihape where we went to see Chrissie and Marty; we had planned to meet them at their coffee bar. I felt guilty because I hadn't gone to see them. Chrissie had another boy who was named after Marty's father Richard. It had been amusing to hear her talk over the phone about the boys' names. Chrissie insists on Ricky because it goes so nicely with Charlie, while Marty refers to the boys as Charles and Richard.

Chrissie was helping Marty in the coffee bar while Grace was at their house, babysitting her grandchildren. She always was a mother in the true sense of the word, and not only to her own. Even William was very fond of the boys whereas in the past he sometimes had given the impression that children around the place were a bit of a nuisance. It was like Nana said sometimes, people mellow when they get older.

Chris stopped work early because she had one of her headaches. Ever since that horrible fall from the cliff, almost four years ago, she suffers from them when she puts too much strain on herself. When we came to their house, she first took some of the medicine she had been prescribed.

It was good to see Grace again and it gave me the chance to introduce her to Dean. She probably had heard a lot about him from Chrissie but she didn't mention anything about the fact that we practically lived together. As was Grace's way she made us tea and offered us home-made biscuits. After Chrissie had her rest, she joined us with Ricky who had woken from his sleep. His big brother Charlie found a real interest in the tablecloth that was on the living room table. It ended on the floor, with the vase that was on top of it. Luckily that was empty, which limited the mess to a few fragments. Grace was quick to clear it away, as not to have Charlie cut his little fingers. I took him on my lap but it didn't last long before he had found another interest: the biscuits on the table.

Grace and Chrissie were eager to learn about my preparations for the trip to Holland. Grace asked Dean if he was going with me, but Dean had no intention to go. I would have liked it if he had decided to come with me but he would be too busy with work. 'Those four weeks will be gone in no time, you won't even have time to miss me,' he had said. I wasn't sure about that, but he might be right. My time in Wellington had flown passed as well. Almost three years with so many things happening, although it appeared I only had kept myself busy with studying and working. The articles for the paper; thinking of something different to write about each week became increasingly difficult. Maybe it was time to move on to new things. But not before I'd finished my thesis. The weeks that followed were rather intense. I stopped writing the articles and concentrated on what I needed to know and do for the final exams. Only weekends were spent at Dean's place, and then he was mostly busy. So, I found myself returning to the house I still shared with Barb, Daniel and Kate. When Kate has passed her tests Barb and Daniel would probably remain in the house, maybe even buy it and start their own boarding house.

One day I had the fright of my life when I saw Paul. He was back at the university to finish his studies. I was glad I Kate was with me that time. He did notice me but didn't attempt to approach me. The incident had me walking on eggs again whenever I had to go to campus. It bothered Dean that there was a bloke out there who had once attacked me but as long as this character kept a distance there was nothing that could be done. He had served his sentence. I wondered when I would have served mine.

After I'd submitted my thesis and the exams were over, all I could do was wait for the results. In the meantime, I moved my things that had been accumulating for three years, to Dean's place. It had crossed my mind to take everything back to my mother's but I soon abandoned that thought. There were still obligations at the paper to be met so for now it was the best solution. Dean had a small spare room where I could keep my things out of the way. He doesn't like his place cluttered.

It was on the day that I was given the results of my exams when Mum phoned to say that Opa Visser had died. Uncle Pieter had received a letter from his sister to inform him about it. According to the letter, Oma was rather confused about the whole matter and kept asking why Pieter didn't come home. Oma was living with Aunt Hetty and Uncle Geert for the time being. Mum said that Pieter was worried about his mother, but concern rang through in her voice as well. I wondered if I should come home but Mum didn't find that necessary, she just wanted me to know what had happened.

Fortunately, the bad news did not put a damper on the good news. I passed. When I told Mum she was very thrilled. She wanted to come down straight away to congratulate me personally. I said there was no rush and promised I'd be home soon enough for her to throw a party. I don't know whether she took the party suggestion seriously but she promised me a nice cake to celebrate. It didn't take long though for the postman to deliver letters of congratulations. It turned out the whole family was more excited about my achievements than I was. My mind was occupied by something else. Even the nice dinner at a restaurant Dean treated me to could not change that. For me, my next goal was more important and one day I went to a travel agency that dealt with overseas voyages. The lady there was very helpful. She told me about what would be the best way to travel to Europe. She suggested PanAm, which sounded familiar. Nana had not only taken that airline to America, but Dean had also flown with them. When she mentioned the price of a ticket, I became apprehensive. It was more expensive than I had imagined, so I asked her about other options.

'You could go by sea,' she said and gave me the details for that option. It would take a lot longer and I wasn't sure if I wanted another boat journey. It only left me with one option and that was to work hard for another year until I had enough money to pay for my journey. The wages I had been receiving from the newspaper had been in dollars since the arrival of decimal currency and some of it was put with the rest of my savings in the bank. But it was still a bit odd. I had put my hard-earned pounds in the bank but would take them out as dollars. It was slightly misleading as well; the amount of money would almost double. Not because of interest, merely the exchange rate.

Not to let the great times I had in the past few years go by unnoticed, I thought a party was in order. So, one evening the friends I had made showed up at Dean's flat. Kate arrived with her new boyfriend and we could only guess if it was serious this time. The party was a great success during which, for old time's sake, a little bit too much alcohol was consumed, but I thought at the time it added to the fun. I didn't hold the same opinion the following morning and I was pleased Dean had gone to work so he wouldn't witness what state I was in.

To earn more money I could either go back to working in a tea-shop or do some more work for the newspaper. According to Dean, it would not be a problem getting a contract with the paper as they welcomed educated workers. Although I wasn't really trained as a secretary I was given an office job at the newspaper, typing out articles others had written. Not what I had wanted, but it had to do.

Europe lingered on the horizon.

7

Grey clouds glide by the small window of the aircraft as it is on its final descent, into Amsterdam. Ellie tries to distinguish land where the clouds meet clear skies, but only the sea can be seen. 'We're not there yet,' the man next to her says. 'North Sea,' he points out.

'Well, it's been a long time since I've seen that too,' Ellie replies and looks out again. The air hostess walking through the aisle points out to her to fasten her seatbelt.

'I bet you're getting all excited now,' the man says. 'Are they picking you up?'

Ellie shakes her head. 'No, I don't think so. But I have their address.'

'Where did you say they live?'

'Arnhem, somewhere around there.'

'Oh, then you can take a train. Trains go that way, but you have to get to the Central Station first.'

'Is that far from the airport?'

'No, but it's too far to walk,' he says laughingly. 'But you can get a bus, I suppose. Unless you want to take a cab. Cabs go there, I always get a cab.'

Ellie's attention is drawn to the scenery that appears from under the layer of clouds. In the distance below, crested waves roll onto the yellow strip of sand that borders the dunes.

'I suppose you're just too late to see the bulb fields, tulips are just about finished,' the man says.

'Are they?' Ellie wonders. 'I thought they would be in bloom still.'

'No, not now. They're a spring flower.'

'Shame,' Ellie replies as she keeps her eyes fixed on the fast-approaching meadows below.

'But there's lots more to see,' the man goes on. 'You'd be amazed. Go to the flower market in Amsterdam, they've got lots of great flowers there.'

As the wheels of the aircraft hit the tarmac, the sound of sharp braking announces their arrival at Amsterdam Airport. The tense expression on Ellie's tired face changes to one of delight. 'Finally,' she whispers. 'Finally home.'

When certain passengers start gathering their belongings an air hostess announces once more to remain seated until the plane has arrived at the terminal.

'So you finally made it,' the man next to her says. 'Long way.'

'It sure was,' Ellie replies.

Cabin personnel open the doors and passengers slowly make their way to the exits. Ellie takes her bag and slides the strap over her shoulder. She mingles with the rest of the passengers as they walk down the stairs off the plane where a waiting bus will take them to the terminal.

Ellie has no problems at Customs when she shows them her Dutch passport, and she proceeds to claim her suitcase.

Some time later, she stands a bit lost among hundreds of people in the arrival hall when the man, who had been sitting next to her on the plane, emerges from the crowd. He directs her to where she can take a bus. Ellie gratefully thanks him and walks to the stand where a bus has just come to a halt. In broken Dutch, she explains to the driver she needs to go to the train station in Amsterdam. 'Hop on,' he says. Ellie drags her suitcase on the bus and gives him the money for the ticket. With a sigh, she sits down.

Not long after, they leave the airport with Ellie gazing out of the window. Cows graze in the meadows that line the main road. In the distance, farmhouses that are surrounded by trees, and beyond the first signs of a city. Traffic quickly becomes more cluttered and crowded when they reach its boundaries. Ellie straightens her back when the bus drives through the streets of Amsterdam on its way to the centre. At one point, the traffic is held up as there seems to be some sort of disturbance. 'What's going on there?' Ellie asks the woman beside her, in English.

'O, eh, relletje … No, riot. Not nice.' She shakes her head disapprovingly. When they see smoke emerging between a group of people, a policeman motions the bus driver to take another street. The drivers behind the bus follow.

'Are we taking a detour?' Ellie wonders.

'Another street, we cannot go right, eh, straight.'

The bus enters a narrow street with small shops on either side. The street eventually leads them close to the train station where Ellie gets off to make her way through the busy, late afternoon crowds. Inside the station, she walks to one of the ticket windows. She doesn't have to wait long and when it is her turn to purchase a ticket, she enquires about trains at the same time, and soon she is at the platform where the train to Arnhem will leave from.

Crowds shove forward when the train rolls in, and a friendly man helps Ellie to get her luggage on. After she has manoeuvred her suitcase between two benches, she slumps onto one of them herself. By the time the train pulls out of the station, Ellie is asleep with her head leant against the window of the compartment.

Almost an hour and a half later the guard comes to check the tickets. Ellie opens her eyes and looks around her unfamiliar surroundings. 'Next stop, young lady,' the guard says and hands her back the ticket.

The following morning Ellie shows the innkeeper a sheet of paper. 'This is their address,' she says. Her Dutch sounds better than it did the day before. The man takes it from her. 'Oh, in Driel … Do they have a telephone?'

'I don't know.'

'Let's have a look,' the man says and takes out a telephone directory. Holding the sheet of paper in one hand he flicks through the pages with the other. ' … Driel … Schouten.'

His fingers slide down the names. 'Schouten, here we are, Schouten, Dorpsweg. One eight three four.' He jots the number down under the address.

'Do you want to call them now?'

'Yes, if possible,' Ellie replies.

'Telephone's over there.' He points to the corner of the lobby.

'Thank you.'

She walks over to the booth but then wonders how she should go about it. 'Do I just pick up the receiver and dial?'

'Yes, Miss. You pick up the horn … do you have a few dimes?'

Ellie searches in her purse for a few Dutch coins. 'Yes. Thank you, Sir.'

She drops a coin in the slot and dials the number.

'Aunt Hetty?' Ellie asks when there is a noise at the other end.

'*Yes?*'

'This is Ellie Visser, I wrote you a few weeks ago. Did you get my letter?'

'*Yes. You said you wanted to visit us.*'

'That's right, I'm in Arnhem now and I wondered if it's all right for me to come over.'

'*Oh, are you? Well, I guess that it's all right. Do you know how to get here?*'

'No, not really.'

'*You have to take a bus, they leave from the train station. Bus 15 to Driel and get off at the first stop.*'

'Bus 15,' Ellie repeats.

'*Have you found a place to stay yet?*'

'I stayed at this small hotel last night, I only arrived yesterday.'

'*You can stay with us for a couple of days, but you have to share a room with Joke.*'

'Oh, if it's not too much trouble,' Ellie replies. 'I don't mind.'

'*Well then, I'll see you sometime today.*'

'Yes, see you then.' Ellie hangs up the receiver and walks over to the reception desk. 'I want to find out about this bus I need to take,' she explains. 'Is it all right if I leave my suitcase here for now?'

'No problem, just put it there in the storage.'

Ellie suits the action to the word and then makes her way outside. She squints her eyes against the sudden brightness of the sun. At her ease, she walks among other pedestrians and follows the street back the way she came the evening before. She glances around and stops at shops to have a look in the windows. When she passes a small bakery, she goes in and asks for a few raisin buns. The shop girl swiftly puts a few buns in a paper bag. 'Here you are,' she then says. 'That'll be forty-four cents.'

She pays the girl, puts the rolls in her bag and continues on her way along the sunny street where she notices a bus number 15 stop not far from her. Quickly she walks towards it and asks the driver if it's the bus to Driel.

'No, you want the one across the street,' is the reply.

'That one goes to Driel?'

'That's what I just said,' the bus driver replies.

'Do you know at what time it goes?' Ellie asks.

'There should be one in about half an hour.'

'Thank you,' Ellie says. A few more people get on the bus that then pulls away from the stop. Ellie walks back to collect her suitcase at the inn and returns to the bus stop to await the bus. While waiting she takes out her purse and checks the change. She looks at the woman standing next to her and asks her how much a ticket costs.

'Where do you need to go?'

'Driel.'

'I'm not sure about that,' the woman replies. 'I live here, in the city, but it shouldn't be more than a guilder.'

'Oh, okay, that should do then,' Ellie says.

'Do you have enough money?' the woman asks.

'Yes,' Ellie replies. 'You see, I just arrived here yesterday and I still need to go to the bank to change money.'

'Oh.'

'I only took a small amount of Dutch money with me.'

'Oh. Where do you come from then?'

'New Zealand.'

'New Zealand,' the woman says with some awe in her voice. 'That's a long way away. But you speak Dutch well.'

'I am Dutch,' Ellie replies, 'but my mother and I left here seventeen years ago.'

'You did? You must have been really young then, and you still remember your old language?'

'Yes, well, we spoke Dutch a lot at home.'

'You did? Oh, there's the bus.'

Ellie lifts her suitcase and follows the woman onto the bus. She pays the driver and takes a seat not too far from the exit. They drive through streets where, in neat rows, small, brick houses with tidy little gardens in front are seen. In the sunny street children are playing with a ball and a few girls skip rope. The bus makes a few more turns into different streets to allow people on or let them off before it leaves the city of Arnhem behind. Ellie peers through the window not to miss anything of the scenery. They cross a bridge over a wide river to follow it a moment later. Sheep with their lambs graze in the forelands, fruit trees on the other side of the road are on their way to produce fruit.

Eventually, they enter a small village not far from the river. The driver pulls up the bus and tells Ellie it's her stop. Ellie manoeuvres her suitcase through the aisle and she thanks the driver.

She watches the bus drive off, leaving her standing by the side of the road. Ellie has a look around in the seemingly deserted village.

A man is weeding his little front garden, and Ellie walks up to him to ask if he knows where she can find the Dorpsweg.

'You're on it,' he says.

'Number eighteen,' Ellie explains. 'Which direction is that?'

'Oh, you want Schouten,' he says. 'They're over there.'

'Thank you.'

Ellie crosses the street and enters through the low garden gate at number eighteen. She rings the bell at the front door. After some stumbling in the hall, a teenage girl opens up. 'Hello,' she says. 'Are you Ellie?'

'Yes, I phoned this morning.'

'My mother had to go to the grocer's,' the girl says.

'Oh, I thought she would be at home,' Ellie replies.

'She'll be home soon,' the girl says and opens the door a little wider. 'Come in. I'm Joke,' the girl explains.

'You're supposed to be in my room.'

'Yes, your mother mentioned that this morning,' Ellie says and puts her suitcase down in the narrow hallway. 'I hope you won't mind.'

'No,' she replies a bit indifferently. 'My mother says that you're a cousin of ours.'

'I am,' Ellie says. 'Although, we never met before.'

'You live too far away, how can we ever have met?'

Ellie follows her into the living room. The girl sits down on the couch and takes up the book she was reading. Ellie looks around the room and notices a photo of her grandparents on the sideboard.

'How's Oma?' Ellie asks after a few moments.

'Alright. She'll be going to an old people's home.'

'Will she?'

There is also a photo of Pieter with Ursula when she was younger.

'Do you know them?' Joke asks. 'They live in New Zealand too.'

'Yes … Yes, I know them well.'

There's a sound of an opening and closing door. Ellie turns when a few moments later the living room door opens and her aunt Hetty enters. 'She's here, Mum,' the girl says.

'So I see.' She shakes Ellie's hand.

'Hello,' Ellie says.

Her aunt looks at her. 'All grown up,' she says. 'I only remember you as that little five year old.'

'Yes, it's been a while,' Ellie replies.

'Won't you sit down?'

'Sure,' Ellie says and sits down in one of the lounge chairs.

'That's Dad's chair,' Joke says.

'It's alright,' her mother says, 'he's not here now.

Would you like something to drink?' she asks Ellie.

'If it's no trouble,' Ellie says.

'Tea? Coffee? I don't know what you always drink in New Zealand.'

'Whatever you are having is fine with me.'

'Alright then,' Aunt Hetty says and she starts preparing the coffee. 'Was it easy for you to find?' she asks from the kitchen.

'Sorry?'

'Were you able to find our house easily?'

'It wasn't too bad. I asked a few times,' Ellie replies.

'So,' her aunt says when the coffee is percolating. 'How are all the others? How's Pieter?'

'He is fine, so is Ursula,' Ellie says, 'and my mother.'

'It's hard to judge when they're so far away. We don't really keep in touch, only at Christmas usually.' When the coffee is finished she stands up to pour it into the cups.

'Mum, can I have some juice?' Joke asks.

'You know where to find it,' her mother says.

'Can you get it for me? Please?'

Together with the coffee Ellie's aunt brings in a glass of juice.

She holds a tin with spiced biscuits in front of Ellie, who takes one out before her aunt puts the lid back on.

'I would like to see Pieter again,' she says. 'It's been so long, I hardly remember him.'

'I brought some photographs with me,' Ellie replies. 'I'll show them to you.'

'That would be nice. Do you think he will come to Holland too?'

'I don't know,' Ellie says. 'He once said he would like to, but … Do you want me to get the photos? They're in my suitcase.'

'It's all right. Drink your coffee first. So uh, what are your plans while you're here?'

Ellie lowers her cup. 'Well, I'd like to see Oma of course.'

'She'll be going to an old people's home.'

'I told her that already, Mum,' Joke says.

'She cannot handle the farm by herself,' Aunt Hetty continues. 'Of course, it would've been different if Pieter were here.'

'Pieter, Uncle Pieter, has his own farm,' Ellie says.

'Yes, we know. It's a shame though. Geert certainly won't take over, he's an electrician not a farmer.'

'Well, I suppose Oma will get lonely, all by herself on that large farmstead,' Ellie says.

'Yes, and it's not safe anymore, to have her there all by herself. Not to mention all the work that's involved. Mind you, Father sold the cows already before he passed away.'

Ellie takes a bite of her biscuit and finishes her coffee. 'Do you sometimes visit my father's grave?' she then asks.

'Your father's … grave?'

'Yes.'

'You mean … Well, I haven't been there for a while. He's not buried here, it's in Beek near where Mother lives.'

'I would like to go,' Ellie says. 'Maybe you can tell me how to get there.'

Her aunt falls quiet for a moment.

'Is that Uncle Klaas she's talking of, Mum?' Joke draws her attention away from her book once more.

'Yes, dear,' and turning to Ellie again: 'I think we can arrange something. Then we can visit Mother at the same time.'

'That would be nice,' Ellie says.

Her aunt gets up to take the cups back to the kitchen as she asks if Joke has shown her the room already.

'No, not yet. I left my luggage in the hall.'

'Right, come along and I'll show you where you'll be sleeping.'

Ellie's uncle Geert is calling out to his daughter Marja to hurry up. 'And where's Gert-Jan?' he asks.

'I don't know,' Marja replies and gets into the car where Ellie already patiently waits.

'Gert-Jan! Where is that boy?' he wonders when his wife Hetty comes out of the house. 'He was out here a while ago,' she replies. 'Gert-Jan!'

Kicking his football the boy emerges from beside the house. 'Why do I have to come?' he asks. 'I don't want to.'

'Get in the car,' his father replies.

'Joke can stay home, why can't I?'

'Joke is older, she can look after herself,' his mother says.

'I can look after myself too,' Gert-Jan says.

'Gert-Jan,' his mother expresses impatiently.

She takes a seat next to the driver's while Gert-Jan gets in at the back with Ellie and Marja.

'Let's get one thing straight,' Geert says. 'I don't want any whining and teasing when we're on the road.'

'OK, Dad,' Marja replies and loosens a piece of string she kept on her wrist.

Her brother stares out the window, an expression of ennui on his face.

'Look,' Marja says to Ellie. 'This is how you do it.'

She puts the string on her little finger and entangles it around her other fingers, she then takes the string off her thumb and, without getting it stuck, she pulls it off.

'How do you do that?' Ellie asks amazed.

'It's a secret,' Marja replies.

'No it's not,' Gert-Jan says. 'It's a trick,' and tries to grab the string from his sister's hand.

'Stop that!' Marja calls out. 'Dad!'

'Gert-Jan, cut it out,' his father says from the front seat.

'Would you kids like an apple?' Hetty asks.

'Yes please, Mum,' Marja replies.

Hetty hands three apples over to her.

'I don't want one,' Gert-Jan says.

Marja takes an apple and gives Ellie one who puts it in her bag.

'Are you sure you don't want one?' Hetty asks Gert-Jan.

'Yes,' he grumbles.

Soon after, his mind is triggered by the things he sees passing by the car window and Gert-Jan's mood changes for the better. He starts telling the rest of the family what he has been taught in school. 'That's where they make the preserves,' he says when they pass a well-known factory.

'And the pastries,' Marja adds.

'No, not pastries,' Gert-Jan contradicts.

'They do too, our teacher said so.'

'And our teacher said they make preserves there.'

'Children – ' Hetty soothes.

'And our teacher says they make both, and he knows better,' Marja says in an angry voice, 'for he's teaching a higher grade.'

'Dad? Tell her they make preserves there,' Gert-Jan says.

'They make both, and can we now have some peace and quiet in this car? Please.'

'See?' Marja says to her brother.

The drive to Oma's farm continues without further strife and Ellie enjoys the flat, Dutch landscape that slides past the car window. A little over an hour later they are nearing the farmstead where Oma Visser lives. A rather opulent looking home surrounded by majestic willow trees amid lush green meadows. The little African marigolds that line the path of Oma's immaculate front garden, pale into insignificance beside the high, rustling treetops.

As soon as the car comes to a halt, Gert-Jan jumps out and runs to the back where a farmhand is taking a few horses to the field.

Yellow clogs sit outside the kitchen door where the rest of the family enters the house. Their stumbling draws Oma Visser out of the living room and into the kitchen to see who is at the door. 'Oh, there you are,' she says. 'Did you have a good drive?'

'Yes, Mother. How are you?' Hetty replies and kisses her mother on the cheek.

'Mother,' Geert says by way of greeting.

'And there's Ellie too,' Oma Visser says. 'How are you?'

'Fine, Oma. I'm doing fine.'

'How's Pieter?' Oma asks. 'Why didn't he come with you?'

'I don't know – '

'Pieter is busy, Mother, you know that,' Hetty says. 'He has his farm.'

'That's no excuse,' Oma Visser says. 'If Ellie can come, why can't he.'

'Mother, I will make us some coffee and then you can catch up with Ellie,' Hetty says. 'Can I have tea, Mum?' Marja asks.

'That's a good idea,' Oma says and takes Ellie by her

arm. They go into the living room when Oma again asks how Pieter is. 'I haven't heard from him for a while. He should write more often.'

'He gave me a letter to give to you,' Ellie says.

'Where is it, child? Show me,' Oma responds impatiently. Ellie takes the letter from her bag and gives it to Oma Visser who immediately tears open the envelope and takes the letter out.

'Is that all?' she asks as she notices the few lines scribbled on the sheet of paper. Within a minute she has finished reading them. 'Surely this is not all that has happened.'

'What does it say, Mother?' Hetty asks.

'Hardly anything, just "we're all fine, just bought more sheep", as if I'm waiting to hear that.'

'It was just a quick note he wrote before I left,' Ellie says. 'There should be something from Uschi as well.'

'Who's Uschi?' Marja asks.

'Ursula,' Ellie replies.

'Oh, yes. There is more,' Oma says and takes a card from the envelope. With delight, she reads the card her youngest granddaughter wrote her. Hetty carries the cups with coffee and tea into the living room and puts them on the coffee table.

'Where is Geert, the coffee will get cold,' Hetty says.

'He went to the barn,' Marja replies. 'Do you have any cookies, Oma?'

'Wait your turn, Marja,' her mother says.

Before Ellie drinks her coffee she takes out the photos she brought with her from New Zealand to show them to Oma Visser, who is delighted when recognising the familiarities and mostly, her son and granddaughter. 'You can keep those,' Ellie says.

'Oh, thank you,' Oma says and scrutinises the

pictures once more.

'Marja, go get your father,' Hetty says. 'Tell him his coffee is getting cold. Mother, we will go to Klaas' grave this afternoon. Would you like to come?'

'To Klaas? I don't know, Hetty ... I haven't been to your father's either.'

'You don't have to if you don't want to,' Hetty replies.

'I don't think I should,' Oma says. 'It's all so ... I can't handle it.'

'Alright then, we can take you another time.'

The children remain with their grandmother when Geert and Hetty take Ellie to the churchyard to see where her father was buried all those years ago. The drive to the graveyard takes them within the boundaries of the town where the brick tower of the church marks the centre. Brick houses with red-tiled roofs line the roads that lead them there. When Geert has parked the car Ellie is slow to get out. 'I should have taken some flowers,' she says.

'You can't buy flowers now,' Hetty replies. 'The shops are closed on Sundays.'

Hetty leads the way as they enter the graveyard through the wrought iron gate. For a while, only the crunch of the pebbles under their feet can be heard as they stroll along the well-maintained gravel paths.

'It's in this lane,' Hetty says as she heads the small group. Ellie looks at the headstones while they walk on.

'Here we are,' Hetty says a few moments later. 'This is Klaas' grave.' Ellie and Geert stop beside her and Ellie looks down at the gravestone. 'Klaas Visser,' she mumbles. 'Born January 1925, died September 1951 ... He was so young still,' Ellie says in a soft voice.

'He sure was,' Hetty says with a sigh.

The treetops are hushed above them as they stand there in silence, surrounded only by the twittering sounds of the birds.

'What did he die of?' Ellie asks.

'Were you never told?' Geert wants to know.

'Mum said an accident.'

Geert looks at Hetty. 'Yes, I suppose it was an accident,' the latter says.

Ellie looks around and walks to the end of the path where she picks a few wildflowers in the side in a ditch. She creates a small bundle and places them on the grave. 'Daddy liked wild flowers,' she says.

Hetty and Geert glance at each other.

'Shall we go now?' Hetty suggests after a few moments. Ellie nods as she watches a bee that has been attracted by the colourful display on the marble gravestone.

'Let's have a look at Father's grave too, now that we're here,' Hetty says. As Ellie follows behind they go into another lane. At the grave, Hetty removes a few dead leaves from her father's marble stone and straightens the flowers in the vase. 'They keep it up nicely,' Geert says.

'Yes ... Well, they should,' Hetty replies. 'That's what Mother pays for.'

In a quiet mood, they walk back to the car. The priest is just about to enter the rectory when he recognises Hetty and inquires after the family. Ellie slowly strolls on to wait near the car. She has a look around the Church square where the other two join her a while later.

'Would it be all right with you if we'd go to where I used to live?' Ellie asks her aunt and uncle. 'Have a look?'

'I'm not sure,' Geert says as he gets in the car. 'It's a bit out of the way, isn't it?'

'I don't know,' Ellie replies. 'Is it far from here?'

'Druten,' Hetty says and gets in the car. 'Do you think we can drive through there, Geert? On the way home?'

'I'll have a look on the map later on,' Geert says and pulls away.

Marja and Gert-Jan are somewhat reluctant to go back with their parents as they enjoyed riding on one of the working-horses. 'Can't we have Oma's horse when she goes to the old people's home?' Gert-Jan asks.

'Don't be silly,' Hetty says, 'where will we put it?'

'There are a lot of meadows around our house,' Marja says.

'Yeah,' Gert-Jan backs his sister up.

'Get in the car kids,' Geert says.

Ellie kisses Oma Visser goodbye. 'I promise, I will tell Uncle Pieter he has to come and visit you,' she says.

'Mum, we can have a horse, can't we?' Marja gives it another try.

'Have you said goodbye to Oma yet?' Hetty asks.

Gert-Jan yells a goodbye in the direction of his oma, who is waiting outside the kitchen door to see them off. 'Bye children,' Oma returns the greeting. They wave at her from the car. Hetty gives her mother a kiss and gets into the car as well.

With the children having had their fun on Oma's farm, they fail to squabble while on the way home. Geert has decided to make a slight detour so Ellie can have a look in the town where she grew up as a small child. They're on the road for almost an hour when they reach the town of Druten.

Geert enquires if Ellie remembers the street.

'It was a bit on the edge,' Hetty answers, 'to the east of town.'

'Waal Street,' Ellie recalls.

The centre of the town shows traces of bygone times and Geert slowly drives the car along the cobble-stoned street. 'This looks slightly familiar,' Ellie says. 'There was a grocer's on this street.'

When Geert has taken them through the street to make a turn at the end of it, Ellie remains uncertain as to where the grocery shop was. All they notice on the same spot is a small supermarket.

Gert-Jan and Marja try their best to read all the street names when they go through the part of town where Ellie used to live as a child. A chocolate bar is promised to the one who first spots Waal Street. Ellie looks around attentively but doesn't see anything familiar. 'Maybe we should get out and walk around,' she says.

'Waal Street!' Gert-Jan calls out.

They all look to see as the car takes them through a newly built area.

'Funny, Gert-Jan,' Hetty says.

'It is Waal Street!' Gert-Jan says defensively. 'I read it on the sign.'

'He's right,' Geert says. 'Look.'

'Now I'll get a chocolate bar,' Gert-Jan states.

'I don't think this is the same Waal Street,' Ellie says.

'I think it is, Ellie,' Geert replies. 'I think they pulled all the old houses down and built new ones.'

'Did they?' Ellie questions. 'But, there wasn't anything wrong with the house we lived in.'

'The council probably held another opinion,' Hetty says. 'What a shame though, they were such lovely old houses.'

'Yes,' Ellie agrees. 'That's all I remember, those small houses made of dark red brick, with the little gardens in front.'

Geert drives the car to the end of the street where sand still covers the newly laid paving stones. He turns the wheel to leave the town, and follows the road that runs parallel to the river.

Hetty hangs up her apron as she has the meat roasting in the pot. She checks the potatoes and cabbage and turns the gas off before she walks into the living room where Geert is watching television with Joke and Marja.

'What is that all about?' Hetty says when she sees the disturbing images on the small black and white screen.

'They shot Robert Kennedy,' Geert replies.

'They did what? Why would they shoot him for?' She sits down on the edge of a chair to watch the news broadcast. 'This is dreadful,' Hetty responds. 'First his brother, and now him. What's that country coming to?'

She gets up and tells Joke to go and see where her brother is.

'I know where he is, he's playing soccer in the street,' Joke replies.

'Well, go get him, please,' her mother says. 'We have to eat soon.' Hetty goes to Joke's room where she finds Ellie writing in her journal.

'Is it time for dinner?' Ellie wonders.

'Almost,' Hetty replies. 'First, there is something I'd like to show you.'

Ellie glances up with some curiosity and follows her aunt up the stairs where the latter pulls out the ladder to the attic. 'I have a few of Klaas' belongings here,' Hetty says as she makes her way up the narrow ladder. 'I have kept them all these years and I think you should have a look at them.' Ellie follows her close behind into the attic. Hetty pushes a few card board boxes aside and removes a children's playpen so she can reach the boxes behind.

'Now, which one was it,' she says.

'I can't believe you kept some of Dad's things,' Ellie says with excitement in her voice. 'I thought Mum threw all of it away.'

Hetty takes out a small, bygone looking cardboard box, the brown paper edges are curled on the sides. She wipes the dust off the lid but hesitates before opening it. 'Ellie,' she says. 'There is something in here, a letter that Klaas wrote to Rita just before he passed away. Rita knows of its existence, but she asked me to destroy it ... '

Ellie looks at her aunt with anticipation.

' ... It might be rather disturbing for you to read, but, I think you should know, so.' She takes the lid off and starts putting the contents on one of the boxes. A few cuff links, a photograph with his father, a watch. Ellie takes the watch from the box and looks at it. 'I remember him wearing this. On Sundays, he wore it on Sundays.'

The envelope Hetty removes from the box next was likely white when it was first handled. By Klaas Visser. There is no indication as to whom it is addressed to. 'This is it,' Hetty says. 'I only found it between his things years later when I finally sorted them out.' She hands it to Ellie who takes the letter from the envelope and reads the letters in faded ink, written on the yellowish sheet of paper. She shakes her head in disbelief when she has finished reading it. 'Are you sure Dad wrote this?'

'Yes,' Hetty replies. 'It's his hand, and it confirmed what I always thought.'

'You mean, you knew all the time that I wasn't ... I don't know about this, Aunt Hetty. Anybody could have written this.'

'I knew you would be upset,' Hetty replies. '... He ... that ... he intended to take his own life.'

'And if that isn't enough,' Ellie says in a soft voice,

'you're trying to tell me that my dad wasn't … was never my own father?'

'I had no idea, Ellie, until I read this letter. I honestly had not, but I always did have my doubts about the way he died.'

Ellie shakes her head. 'No, no, it cannot be. Why … How could you have had doubts? It was an accident!'

'He drowned, Ellie. He was found drowned in the river. He could not swim.'

'He could not swim.' Ellie slowly repeats the words, disbelief shows in her face. 'All Dutch people know how to swim!' she then adds in a loud voice.

'He hardly came near the river,' Hetty says gently. 'I think he must have jumped from the high bridge. You might have been too small to remember, Ellie, but Klaas was a troubled man. Ever since he came back from that German labour camp.'

Ellie lowers herself on the dusty attic floor, and hides her face in her arms.

'This letter explains it,' Hetty says.

Ellie shakes her head to silence Hetty's voice.

'I wrote Rita about it, years ago,' Hetty continues. 'She must have known it was a suicide, I mean … with the knowledge, the secret she was carrying … '

'How many people know about this?' Ellie asks in a muffled voice.

'I'm the only one in the family who knows that Klaas is not … that he was not your biological father, apart from Rita of course. I never told anyone, not even Mother. I wrote Rita about the letter and she replied, begging me to destroy it, never to let anyone know.'

Silence sets in after Hetty's voice has faded into a mere whisper. She looks down at Ellie's distraught face.

'What a … ' Ellie utters. 'How could she? I can't

believe she would do such a thing!?'

'I'm sorry,' Hetty says. 'But I thought you should be told, if not by Rita … '

'Do you think, do you know whether, Uncle Pieter knows?'

'I wouldn't know, unless Rita has confided in him.' Someone calls Hetty's name from downstairs. When Hetty doesn't answer there are footsteps on the stairs. 'Where are you two? Dinner is getting cold,' Geert's voice sounds.

'We're coming!' Hetty replies through the stair opening.

She looks at Ellie who is still sitting on the floor. 'It must be hard on you to come to terms with this. But, at least you know the truth now.'

Ellie remains silent, her face hidden in her arms.

Hetty starts going down the ladder. 'Won't you come for dinner?' she asks.

There's no answer.

'All right then,' Hetty says. 'I will keep some warm for you.'

She disappears through the opening, leaving Ellie. Alone in the dusty attic.

《 》

Almost all my life in New Zealand I had been looking forward to going back to where I once was born, and finally the day was there that I could board a plane for the long flight that would take me to Holland. Mum still wasn't excited to see me go. She didn't come with us to the airport but said goodbye to me at home. Uncle Pieter and Ursula on the other hand were very thrilled for me. When Dean and I visited them, on the way to the airport in

Auckland, Uschi could barely drag herself away from me. She wished she could come as well. Uncle Pieter promised her that one day she could go to The Netherlands. They gave me all the details of the whereabouts of Uschi's uncle in Germany, although it might be hard to contact him as he didn't speak any foreign languages. Dean and I spent one night in a hotel before he dropped me off at the airport for an early flight the day after. For a moment, I wished he would have come with me, but when I waved goodbye at him while going through the gate, I felt it was all right. Although I was hoping the four weeks that were to come, would keep me so busy I wouldn't have time to miss him.

The journey was long and exciting; I was a novice at travelling by plane. There were a few stops in America and a final one in London before we reached Holland. Even after almost forty hours of travelling, I was still excited when we landed for the last time, in Amsterdam. It had been a good journey with quite a few interesting people to talk to, but I was happy to be landing on Dutch soil at last. The American, Keith, who had sat next to me on the last flight, had made me question whether I should stay in Amsterdam for a few days before visiting the family. But I felt too tired to make changes to my itinerary and took a train straight to Arnhem. Be it with mixed feelings. Mum had persisted in saying that the contact with the Dutch relatives was not good. For a while, I thought she might have been right as Aunt Hetty never sent a reply to the letter I wrote her. Uncle Pieter however assured me that there wouldn't be a problem at all. When I finally stood on their doorstep and was invited into their house I thought Mum had probably been right. I didn't feel all that welcome, they seemed to be rather distant. Not what I was used to, but maybe it's just their way. After a few days, I realised it could've been a matter of waiting to see which way the cat would jump. Aunt Hetty and Uncle Geert had only seen me as a small child and didn't know what to expect. My cousins, who didn't know me at all, changed their attitude towards me as well when I'd been in their house for a few days. As if they were getting used to having me in their midst.

Holland has a different atmosphere from what I remember, and entirely different from New Zealand. There seems to be a great sense of freedom, not that New Zealand is not a free country. Maybe it has to do with the people here, they are a lot more outspoken, which is not always a good thing, judging by the riots in the cities. But then, in New Zealand people demonstrate as well.

Although Holland lacks the mountains that we have, the scenery here is beautiful. Maybe I was lucky to arrive in late spring with everything covered in fresh greenness and flowers everywhere. Walking in the small village of Driel was like walking down memory lane. As a child, I had never been to this town but the flat Dutch landscape was rather similar to what I had kept hidden in my memory. The drive to Oma Visser's home was like a movie that had come to life. Oma was pleased to see someone who knows her son Pieter well. I hardly remembered the farmstead they had always lived in and was amazed when I saw it. Only now it struck me how wealthy they've always been.

They must have had quite a shock when they saw our humble abode on their visit five years ago. And maybe that was the reason why Opa Visser was so condescending about Uncle Pieter's farm. It wasn't affluent enough.

I suppose it is to have some kind of closure that people want to visit graves of loved ones. I know I had that feeling and was glad Aunt Hetty and Uncle Geert took me to the graveyard to see my father's final resting place. I didn't know what to expect when I would finally be standing at the foot of a grave. My Dad's, a person I had looked up to as a child and even later on when I knew he wasn't there anymore. A feeling of acceptance came over me when we were standing there. After all these years I could finally see for myself Dad had found a peaceful place to rest. But it was a strange awareness to know that in a few years I will have outlived him; he never lived passed the age of 26. I picked a few of his favourite flowers to leave behind, next to his engraved name on the black marble.

When my cousins had to go to school on one of the last days before their summer holidays, Aunt Hetty suggested she and I could go to Amsterdam for the day. She hardly ever goes there as they have Arnhem close by, and I hadn't see much of Amsterdam when I arrived. So, while the children took the bus to school we took the bus to the train station in Arnhem. This time I was aware of the journey that took us from the forested area to the flat farmlands. From the smell of pine trees to the smell of cow dung. Not long after, the natural smells were replaced by the artificial as we reached urban agglomeration. I hadn't realised when I first arrived, that Amsterdam has rather a large harbour. Not to the open ocean like in Wellington or Auckland but in the wide canal that divides part of the province of North Holland.

When we had made our way outside the train station I couldn't believe my eyes at the sight of so many bicycles that were parked out there. Even on the bridge that we crossed to walk to the Damrak. We took our time as we were looking at the shops and I couldn't resist buying a few Dutch souvenirs for the family at home. We couldn't believe some things we saw in certain shops.

The Dam was another experience, a lot of hippies sat around the National Monument. New Zealand has people like that as well but I don't think they are ever allowed to violate a National Monument. The atmosphere was so relaxing and laid back on this warm and sunny day as if there was no worry in the world. No war in Vietnam, no hunger in Biafra, no ferries capsizing with dozens of people drowned. Even rioting against social mishaps seemed to have been abolished for the day.

Aunt Hetty and I bought an ice cream and sat between the rest of them. Dean had given me a camera before I left. 'Never leave home without it,' he had said and gave me tips on how to make a good photo.

'Some things are better said with the still image of a photograph,' he sometimes said.

We had a delightful conversation with a Frenchman who had strayed up here. With the little English he spoke and the few Dutch words he had picked up we managed to fill an hour of sociable talk in which he told us his life's philosophy. Most of it has slipped my mind now, but it had a lot to do with living a carefree life. We asked a passer-by to take a photo of us with the Frenchman. We could have stayed there all day but as we wanted to see more of Amsterdam we thought it better to move on.

We strolled along one of the narrow streets with even more shops, and at the end, there was this beautiful bell tower, and right behind it, the Flower Market. An amazing sight to see, those boats on the canals selling all sorts of colourful flowers. Hetty purchased some tulip bulbs, she said she always wanted to have "tulips from Amsterdam". I followed her example, hoping they would catch on in the generally hotter New Zealand climate. I wondered if I could send some to Nana in Boston, I was sure she would love them …

Aunt Hetty gave me this letter … a few days ago … Aunt Hetty, who is not my real aunt at all, gave me a letter … My mind is still in turmoil … The letter was meant for Rita, years ago, my father … my … Yes, he was my father. He raised me. He took me to the beach. He made toys for me. He called me his favourite girl. Until … until he found out what Rita had done to him. My mother, I thought I knew her. Why would she do such a thing? All those lies. All my life. My dad was a sweet man. Until … It was her fault, she caused the most harm!

I don't know how long I had been sitting on that floor in the attic. My thoughts were disturbed by Hetty when she came to see if I was still there.

If my mother had only told me. If she would have only let people know. There wouldn't have been a reason for me to be living a lie all my life. She herself had lived the biggest lie. I wondered how it made her feel. What was she thinking of? Even when she knew there was this letter she never bothered to tell me. Did she think Hetty would burn the letter? Was she hoping that the only other person who knew would die before her time? Is she so artless that it made her believe no one would ever find out?

It explains a lot about her behaviour, her reluctance to see me go on this trip. Even more so, a fear. I know now, not a fear that something would happen to me. No, rather a fear for the person who could tell me the truth. Why did she never tell me?

I wonder if Uncle Pieter knew. But he was happy to see me go and visit the relatives in Holland. Even gave me some extra money. I wonder how he would react if he found out I never was the daughter of his brother he had been kind to all these years, as a substitute father.

My father, my dad, never was, disappeared when I was too young to understand. Had he been kind to me because he was left unaware? He must have found out sometime, according to the letter. It wasn't just the harm the Germans had done to him. Rita had done the biggest harm. How could she live with that on her conscience? Hence the escape to New Zealand, away from the reality of the situation. Went there where she could be the sad widow, left behind with a six-year-old. It makes me doubt the mother-daughter love and relationship I thought we had. Was it just love out of guilt for her? Poor thing, if she only knew? Or is it genuine?

Suddenly I felt I didn't belong in the house of this aunt and uncle, who were just strangers in fact. Told Hetty I was leaving. Started packing my suitcase. She said there was no need, not because of that. She offered to help. There were authorities that might be able to assist. I didn't know what she meant. Assist with what? My father was gone.

'Find out the identity of your real father,' she said.

My mind was still blurred by the latest knowledge. What on earth did she mean? Hetty said that there very well could be a man still out there. A man Rita had been seeing when Klaas wasn't home. Another man?

Hetty made us a cup of coffee and took out a notepad.

I told her I didn't see the point. My father had died. What was the point in looking for another? An unknown man? She said a lot of people find lost relatives after many years, through the Red Cross.

I didn't lose a relative that needed to be found, I told her.

'Think, Ellie. Maybe this man has been looking for you all these years. His daughter.'

Why would someone look for a daughter he doesn't even know exists?

'Are you sure? Did Rita never keep in touch with the true father of her child?'

I wasn't sure. I wasn't sure about anything anymore. I wasn't even sure whether I knew my own mother.

She wanted me to tell her exactly when I was born and she tried to remember what Rita was doing at the time. I told her there was no point in going through the effort.

I would never want another man playing Dad to me. I had loved my dad.

'Ellie. Ellie, be realistic. I know you must be hurt, but aren't you idolising Klaas a bit now?'

What has loving your father to do with idolising?

'Klaas was my brother. I loved him too. But we cannot turn back the clock.'

I told her to stop it and ran out. Away from their stuffy Dutch house. I had to clear my mind. I ran out and soon I found myself walking in the fresh winds, alongside the river.

I missed home, I missed New Zealand. Wished I could talk to someone.

Uncle Pieter? He's not my uncle, really. But he would listen.

Dean? Dean would help me with anything. I missed him. I wanted him with me.

Grace? Grace is the sweetest person. She would be shocked. Just like I was.

And Chris. Chris is always a good friend, but wouldn't make a big deal out of it. 'You're a big girl now,' she would say. 'You don't need a daddy anymore, you've got your man.'

I had to smile about that thought. Yeah, that's what

Chrissie would say. And she would be right. Was I truly exaggerating my behaviour? But that's what my feelings were for this man who had been my father when I was young. I'd loved my father.

Rita. I thought of her. I don't think I want to see her for a while. I don't think I would want to hear her excuses. For there was no excuse.

She would only tell more lies.

I let the wind push me along. It was getting chilly, but I didn't mind. I enjoyed its freshness.

Maybe Hetty was right. Maybe … Well, she *was* right. If Klaas was not my biological father, there might be someone else out there. But I did not want to know.

I sat down on the grass and watched the lambs frisking in the green pastures, under the watchful eyes of their mothers. I wondered where the father was in this peaceful scene. I picked some grass and tried to lure a daring lamb to come closer to me. But she didn't fall for it. With a playful jump, she ran back to the others.

What could I still do in this country? I'd seen what I wanted to see. Met the people I wanted to meet. Didn't feel like going to Germany.

I missed home.

I strolled back through the meadows. Maybe I could change my flights, maybe I could go home sooner.

A few horses turned their heads and looked at me with their dark, faithful eyes. Those animals didn't seem to have a worry in the world.

I kicked some dry mud. Yes, I would go home.

In the evening when I was lying in bed my thoughts wandered to the dear friends in New Zealand. I don't recall how long I had been slumbering, but for some reason, I was wide awake all of a sudden.

It was Tine, Tine and Henk I had thought of. That rainy day in Auckland when Mum and I met her when they were telling each other about their volunteer work in the war. That reminder made me jerk upright in my bed.

'Are you awake still?' Joke asked me. She was covertly reading a book by the light of a torch. 'I thought you were sleeping,' she said and went back to her reading.

That day when Tine invited us over to their place and showed us those photographs. The photographs with the soldiers! Maybe Hetty was right, maybe Rita did keep in touch. Perhaps ... I suppose it was my "journalist instinct" Dean said I had, that made me inquisitive about the man in the photograph. Rather that, than the possibility that he could be my real father. In the morning I told Hetty about this and that I was thinking of going home to talk to Tine. Hetty tried to discourage me. I had hardly been here for two weeks, a shame after all the money I had spent. But she was very interested when I mentioned the photograph of my mother with that soldier. She said that might be of help.

《 》

On a chilly, misty morning the plane touches down in Auckland and after a while Ellie is outside the airport, waiting for a bus to take her to the city. Standing alone, absorbed in thought, she is surprised to hear someone call her name. Her face lights up when she sees Jody approach, with a young man in his company. 'Ellie, it is you,' he says. 'I haven't seen you for a long time.'

'How are you?' Ellie asks. 'And you look so handsome in that uniform,' she adds admiringly.

'Thanks. Chris told me you were in Europe.'

'Yes, I just arrived back in fact.'

'You did, did you? You must be tired. Long journey,' Jody replies. 'Oh, let me introduce you, this is Michael.'

'Hi, how are you?' Ellie says and shakes his hand. 'So, how is life with the Air Force?'

'Interesting,' Jody replies.

'And how is everybody at home?' Ellie asks, seeing the bus approach.

'Oh, fine. Same as always.'

'Well, this is my bus. Have to go. It was good to see you.' She hugs him before she boards.

'Take care, Ellie.'

He helps her with her suitcase. They wave to each other as the bus pulls away into the mist.

Ellie gets off in Balmoral and walks the last block to Tine and Henk's home. With a sigh, she puts her suitcase down on the front steps and pulls the ringer. Tine is amazed to see it's Ellie who comes to visit. 'I thought you were in Holland!' she calls out.

'I just arrived back,' Ellie explains, 'and … I would like to talk to you.'

'Sure, come in. Why didn't you call? I could have collected you from the airport!'

'It's OK, Tine, I managed. There was a bus going.'

Tine takes the suitcase from her and leads the way into the living room. 'Sit down,' she says, 'you must be tired.' Tine goes to the kitchen to make something to eat and puts the kettle on for a cup of tea. 'How was Holland?' she calls from the kitchen.

'Fine, warmer than here at the moment,' Ellie replies. She has a look at Tine's books on the shelf. 'Is Henk still at work?' she asks.

'Yes. He won't be back until tonight.'

Waiting for the kettle to boil, Tine comes back into

the living room. 'Are you looking for something in particular?' she wonders as she spots Ellie in front of the bookshelves.

Ellie turns to face her. 'Tine, I think I had better explain why I came straight here from the airport. I found out something when I was in Holland, something about Rita. And I was hoping you could help me, get some more answers.'

'About Rita? What about her?'

'Well, you knew her before I was born and I wondered, if you remember if she saw any other men. Besides Klaas.'

The kettle starts making a whistling sound and Tine goes to the kitchen to make the tea. Ellie follows her there. 'You see,' she says, 'I've discovered that Klaas is not my real father.'

'What? Come on Ellie.'

'It's true, Tine. And Rita didn't want me to know. Didn't want anybody to know.'

Tine puts the tea on the kitchen table. 'I can't believe that,' she says. 'Rita wasn't one to be involved with any Tom, Dick or Harry.'

'I'm serious, Tine.' Ellie's voice sounds tired. 'I have this letter, Klaas wrote it before he died. It explains it all.' She takes the envelope, which is carefully wrapped in a piece of paper, from her bag. 'This is it,' she says and takes out the letter to give it to Tine.

Tine looks at her before she focuses her eyes on the sheet of paper. 'It's an old letter alright.' Her face becomes more and more serious as she reads on.

'This part,' Ellie points out. 'This part explains it.'

' … You run away with your daughter,' Tine reads out loud, 'maybe one day, she will find out the truth. Maybe one day she will know which one of the hundreds of soldiers that were here … is her real father.' She glances at Ellie briefly. 'Maybe she will never know. But I know one thing,' Tine strains her eyes, ' … I wo …won't be there anymore to witness it … ? Signed, Klaas Visser,' Tine concludes. 'But this is, where did you get this letter?'

'Hetty, Pieter's sister. I stayed with them when I was in Holland.'

'Hetty?'

'Rita's sister-in-law. She kept a few of Klaas' belongings, including this letter. Rita knew about this letter. She wanted Hetty to destroy it.'

Tine looks at her. 'And now … you know, the truth. You must have felt … What did it do to you?'

Ellie shrugs her shoulders. 'Like … Oh, I don't know,' she sighs. 'At first I felt like my whole world was swept away from under my feet. It's all so unreal, but … I thought about it a lot.' Ellie sips her tea and then continues. 'According to the letter, Klaas seemed to think, one of those soldiers … Well, you and Mum were nurses.'

Tine listens to her calmly.

'I remember, years ago, you showed us some photographs of you and Rita with these American soldiers.'

'Canadian, they were Canadian,' Tine replies. 'I did too,' and she walks out of the kitchen. Ellie follows her to the living room where Tine takes the photo album from the cabinet. They sit down on the couch and Tine flips searchingly through the pages.

'Here, there they are, your mother with Greg. And this one,' Tine points at a portrait photo of the young soldier, 'this is one he sent himself.'

Ellie has a closer look and takes the album from her. Tine lets her eyes drift from the face in the photo to Ellie's face. 'Well,' she utters. 'Let's have a closer look.'

'It's him, Tine,' Ellie says. 'I know it's him.'

'Ellie, you can't be sure – '

'Look at his nose.' Ellie follows the lines on the photograph with her finger.

'Let's take that photo out,' Tine says and carefully removes it from the album. She holds it next to Ellie's face. As Tine compares the two faces, amazement shows in her eyes. 'Well ... But, we can't be sure. The only one who knows for sure is Rita.'

'I don't want to talk to her,' Ellie replies resolutely.

'Ellie,' Tine says with a soothing voice. 'You have to let her know.'

'I have a feeling she knows exactly what happened when I was in Holland,' Ellie says.

Tine is quiet for a moment. 'All right. I must say, I do see a likeness. We'll ask Henk when he comes home, see what he thinks. Oh, Ellie. I don't know what to say. And Rita ... who'd have thought?'

'Yes, Rita,' Ellie replies, fatigue ringing through in her voice. Tine puts an arm around Ellie's shoulder. 'Rita was rather close to Greg, but I didn't think much of it at the time, knowing Rita was married.'

'Well, that never stopped her,' Ellie says. 'She's had an affair with Pieter for years. I wouldn't be surprised if it was going on even when Pieter was married.'

'Don't jump to conclusions, Ellie. You don't know that.'

'No, I'm sorry. I'm just, tired.'

'I think you're right,' Tine replies. 'Have a rest first. I'll show you to the room.'

A few minutes later, Ellie rolls onto the bed and pulls the cover over her.

《　》

I slept like a log, all afternoon. Had strange dreams, about Uncle Pieter, beckoning from a shore while I was moving further and further away. Uschi standing next to him, calling my name until only an echo sounded. The echo changed to a knock, a harsh knock on the door that woke me. Tine came to see if I was awake and if I would like to have some dinner. She is a sweet person, so is Henk. Strange, that they never had any children, they would have made great parents. Henk had noticed a resemblance between the man in the photo and me as well. We saw his name was written on the back in full, Gregory Williamson.

In the evening I wrote Hetty a letter. Henk offered to have an extra copy made of the photograph so that it could be sent as well. Tine had a long conversation on the phone with Rita, I think my mother was in tears at one stage. Tine tried to make me talk to her but my mind was made up. I knew the truth, there was nothing she could tell me anymore. Nothing apart from excuses and I wasn't willing to listen to those. She was too late with explaining something she should have told me years before.

I will send her the letter, her husband wanted her to have seventeen years ago, hoping she would understand, for now.

There was only one person I wanted to talk to. Dean was surprised when he heard my voice on the phone, he thought I wouldn't be back until a few days later. Maybe I should have let him know that I had changed my flights. He wanted to know if I had come back because of what I had found out in Holland. 'Your uncle came by one day and told me the whole story,' he said.

So Pieter knew all along. Rita had confided in him after all. Dean was flying up in a couple of days and said we could talk about the whole matter then. He had some news that he didn't want to keep from me until then. He had accepted a job as a foreign correspondent in America and asked if I would like to join him when he went there. I didn't need a long time to think about it. I explained to him I wasn't ready to talk things over with Rita and had no intention of going home at this stage. Dean offered me a perfect way out.

I was torn between whether I should talk to Pieter or not. After what Dean had told me, I was in doubt. If he had known, why had he not been the one to tell me? I heard his voice echoing in my ears "talk to your mother". I was apprehensive about contacting him. Afraid of his reaction. I thought of Ursula, who had no part in all this, I should at least make an effort to contact her before I went off to yet another country.

Tine offered to go with me to collect Dean from the airport, but she understood when I said I would rather go by myself. I was walking to the bus stop when Pieter drove up. I felt a bit confused when he got out of his car and came towards me. But soon I noticed there was no need, for the first thing he did was apologise for the fact he had never told me about Rita's secret. He had known for years. He wanted to talk about it but I told him I didn't have time, that I was meeting Dean. He persisted, it was important to him he said. 'We can talk on the way to the airport,' he suggested.

I felt I owed him that much and got into his car. He was silent for a while which made me wonder if he wanted to talk at all. But then he said that there had been a time he wanted to marry Rita. It was at that time Rita had told him that his brother was not the father of her daughter.

'I tell ya, that came as a big surprise to me,' Pieter said. 'And the fact that she kept it hidden. I told her "you tell your daughter or there's not going to be a wedding".'

Rita had not been pleased with that dilemma and it had even caused a fight with Pieter because she did not want me to know. 'She just wanted to protect you by not telling,' Pieter assured me.

'You could have told me,' I said to him. He admitted regretting never having done that, for instead of marrying, they had an on-again, off-again relationship for years and in the end, their love for each other just withered and died.

'So, you jeopardized your own happiness,' I told him.

'I never realised that, until it was too late,' he said.

Silently he drove on. A feeling of compassion came over me, for, even though he had had a hand in it himself, I couldn't help but think that Rita, in a way, also had destroyed Pieter's chance of happiness. The thought of that made me feel even worse about her. It was as if Pieter noticed. He said Rita only did what she thought was best but he had to admit, she was paying for that now.

He walked with me to the entrance of the arrival hall and wished me all the best. I hugged him and told him that I loved him, told him he was still my favourite uncle. I promised him to send Ursula a letter from America.

'She will like that,' he said.

When he walked back to his car, he called out to stay in touch. Typical for Uncle Pieter, it seems he can never *say* he cares.

I was so happy to see Dean walking through the entrance gate into the hall. I ran and threw my arms around his neck. He was pleased to see me happy and asked if I was all set. The two tickets to America he had in his pocket, were for the next day.

That evening, when Dean and I were getting ready for

our stay in America, Henk gave me two copies of the photograph. One was enclosed in the letter to Hetty, the other I put in my bag with my passport and airline ticket. You never can tell.

Some things are better said with the still image of a photograph.

တ

If you enjoyed this book, an honest review would be appreciated as it will help others discover the story.
Thank you !

ᘓ

Dutch words explained:

Oma – Granny, Grandmother
Opa – Grandfather

You can join the Readers List here and get your free Ebook: https://cmuntjewerf.com

Printed in Great Britain
by Amazon

26282968R00162